PRAISE FOR THE ALFORD SAGA

"For adventure seekers...a journey full of promise and danger." *The Globe and Mail*

"Can you talk about thrill-a-minute Canadian history? You can now. Paul Almond has worked for many years as a TV and film director, and his skill shows in the drama and pacing of this first-rate read." *Carole's BookTalk*

"I believe this one should be placed into the hands of every young student learning the history of Canada.... Paul Almond's portrayal of the Mik'maq is very accurate, he embraces the true circumstances and includes the significant legends of the people." *Mrs. Q Book Addict*

"Paul Almond...has created characters with great finesse. The readers will find themselves rooting for this likable and inspiring hero." *The Gaspé Spec*

"Readers will find this book an easy way to learn more about the English and French pioneers, and the Micmacs indigenous to the area, as they begin to create a new society incorporating all three." *Suite 101*

"The Alford saga is epic and historical...[with an] easily accessible prose style employed by its nationally prominent author" *Westmount Examiner*

Also by Paul Almond

THE
PIONEER

BOOK THREE of the ALFORD SAGA

PAUL ALMOND

McArthur & Company
Toronto

First published in 2011 by
McArthur & Company
322 King Street West, Suite 402
Toronto, Ontario M5V 1J2
www.mcarthur-co.com

LIBRARY AND ARCHIVES CANADA CATALOGUING IN PUBLICATION

Almond, Paul, 1931-
The pioneer / Paul Almond.

(The Alford saga ; bk. 3)
ISBN 978-1-77087-123-6

I. Title. II. Series: Almond, Paul, 1931- . Alford saga ; bk. 3.

PS8601.L56P56 2011   C813'.6   C2011-904295-9

 Canada Council   Conseil des Arts
for the Arts   du Canada
 ONTARIO ARTS COUNCIL
CONSEIL DES ARTS DE L'ONTARIO

The publisher would like to acknowledge the financial support of the
Government of Canada through the Canada Book Fund and the Canada
Council for our publishing activities. The publisher further wishes to
acknowledge the financial support of the Ontario Arts Council
and the OMDC for our publishing program.

Cover design by Jelena Reljic
Typeset by Kendra Martin
Map design by David Stansfield
Printed and bound in Canada by Trigraphik LBF

10 9 8 7 6 5 4 3 2 1

For Joan
as always

The Alford Family Tree

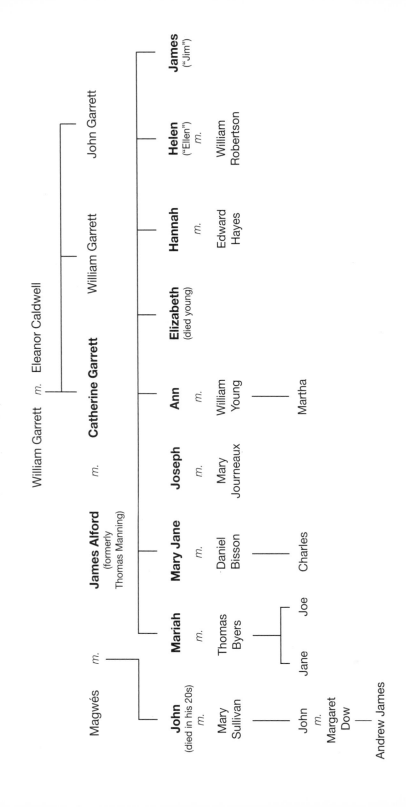

CANADA EAST (QUEBEC)

ST-LAWRENCE RIVER

SHIGAWAKE

MATAPEDIA RIVER

NEW CARLISLE

QUEBEC

MONTREAL

Chapter One: 1853

James Alford pushed back his chair and looked up at his wife, Catherine, pouring a cup of tea by the open fire for her eighty-year-old mother. Their eyes met for a moment. James saw the worry written in her eyes and across her features, so loved but now so harrowed. The long snow-bound winters and toiling summers had marked both of them.

"There's nothing wrong," James assured her, "Jim's just working late, that's all."

But his words sounded false. Their youngest son and only heir was missing. He paused, then rose. "I'll go take a look."

Catherine nodded. "Good." Strong as a birch and hair as white as the snow soon to fall, she put the teacup down by Mrs. Garrett, sitting straight as a pine in her chair.

"It's going to be just fine." James reached for his wide-brimmed hat, threw on a heavy coat, and went out through the back kitchen.

"When has Jim ever missed his supper?" Catherine called after him, as she began clearing the dishes from the large homemade pine table in the centre of the room with its open stone fireplace.

The tall, gaunt, old man with his large, frayed moustache hurried up the ox-track on the hill behind, scarcely looking back down on the farm he had hewn out of the raw forest. His whitewashed farmhouse with its black tarred roof, back kitchen added on, looked relatively prosperous and well kept. Next farm over he'd given to his eldest daughter, Mariah, on her marriage to Thomas Byers, and next to that stood another house and barn that James had given to his eldest son, John, carried off in his twenties by diphtheria ten years ago. Beyond the houses, the blue Chaleur Bay twinkled in the late sun.

Over the brow and onto the flat field James marched, his forceful stride belying his more than seven decades on earth, a long time for someone on this harsh Gaspé Peninsula jutting into the storm-filled Saint Lawrence Gulf. With a sense of dread, he strode across this first acre, cleared some thirty years ago after his land grant of 1819.

The *padda padda* of the mill's giant water wheel echoed across the Hollow — about time they used that brook for something useful! Harvey Manderson had bought the strip of land from James four years before, and what a blessing the gristmill had been for Catherine and the other wives in this young and growing community. Forty years ago when James had arrived, only the Micmac knew of the brook. They had named it *Shegouac*: "nothing there," presumably because no spring salmon came to spawn. But James had seen quite enough fresh water for cattle and eventually to run a mill, so had stayed to settle the land.

Frozen ruts squashed up by oxcarts slowed his progress. Another year almost over. Soon blizzards would lock them into their houses and barns for months. Would this year now be ending in what he feared — another disastrous accident? He drove off images assailing him: an axe wound draining life's blood, or the body of Jim twisted under a fallen trunk — no! Nothing could possibly have gone wrong with his youngest son — he was just working late, clearing a pasture.

Jim would inherit the farm, no doubt about that. James had originally expected it to be his first son, John. But one day ten years ago, John had complained of a sore throat, in itself not worrying: he was a healthy young man in his late twenties, married, with three children. He'd been helping his father haul in the last of the oats: only Catherine had interpreted the dreaded signs. For soon, with a rising fever, John had declared he was having trouble swallowing — diphtheria, the kiss of death.

Perhaps with his Micmac blood from Magwés, the hidden first wife of James, he'd not developed the means to avoid white settlers' diseases. Catherine remained with him night and day. James kept hovering near, but soon it became too much. He prayed in the barn, on the cliffs, at his harrow turning up the rich earth, out loud and in silence, everywhere, over and over. But slowly, it was harder for John to swallow. And then, one morning, he cried out, "I can't breathe! Lord help me, I can't breathe." Mercifully, the end came soon: they had laid John to rest up in Paspébiac, the nearest churchyard, and marked the grave with a wooden cross, which even now was beginning to rot under the savagery of the seasons.

The rest of James's offspring, save for Hannah, were all married and scattered up and down the Coast. All had their own farms, so young Jim, at nineteen, was the only one left to inherit and farm the Old Homestead.

And now this last-born son was late for his supper, so very unusual. Would he, too, be snatched by that familiar figure in a dark cloak who carried such an impartial scythe to cut down no matter whom: babies, the aged, and worst of all, young men in their prime? James quickened his pace.

A shout made him raise his eyes. On the next rise, four dark, misshapen creatures with hunched backs came at him, silhouetted against the brooding sky. His pace faltered — his eyes were not what they were.

Carrying great sacks on their backs, the brave Byers boys loomed into his vision, following their father, Thomas. "Ol' Poppa, look!" Bobby, the youngest of the rascals, came running up to his grandfather with the sack bobbing on his back. "Just look at all this here birchbark we got!" He had always been a lively child.

"Hello there, Mr. Alford," Thomas Byers said. In a land that honoured older folk, even in-laws called seniors by surnames. Farmers all, they possessed that Old World courtesy instilled by frequent Bible readings. "This bark is for young John here. Mariah said we better honour her brother's memory, and keep it in shape for the little fella."

Grandson John frowned. He didn't like, at fourteen, to be called a little fella. Dark features and shiny black hair inherited from his grandmother, Magwés, made him exceedingly handsome, but he was short for his age. When his father had died, his mother, Mary, after five years of bringing up her children alone, had married and gone to live in Gascons with her new husband, an Ahier, leaving John behind with the Byers beside his own strip of land.

"Good for her! But still and all, kinda late for barking, no?"

"Well, tell the truth," Thomas went on, "soon as it started to cool down this autumn, Mariah, she kep' at us.

I got no time fer insulation, I told her, but she said, well, you got time tonight! No dinner until yez come back with a load of birchbark. She's a tough one, that." Thomas was not overly handsome with his bold, angular features and a large moustache, but one thing for sure: he was good-hearted, with a love of children.

James smiled. "Well, I guess young John will be pleased when he gets old enough to live in that warm house all barked up by his uncle!"

"Soon, Ol' Poppa," John said with his usual bravado, "I'm gonna find me a wife, and I'm gonna move in!"

James smiled — same spunk as his wonderful father, now long gone.

"But you, sir," Thomas asked, "what are you doing back here so late yourself?"

"Oh, nothing," mumbled James, and then his anxiety got the better of him. "Well, you know Jim went back to clear land — you didn't hear no chopping when you were barking?"

"Not a chop." James dropped his eyes. Just what he dreaded. Thomas hastened to add, "Oh, I s'pect he's twisting out roots."

"I s'pect so," James replied. With a wave, he took off. If there had been an accident, they'd all know in very short order. And why harbour such thoughts now? You have so much to be thankful for, he reminded himself. Just count your children: nine, eight living, and fourteen grandchildren: all healthy. The Good Lord above, to whom he prayed daily, had given him more than his share of happiness.

So James pushed aside these ominous thoughts as he hurried back along his fence made from huge, upturned roots dragged off the land by him and his boys. Lucky with his oxen too: Smudge and Keen had worked so very hard without complaint. Keen was less "keen" now at twelve years old, but Smudge, whom Keen had trained, had many more years in him. Yes, so much to be thankful for.

How he loved walking through autumn woods! The leaves were feeling their last taste of an Indian summer sun before they shrivelled and fell. The birch had been the first to turn, brown and russet hues, while the maple were blazing with their last flames that engulfed the whole countryside: bright vermilions and crimsons that graced the Gaspé in October. It reminded him nowadays of his home in the North Country (as northern counties in the Old Country were called), though the autumns there were only filled with browns and sandy rust, the colour of the hull of the naval vessel on which he had served and crossed the Atlantic. The poplars here were bright with autumnal yellow, contrasting the glorious maple. Often, while other trees descended into their dotage, a young maple remained glistening green, a melody of shades when the wind rustled its leaves. Vivid red clumps of rowan berries brightened the fluffy green pines among the darker green of the ageless spruce.

As James dipped down into a gully, he saw such lovely ferns doing their best to out-colour the trees above, ferns that in spring produced for him their succulent fiddleheads. A raucous flock of crows could be heard gathering for their southern journey, and he picked out the knock and clack of ravens signalling imminent departures. The colourful woods were emptying of their birds, though here and there he heard a warbler dropping down briefly from the North to grab a few seeds before migrating south. All around, foxes and skunks were fattening themselves for their long hibernations and, in spite of frosty nights, a few wild flowers cast up their yellow and white faces in search of the last rays of the sun as it spiralled lower. The whole countryside sang in a symphony of colour before it shaded into those ominous greys and blacks of bare trunks and bark, relieved only by perching tufts of early snow. Then, these stark sentinels of winter, soon shorn of leaves, would speak loudly of the death of another season: so many he'd seen, coming and going.

The back section of farm was divided by a sloping gully. He reached the shallow bridge built of stones picked from the field one by one and hurried over it. Beyond Shigawake Brook, he saw the partly cleared pasture Jim had been working on, and paused. Did he really want to cross the log bridge and find an awful truth?

He allowed the familiar sound of his brook to have its calming effect. How he had enjoyed that gentle gurgling long ago while at his cabin down at its mouth, so comforting when loneliness struck, as it often used to. He had made his way here from Port Daniel estuary where the *Bellerophon*, one of the finer ships of the line in His Majesty's Navy, had pulled in for shelter during a savage spring storm. Seizing what was undoubtedly his last chance to escape the Navy and try his hand at being a settler, James had jumped off and swam ashore, so becoming a "deserter." Such tortured years on the run, keeping one jump ahead of the marines who meted out the inevitable punishment for deserters: death by one thousand lashes.

Once, they had very nearly caught him. He had gone looking for work in New Carlisle and, as was the custom, had been invited by the Garretts to stay the night. As soon as they had guessed his true identity, the feckless Garrett sons had left to inform the Justice of the Peace of his whereabouts. But dear Catherine, she had saved him. Such a quick thinker, even then.

As he remembered, a smile tweaked his lips: how great had been the future that lay ahead of them, though he had not known it then. He had won her, and brought her here to his cabin by the brook, then built his house and cleared his farm, and they'd had thirty good years together, thank the Lord. Now, this would all pass to his youngest son, Jim. Oh yes indeed.

Thus cheered, he stepped resolutely forward, crossed the brook onto a rolling half-cleared pastureland, and stopped, afraid. Summing up strength, he called loudly, "Jim. Jim!"

"Over here," came the rejoinder.

His son was safe! James strode forward: how much Jim now resembled himself at that age. Wiry and thin, his childhood blond hair inherited from Catherine now dark brown, though last summer's sun highlighted it with bronze, his brown eyes frank, striking, set in an unconventionally handsome face, bold rather, even audacious. Just as James himself must have appeared on the *Bellerophon*, before he deserted.

But now, he began to remonstrate with Jim for his lack of concern: how worried his mother had been at his missing supper. Then he heard the awful reason: "See, Poppa, I wanted t'git all this here cleared fast, 'cause I've come to decidin' something." He looked down, not wanting to meet his father's direct gaze. "Y'see, I've been thinking... I've a mind to take off."

James stared at him. What was he saying?

"You see, Poppa, you growed up in England, you've sailed the high seas, God knows what else you did when you was my age, but you sure didn't sit in one place, small as this one here, and then all your life have nothin' to remember. I think I'd die if I never went anywheres..." James opened his mouth to speak, but words failed him. "Maybe it's your blood, Poppa, beating in me heart," Jim made a half-hearted attempt to smile, "but you showed me the way, I want to go, I've got to go, I *am* going, right after I get our ten cord o' firewood felled for winter, I'm makin' tracks for the big city. For Montreal."

James stood stock-still: Jim leaving! Leaving all of them, and the farm that, one day, would have been his own.

And James saw there was not one thing he could do about it.

Chapter Two

Six weeks later, Jim Alford struggled anew with his decision to leave home. At the end of the fifth day of his long trek to Montreal, he found it more gruelling than he had ever imagined. For the first time, he worried that he actually might not make it through. He had taken care to leave when the weather signs predicted a stretch of clear sunshine, but this afternoon louring blue-grey clouds had shrouded the bay in flurries whipped by a manic wind into whorls of snow flung at his face, forcing him to squint. Fatigue gripped his youthful bones and weighed them down like an anchor. Nineteen and healthy, he was used to years of hard work, but not to trudging on snowshoes with a heavy pack for days on end.

Summoning up a reserve of strength, he forced himself onward toward the tip of the bay where he'd heard the settlement of Restigouche could be found. This stinging snow was worse than the harsh sun that had bled his vision into whiteness, dazzling him the last few days. Thank heaven his old father had whittled him a pair of goggles with only a sliver to see through. He must have learned that from the Indians. Funny, Ol' Poppa had learned so much, but seldom spoke about his past.

But in all, a pretty understanding father: over the past month, working in the woods together cutting their winter's firewood, the old man had never once brought up this coming departure. Jim was grateful for that. They worked together as a team as always, but he had noticed the old man slowing down. Jim doubted he'd see his father spending many more winters in the woods, much as he said he loved the clearing and cutting.

Forsaking the farm for the big city had caused considerable grief, not only for his father but also his mother, and of course his grandmother, the sharp-tongued Eleanor, who made very certain to voice her disappointment. Strong old lady, he thought, and then realized that the next time he came back, if ever, she'd likely be gone.

Early that cold dawn a week ago, they had gathered at the door to say goodbye. The night before, his grandmother had kissed him and given him a small pouch of shillings to fend off any unforeseen obstacles: hunger, lack of lodging, or the means to return, if he failed in the big city.

His mother had kissed him and hugged him as tightly as he had ever been hugged in all his life. The old man with his walrus moustache shook his hand, grief written all over his features, but never a word of admonishment. They both wished him well, but as they turned and shut the door against the cold, Jim felt a lump rising in his throat. Was he such a fool? A hundred perils lay ahead that indeed might claim his life before he even got to Montreal.

Jim carried his pack by means of a tumpline, a strap round the forehead that his father had demonstrated. Wearing new Micmac snowshoes, he had long ago learned the special gait needed to manoeuvre this awkward footwear, but still, the endless walking had taken its toll. This morning he had passed a few houses before the snow started; what if the others lay too far ahead, what if they were several hours away? He'd better find shelter quickly, or tomorrow's dawn would see his youthful body stiff in a snowdrift.

To divert himself, he conjured up his last night cleaning the stable. Ethel, his pretty, brown-haired friend, had burst in the stable door. Closing it and leaning back, she announced, "I've come to say goodbye."

Jim put the manure shovel aside. "Well, well, this is a surprise!" He went directly to her and they stood, looking at each other, no hug or kiss but the air between them pregnant with anticipation. Now that she had come, did that mean she was prepared for something more than just a kiss?

"Weren't you planning," she eyed him, "on coming to see me, to tell me goodbye?"

"I guess... maybe I was afraid of your giving me a right old tongue lashing." After all, they'd had a lot of fun in the last few months, when they'd gotten time. He certainly liked her and felt badly about leaving. But then, as he'd reflected, something about her and their relationship had held him back from any real commitment.

She lowered her eyes. "So that's why I haven't seen yez the past month, like I used to."

"I reckon so."

She opened her heavy coat suggestively and Jim looked down at her tiny form. Again he was gripped by that familiar urge to grab her, hug her, just kiss her to death. But the last time he had tried, a month ago, she had pushed him away, almost angrily. "You think now you're going, you can have your way with me?" Her eyes flashed angrily.

"No Ethel, no. I just want to hold you, so badly."

"You'll hold me as long as you want, once we're married. And I guess that's not to be, now."

Jim felt sure he saw that her large brown eyes held a similar yearning. Yes, but anger, too, mixed in with the desire. "Ah now Ethel, don't say it'll never happen. It's just... well, I don't know what lies ahead o' me. I don't know what the big city'll be like. Who's to say I won't like it?"

"Why go then?"

Jim had to think for a moment. "I guess Ol' Poppa saw a lot of the world when he was on the high seas. Us young folk are not getting anywheres at all. I guess I figured, why not see something, afore I settle down."

"We got lots here. If you're not satisfied, then good riddance!"

He reached out to take her again, seeing that she did seem hurt.

She slapped his hand away. "Let's have none of that now, Jim. If we go any further, I know you fellas, you get all riled up. And I'm not ready for nothing like 'at. Not till I get married. And that's final. Ask other girls. They'll say the same."

From what he'd heard, Jim knew that was mostly true, but on the other hand, not entirely: one or two would open their charms in the comfort of a hay mow. But although he knew who they were, he'd been mostly too shy to ask them for walks along the hot country road in summer, as the obligatory prelude to an evening's lust.

The showdown did not end well, though she finally had placed her face up to his, scrunched her eyes shut, and offered those delicate lips. He pressed down on them, but again, something held him back.

She pulled away hurriedly, buttoning up her coat and tugging open the door. "I'll be here waiting." Blowing him a kiss, she was gone into the night.

Funnily enough, as the door shut, some resolution from deep inside came surging up again. No matter how long she claimed she'd wait, he just knew she was not the girl for him. Was it because, living as she did back on the Second, she would just love to be the mistress of this, the largest farm in Shegouac? Well, that question would forever remain unanswered. Jim finished the stable and returned to the house to prepare for his long journey ahead.

And now, late this morning when blowing snow had made his trek so hazardous, he'd seen the rough track veer inland through the woods. Would it come back out to the bay again? He had decided to head down onto the flat ice and follow the shoreline. Once there, however, the wind had whipped into swirls along the cliffs and hurled itself down to smother him, biting at his cheeks with fangs of freezing sleet. Now, after four more hours, his strength was failing, his knees weak, his neck in agony from the tumpline. Damp snow kept his snowshoes clogged so that every few hundred feet he had to sit, remove them, and bang them together. Worries tormented him. Had he ever felt so tired? And where might the next house be found?

Out here on the bay, he couldn't even see what habitation lay up on the banks. So once again he struck in toward the shore and, at the first dip in the low cliffs, clambered up onto a bare strip between forest and cliff. Summoning strength, he pushed on. Yes, tree trunks sheared, branches lopped off, here was a travelled path. Surely to God that led to some habitation? But dusk had begun to obscure everything. Getting dangerous? For sure. Would he ever find his way in the utter dark descending with this cloud cover and heavy snow?

What else could he do but push on? When night closed in, his father had warned him never to stop, never give in to that urge to relax, to take a breather in a snowbank and rest. It would feel so good and comforting — such a temptation — but that sleep from which no traveller awakens was sure to put a big grin on the old fellow with the scythe — "Son, don't stop, don't rest, whatever you do!" Ol' Poppa had said.

But was the warning accurate? Or was his father just a worrier? He tried to think of when his father had been wrong before. Not often, if ever. Better heed his advice and keep going. But in this murky dark, he found he was straying, tripping over buried stumps, falling and rising, more tired at each step. What humiliation, he told himself, to be found, frozen stiff, so close to home.

His mind wandered and he slowed his tramping, but did not entirely falter. The big city lay ahead, with all its excitement, its thrills, the possibility of money, lots of it, wealth even, oh yes, keep on going, keep going for sure. And finally ahead, was that a small light? No, his imagination. But keep going. Keep trudging. Another fall. Would he get up? No, maybe not. He just lay there, but then his father's face loomed large, eyes blazing, urging, urging him up, and up he got. A few more steps, and yes, it had been a light! In a gust of clarity, he saw even the outline of a building, yes, a stone building, was it? Ahead, through the flurries, a large, stone house.

Would it be empty? Would the settler be friendly? Was there a barn he could seek shelter in? He couldn't see one. He drove himself forward, his breath coming in gasps; his neck ached, his legs deadened from lifting snowshoes heavy with snow. He reached his hands behind and hefted up his sack of belongings, and leaning forward, gave a last lunge.

He reached the door and banged hard.

It opened and a sturdy face, about forty years old, swam into his vision. "Come in, come in." The settler, Robert Busteed, a heavyset man in clean breeches, a well-tended jacket over a clean shirt, and fine slippers, motioned him in.

Out of the icy elements, Jim flopped on a bench and let fall his sack. Mr. Busteed helped him out of his heavy coat, his snowy leggings and moccasins, and brought them to the open fire. Jim just sat, head bowed, panting. How tired he was. But now, safe.

* * *

The next morning, he woke much refreshed. He vaguely remembered that two young women had helped him upstairs to a bedroom and brought him a bowl of soup. With that, he'd apparently fallen fast asleep.

He got up to look out the window. How lucky he had been: the blizzard was still bleaching out any view. With the resilience of youth, he had survived. Then he saw himself in the mirror: he needed a shave, no doubt. Three days' growth — he looked terrible. Finding a jug of fairly hot water outside his bedroom door, he set about giving himself a good wash, and then, a delightful shave.

At breakfast, the master of the house, Robert Busteed, introduced his two sisters, Helen and Elizabeth, in their thirties, well attired and vibrant. Helen, the eldest, had the definite look of a spinster whom life, or rather, adventure, had passed by. Her younger sister, Elizabeth, had the robust appearance of a worker, smouldering with energy, though not in any sense beautiful. Handsome rather. "Where are you heading?" she asked. "Up the Kempt Road?"

Jim nodded. "I'm hoping to get to Montreal, ma'am."

Robert frowned. "Not too many pass this time of year. And usually in a group. You sure it's wise to go on alone?"

"Well sir, Ol' Poppa told me they built this here new road a few years back."

"I remember, I was a child," Elizabeth said. "The army did it."

"Yes, Major Wolfe," his host continued. "They wanted a military road that wasn't too close to the American border like the one from Edmunston, so they picked the Matapedia Valley. But you know, I'd hardly call it a road," Robert said. "Even now. Most of the way you couldn't follow it without an Indian to guide you. Especially in this weather."

"No, Robert, some of the trees have been blazed," his sister Helen said. "Mr. Doucet told us when he came through a month ago, remember? Though it's growed up, not well kept, I heard."

But Jim read concern in their faces. Well, as his father used to say, a challenge is good for a fella. He changed the subject. "Mighty fine house you have here."

"Grandfather built it in 1801. The family has lived in it ever since. You have a farm down the Coast?"

"Yes sir, in Shegouac, all wood though, my father built it after he landed. Before that, he was a Midshipman in His Majesty's Navy."

Robert and the sisters seemed impressed. "You're the first person from down that way to come by in a long time.

Of course, that mail fellow, he comes twice in winter, usually with an Indian guide. And frequently in the summer, but only from up Carleton way."

"Well, sir, 'twas my father first settled at Shegouac Brook," Jim quoted immodestly. "We got us lots of cleared land; my aunt Mariah lives next door, and next comes my uncle John, now long dead. Across the brook, we got a pile o' neighbours. In fact, most of the farms are pretty settled between there and Paspébiac. Big patch of forest in Hopetown with no one, but Poppa says that'll soon fill in the next ten or twenty years." He changed the subject. "Now how far d'ye think it is up to the banks of the great Saint Lawrence?"

"Hundred miles, give or take. Then you've got a long way, probably double that, to Quebec. First part is pretty desolate, I've heard. But getting toward Quebec you might pick up some sleigh rides. That paddle steamer's not working this late in the fall."

"Then how far from Quebec to Montreal?"

Jim saw the girls hide smiles. Was he so ignorant to be setting off on such a trip? "Another two hundred miles or so."

The figures chilled Jim. Oh Lord, had he bitten off too much?

"Well, in any case, you'll have to spend the day here," Elizabeth, the younger sister, pronounced firmly. "We can't let you go out in this blizzard."

She was right, stay he must. And he had noticed her watching him oddly through the breakfast. What did that mean? Was there a hint of attraction? Perhaps even some amorous adventure? Or was that too much to hope for? Well, as their guest, he'd have to wait and see.

Chapter Three

Jim napped again in the morning and woke feeling better after his two good meals. By afternoon he was ready to take off again; the weather had cleared. But the distance to the next stopping place was a good day's walk up the Kempt Road, so Robert pressed him to stay.

He had time to oil the moccasins his father had given him, his heavy boots being inappropriate for the snow-shoes made by the Micmac tribe in Port Daniel, whom his father somehow knew. Made of ash that looped around the front, ending in long straight points behind, they cradled a webbing of *babiche*, strips of dried moose hide. Somebody knocking?

Jim frowned and then decided to go down. Robert and Elizabeth were out in the barn, some hundred yards away, and Helen had gone off for the day. He opened the door.

"How do you do. Daniel Busteed." The man put out his hand, and Jim was struck by his likeness to Robert. "I was just calling in to see if my sister Helen wanted a ride into Restigouche. I have to pick up medicine at the hospital for a sick woman back in the woods." Unlike his brother Robert, Daniel seemed slight, almost ascetic, with the air of a scholar, and a slight British accent.

"Helen's off at a quilting bee," Jim said. "I'm Jim Alford, from Shegouac." He hesitated. "But if there's room in the sleigh, I'd like to see the hospital. I heard tell there was one up at the head of bay."

Daniel seemed taken aback by his eagerness, but perhaps out of good manners replied, "Come right along." He waited while Jim put on his heavy boots and clothes, and out they went.

"Not often I get to ride behind a horse!" Jim confessed, as he swung into the sleigh after Dan.

"Not too many down your way?" Daniel sounded a bit supercilious as he slapped the horse with leather reins. They set off at a good pace through the bracing air that had now turned colder.

Jim was glad of his heavy tuque. He noticed that Daniel wore a fur hat in the manner of a Londoner. "Robert told me you studied in London to be a doctor."

"I did. But it all got rather too much. Amputations, cutting off arms and legs, not for me, I'm afraid. I came back."

"Weren't you afraid of your friends making fun of you, I mean, coming back after a big adventure like that? You obviously thought you'd be staying."

Daniel cast him a surly glance. "Not at all. I worked at Saint Thomas's Hospital for a time, but I didn't like it so I came back. Where is the failure in that?"

Aha! Good, an escape hatch, thought Jim, if his own trip to Montreal ended badly. He'd been worrying what to do. Now having upset his host, he kept quiet and just gave in to enjoying the journey.

Such a lovely thing to race over the ice in a sleigh hauled by a horse, bells ringing on its hames. Daniel headed up into the narrows to find safe ice for crossing. The dark spruce were fluffed up like roosters with coxcombs of snow, their branches piled with great perching tufts.

Soon the horse headed out across the smooth ice of the bay, and Jim called to mind the grinding, bumpy, muddy miles over roots in their oxcart with his mother, trekking each autumn to the gristmill in Paspébiac for their wheat to be ground. Now, with Manderson's mill in the Hollow, no need for that boring trip. He remembered that one year they had decided to grind on their own with a mortar and pestle. He used to help his mother; in fact, all the children took turns. That was even more tedious. He made a mental note: the sooner they bought a horse at his farm, the better. But was he not going away? Put the farm out of your mind, he told himself.

"I guess they got a lot of them hospitals in London, then?" Jim asked. "Lots o' people too, I would imagine."

Daniel glanced sideways, scorn written in his eyes. "St. Thomas's built a new operating room up in what they called the Herb Garrett. Mainly for amputations. I watched a couple. That was it." As they reached the other shore, the horse shied at something in the woods and both men grabbed their seats. "I picked up all I could. Pretty interesting: medicine. Lots of developments recently."

"My father, he saw lots of blood and gore. Fought against Napoleon on the high seas, over in Europe. But he don't talk about it much."

Again, he seemed to have said the wrong thing. Daniel pursed his lips, and then went on, "Since that time, they've made quite a few discoveries. Ether's coming in; you can put a patient to sleep while you saw off his leg. Big help. I just read about it in the *New England Journal of Medicine*, a magazine just for doctors."

Jim was suitably impressed. "So you still keep up with the latest?"

"Of course," snapped Daniel. "The journal began almost forty years ago, and I get *The Lancet* too; it started around that time. You can even get a full degree in medicine, if you've a mind, at King's College. That's been going since the thirties."

"None of them doctors down on the Coast, that's for sure."

"Pretty small potatoes hereabouts." Daniel lapsed into silence, then broke it with a hint of excitement. "You know, nowadays they can vaccinate children against disease? Stops the pox. Been doing it in England for some time. I read that it just became compulsory for babies there. Vaccination, it's going to arrive over here some day."

"We got no small pox on the Gaspé, for sure. But we have diphtheria. My uncle died of it."

"No vaccination for that. Nor cholera, which is taking a terrible toll."

"My father's mother died of it coming over the Atlantic. Lots of that over in Europe and England, I heard. They bring the plague here in ships, but make them stop outside Quebec."

"Yes, Grosse Ile." Daniel slapped the reins as they turned onto a more beaten path. "When I was leaving England, they were coming to the conclusion that it was the squalor caused those epidemics. With all the space we have here, we avoid that. You have no idea of the overcrowding in London, and in the North. All that dirt and filth — the report claimed that was the cause. It's probably what got those Poor Laws passed, not so long ago."

Jim found himself enjoying the ride in spite of his companion's frosty attitude. "Pretty rough time if you're poor in the Old Country. Poppa told me when he came down from the North one time, people were hanged for stealing a loaf of bread. I could never believe that myself."

"Well, perhaps not for a loaf of bread, but for five loaves, or anything like that. But they stopped most of the hangings thirty years ago, and fifteen years ago they stopped it all, except of course murderers and those with treason on their mind."

So times were improving, Jim thought. "Did you work among the poor?"

"My intention precisely. I wanted to end up at St. Thomas's Hospital as a general practitioner. But then, I found out that a patient had to have money to get admitted!" Daniel snorted. "And you have to be adjudged curable, and what is more, you must prove that you have enough money to buy your own burial shroud!"

Jim whistled.

"Yes, that did it for me. I didn't go across and do all that studying just to look after the rich."

Perhaps he was not such a bad sort after all, Jim was beginning to think. "So now, you look after the likes of us on the Gaspé Coast? You still get paid, though?"

"Well, they bring me eggs, they bring me flour, whatever they can, so I don't do too badly. In England, they brought in laws stopping the Truck System, you know, trading jobs for goods and so on, back around thirty-one, I believe. Certainly wouldn't work here, that law."

Jim chortled. "That's for sure."

"Probably better it doesn't, for a while," Daniel murmured.

I can write all this to my father, Jim said to himself: medical journals, ether, so many changes. When I get to Montreal, that will be my first letter. He thanked heaven that he'd applied himself when his father had schooled him and his brother Joseph; his sisters could neither read nor write.

They reached the hospital and after what he'd heard about St. Thomas's in London, the plain square wooden building in Restigouche seemed to Jim a bit of an anti-climax. But Daniel was anxious to get to his patient and come back home before dark, so he did no more than show Jim one of the wards. Jim was happy just to glance in at the door, afraid of those epidemics he'd heard about. The hospital could be full of disease after all. Better get back to the sleigh ride he loved so much.

* * *

The next morning Jim would be setting off, all alone. So why not throw himself into enjoying this last evening with his hosts? "That was one of the best suppers I've ever been served!" he said as he finished his bread pudding. "You're a fine hostess, Helen."

Across the table through the candlelight, Helen smiled. "I've had a lot of training, I suppose. As you might imagine, being close to the Kempt Road, we do get a goodly number of visitors."

"You should open a hostel."

"Oh no," Robert replied quickly. "This way we can refuse whom we like, and invite in only those we feel partial to."

Jim accepted the compliment with grace. "Well, our family in Shegouac will always be in your debt."

"You do seem to have a distinguished father." Elizabeth finished her pudding, and sat back.

Jim looked up quickly. It was the first word she had spoken, though she had been watching him closely all through their supper. Not a greatly pretty woman, but striking, with broad almost manly features. She apparently helped Robert with the barn work, leaving the cooking and quilting bees to her unmarried older sister, now nearing forty.

"And I'm very grateful to your brother, sir, for taking me on his sleigh. I did learn much about England, and saw a little more of your countryside up here. Fine way to travel. Nothing as pretty as a horse in harness. I hope one day, the Alfords will bring the first to Shegouac."

Elizabeth wiped her lips with her napkin, put it down, and looked boldly across the table. "We have two fine horses and one young filly in the stable. Would you like to see them? I've got to go out and do the chores."

"I surely would, ma'am," Jim said. "Nothing'd suit me better than giving you a hand. Least I can do, after this fine day, with all the food and lodging. If only there was something more I could offer."

"Not at all," Robert replied, "you've given us quite enough. We get little news from down your way. Most travellers come through from Halifax, or Fredericton, and perhaps from our own New Brunswick coast."

Once out in the stable hanging their heavy outer coats on pegs, Jim was mildly shocked to see Elizabeth wearing a pair of rough trousers. She noticed his look. "I can hardly muck out a stable with a skirt on, now could I?"

That said it all for Jim. She stood squarely, taking in his tall form. Could it be that she had eyes for him? After all, they were alone now, with little chance of being interrupted.

She must have read his mind, because she said roughly, "First we'll need some straw down from the loft for the cows and a bit of hay for the horses. If you climb this ladder and fork it down, I'll feed them."

Up in the loft forking down hay came so naturally, he realized how much he would miss the farm when he got to the city. But he put away any doubts; now was not the time: he had a long trek ahead. So he enjoyed helping and in short order they had the animals fed.

Elizabeth threw some grain in to the chickens and got dishes of oats for the two horses and filly, which Jim duly admired. She spent some time giving one a bit of a brush down, and encouraging him to start on the other. He enjoyed it. "Guess I'd better learn how to do all this if we're gonna have a horse one day. We sure don't brush down Keen and Smudge."

"Keen and Smudge?" Elizabeth laughed. "What delightful names for oxen! You know, you're one of the first travellers recently who knows what he's doing in a barn. I like that." She came out of the stall to put the brushes and curry combs on a ledge. Then she faced him.

Did he see desire in her look? Well, give it a try. He grabbed her, just the way he did with other girls.

She froze. Then she smiled. "I forgot. You're from way down the Coast. And probably, a bit new to all this, from what I've heard."

Jim didn't know what to make of that. He dropped his hands to his sides. She turned, took his strong fingers in her no less leathery hand, and led him to an empty pen at the back of the stable. "We butchered our yearling bull a month ago. This is empty." She opened the large, wooden plank door, and ushered him in.

"Now," she said, "is there any reason to be in a hurry?"

"I'm going nowhere tonight." But then Jim added, believing it was incumbent upon him, "In the morning I have to be off for Montreal, ma'am."

She looked at him boldly. "Ma'am? Don't you think, in these circumstances, you should call me Lizzie? Or even, my love?"

This was certainly a new turn of events. Jim couldn't for the life of him say "my love," but he certainly could blurt out, "Lizzie, I think you're some attractive woman."

"Good," was all she said. She took a step forward and then pressed herself firmly against him. He grabbed her again. "Uh-uh!" Firmly, she placed his hands at his sides. "I thought we weren't in a hurry."

Maybe not, but he felt such a rush of blood he found it hard to restrain himself.

"Are you cold?" she asked

Jim shook his head. Stables were even warmer than the house, with all the heat of the animals and the low roof insulated by its loft of straw.

"Good." She took off her own garment. He doffed his heavy shirt, and stood, uncertain, in his woollen underwear.

She pulled him down in front of her. Then she admired his body with big, appraising eyes. Oddly, he felt no shame, only curiosity.

She eyed him. "Have you done this before?"

Jim shook his head.

She smiled, nodded to herself. "Not often I get, well, one so young, and so alone." She fondled him. "Something very special, you know, your first time. You're likely not to forget this."

"I guess I won't, ma'am — I mean, my love." It sure

sounded funny, but right now, he'd say anything to please.

She undid her own clothes and underthings. With wonder, Jim watched her white body as she lay back in the shadow of the wooden partition between the stalls. She reached up to his face, fondled his cheeks, and then brought his head slowly down, pressing it against her breasts. "You may kiss me — but gently."

And kiss her he did. That, and much more.

Chapter Four

James Alford roamed the large kitchen, striding back and forth like an animal from the Chic-Choc Mountains with nowhere to go. East wall. West wall. Change. Diagonal, this corner, that corner, all the while eyed by a silent Catherine at her weaving, another silent Eleanor at her knitting, and Hannah, busy as always about the open fireplace, making their next meal.

He raged. For three days they had been shut in by the most unholy blizzard. He felt confined — confined by the high drifts of snow that reached over two of his windows, confined by the prison of his ever increasing years, which led to such unexpected surprises. Like yesterday.

Such a simple task. Go out, fork down straw for the cattle, a bit of hay for the two oxen, collect the eggs, though only three chickens were laying, bring out slops for the pigs, all tasks he usually did by rote. The old barn only lay a hundred and fifty feet away. Had that been badly planned? Young Jim had always gone on about needing a new barn. But then, who would ever dream up that great unbinding catastrophe that had befallen, one that had shaken him to his roots, that had forced him to face his increasing age. Whoever would dream that so close to the kitchen door, with the raging wind and bleaching snow, James Alford would ever come over dizzy, and fall down?

James, the young sailor, the Midshipman who had himself helped haul out the heavy cannon through their gun ports, the settler who had shot moose even as they thundered down upon him, who had faced the worst that Gaspé weather could ever invoke, would now, suddenly, within thirty feet of his own house, find himself thrown down, and anchored by the chain of just too many long years of hard work. Whenever had he not been able to bound up and stride on? Whenever had his muscular limbs failed to respond?

His brain, so alert always, so focussed, now spun out of control, dizzying, forcing him to thrash wildly as he tried to lift his addled frame up onto once-sturdy feet. How long must it be before this body would again respond, smart as a sailor's salute, agile as that Midshipman who manoeuvred so well on the topmost spars of the *Bellerophon*? Maybe if he lay still and waited, the necessary strength would come back. He knew too well the white, looming extinction that overtook the unwary, once they succumbed to this icy numbness now threatening.

So don't wait too long. You know what might happen. Imagine, a few feet from your own front door! What would Catherine and her mother do without him? What about young Hannah? Could the women feed the animals alone? Would the animals survive? Who would ever have thought such ridiculous questions might teem in his spinning mind?

James felt his will to rise evaporating, as snow fell on his black, huddled form. And after all, was it not comfortable here? Why struggle? Hannah could feed the cattle, she'd done it before. Instead, he'd let her continue the housework, make the big breakfast awaiting them all inside, while Eleanor knitted and Catherine loomed?

Maybe if I can just get my hands down onto the solid ground, I can lift my shoulders, James thought. But this seemed another world: no ground could be felt, only soft snow, liquid as the sea. To drown him. To sweep him under. No rising today, no heaving up on waves of power. Would they worry inside? But he lost that thought in another welter of images: son Jim leaving the house — how long ago? It seemed years. Or just yesterday? His baby daughter Elizabeth, dying at three years old, oh so many years ago. And how many others? Two grandchildren, also snatched away — well, was he not this minute on his way to see them again?

The images whirled round, the thoughts circled, but not one of them capable of lifting him from the deep drift and throwing him up against the door to call for safety.

The door. Yes, the door. And all that lay behind...

* * *

Someone was bathing his face in hot water, someone else was pulling off his clothes. He opened his eyes. Such concern on Catherine's face. Tears. He wanted to comfort her. But no limbs responded.

"I told him not to go out alone!" Eleanor's dry voice cut the murmurs of concern burbling around him. "I don't know what possessed you, Hannah, but you did right with that hunch of yours, going out there after him!"

Hannah was far too busy caring for James to respond. And as his strength and sanity returned, James forced himself unsteadily to his feet. "I'm fine, I'm perfectly fine."

"You'll go right upstairs and lie down," Catherine ordered.

"I will not." James walked unsteadily over to the table and sat. "I'll have a nice cup of tea and then some of that breakfast Hannah's been making. Then, who knows," he wavered, "I might just take your advice."

And so, the episode had been closed.

And now, he was pacing the room. Was yesterday's fall anything to do with his present rage? Of course. Everything. And now, the women had not let him go do his chores this morning. Hannah had done them, and apparently with ease. She'd make such a great wife for someone, and he had an inkling who that someone would be. Already the man was building his own house down the coast in east Shegouac, over by her siblings Mary Jane and Joseph. A fine worker, Ned Hayes, but so shy. James had noticed him around women. Never opened his mouth. Well, James would encourage his daughter Hannah to open hers, no doubt about that. She may not be the prettiest of daughters, with her brown hair so plain in a bun, her brown eyes rather small, but she was a thorough worker and would make a great wife and mother. So proud of her, and Jim — yes, Jim, oh dear! Back swooped the vultures of depression that he had fought ever since that departure. Yes indeed, was that also making him rage?

His farm, their farm, what would become of it now? Apart from Hannah, his daughters were happily married with their own farms, so no need of this. Of his two sons, Joseph had married, which left Jim as sole inheritor. And now, would his farm just give in to the relentless Gaspé growth, the bushes which crept in from the edges of the forest to take over fields, spring after spring?

Yes, James thought, that was it: his growing age, and Jim's departure, what two challenges, what two catastrophes, could ever compare with these? And what could he do about them now?

* * *

Late that night, James thought he was awake. He saw great throngs of hooded spectres surrounding the house, throwing their insubstantial but massive shoulders against the wood frames, jostling the joists, heaving their shoulders at the walls with the strength of giant moose. Did they intend to drown the creaking house in acres of unfathomable snow, buried icebergs, wastes of ocean under depths of ice? Yes, if he could howl like a wolf, like a hundred wolves, howl he would.

This great gulf, between the onset of everlasting dark approaching so quickly and an immensity of light dazzling the house with its drifts and ice caverns, was this the divide that one day he must cross? Now, again, he heard the phantoms flap their ghoulish sheets against these upper windows, lacing the panes with harsh whips that seemed everywhere assaulting him. Oh to end all this — put off his uneasy flesh and take on a garment of light, to allow the blinding whiteness of snow outside to smother him in its downy cloak, pierce his brain with flashing shards to illuminate happy dreams at last.

With their monstrous clubs, the giant trolls of weather battered the icicles beneath the eaves and bludgeoned the walls with heartless abandon. But downtrodden though he might feel, stamped on by the heavy and unbearable tread of years, this headlong leap into an eternity was not to be any time soon. So, dream on: let this phantom wind prowl the house on padded feet and fling its gusts against the eaves. He'd lurch through the rooms, tread the worn boards in slippered feet, a gaunt form moving idly from room to room, down the stairs, finally to crouch by the open fire, upon which he threw more fuel. Let them sleep on upstairs. He'd huddle here awhile, and sip some warming soup, and think a spell.

* * *

Catherine didn't hear James get up. She was off in the fields of childhood, playing tag with her brothers. And then, watching wide-eyed at the table the night the young Midshipman arrived from his Waste Land down the coast, so polite and straight with military bearing, his blue eyes and smooth cheeks and fair brown hair bleached by the sun; she had known at once that she would be his wife. That engagement to Billy Brotherton, well, that had just been to rile him up, so angered had she been by James's failure to return as promised. And how she almost swooned that awful day when he had brought her the young Portuguese laddie, Benvenuto, whose mangled arm he had sawn off and then cauterized to save his life. What a husband he would make!

Now again, she rocked in her canoe on that trip down the Coast with Mariah in her arms to bring the baby to her new home. And then, such glorious lovemaking after, and even now, infrequent but still good. She wondered how her husband could still love this old withered body. But love it apparently he did, and her spirited core no less. She felt keenly, even more keenly than he did perhaps, this rage at his increasing incapacities. Worse for him, she thought, even though her back troubled her so that she

34

could not sit long at the loom without getting up to stride around, tidy the room, dust the bowls, even empty the slops — anything to keep moving. Must be hard for a man to lose the muscular strength he once employed so happily clearing woods, ploughing lands, hauling yellow grain into the darkened barns. And now, as she caught a glimpse, in their one mirror with its own wrinkles, of her reflected face, she would even smile at how she had outwitted Fate, for she had a man who loved her, long after she would have thought herself desirable.

*   *   *

Eleanor's soul, as upright as her body, was sunk in deep repose. She had grown used to the gales of wind that rattled the panes and shook the foundations and rafters. She had never felt such shakings and heavings in New Carlisle, where their house nestled in a clustered settlement. Comfortable lives, she and William had made for themselves and their children in the United Empire Loyalist village, beginning with their arrival in the Brig *Polly* back in 1784. Yes, and now William was gone. She no longer mourned the bluff, gregarious husband whom she had loved and put up with — and guided, yes, over many years. She was even thankful that he had gone to his rest. He would never, had he lived, accepted this life in another's house, with another's rhythm, that of her son-in-law James, much as her daughter Catherine had tried to make it pleasant.

Such a daughter. And what great-grandchildren! It was their faces that nightly populated her dreams. One after another, too numerous to recall in her waking hours, each childlike face and then teenage rascal would swim into her consciousness. What delight as she presented them the socks she had knitted, or scarves, or little *chapeaux*. What a delight this last new one had been, another Joey, born next door to Mariah and Thomas the twenty-ninth of November. His little cap she had just finished before coming to bed. She had even added blue ribbons cut from a frock she had worn herself in better times.

The nightly litany lulled her into a lazy dreamland. The first: Henrietta Eliza: "Thank you, Grandma." Janey: "Oh byes, Grandma, you make the best socks!" John: "Now Granny, will you make me a pair of red ones? I seen some fellas in school with red socks. They look terble fine." Yes, red socks she had made for him, dying them carefully from old red material she herself had worn as a young girl. Lucky she had not passed that skirt on to anyone. Shorn of its colours, it now lay on a bottom shelf of her armoire. So many mothers, so many children, and how polite they had been to their great-grandmother. She smiled in her sleep. Not many great-grandmothers around these days, for sure.

But when the Good Lord above decided to lift her in His strong arms and carry her off to his Heaven, who would make their little sockettes, their scarves, their wool-lies, their sweaters, then? And on into the night, her great-grandchildren arrived and drifted by, waving and smiling. Always satisfied, mostly well behaved, just as Eleanor preferred.

* * *

Hannah ached all over! Every time she thought of her Edward, she felt like this. How she longed to be with him right now. Perhaps if she thought hard enough, he might materialize right there, next to her, on the lonely bed of her tiny room. She could just feel his hands holding her tight as he whispered his cuddly words. Oh why had she picked such a shy man — two kisses, that is all they had ever shared.

But why else was he building his house? Surely it must be for a wife. She had been careful to keep her ear to the ground: no rumblings of another taking his fancy. No, so it must be her. Momma had told her, "Hannah, just wait, dear, just wait another year. And then, if he hasn't asked you, I will tell you how it is done. For you know, my dear, such things are best left in the hands of women."

But how? Ask him into the barn? Show him the loft with a gentle smile, and then climb the ladder first and, from the top beam, motion him up? Ridiculous. She was not that kind of girl. So how to get that shy man into a position to ask the all-important question, even with his slight stutter, perhaps on a bended knee? What frustration! What a hard time a girl her age had — how she wished, but in this case only, to be a boy so that she'd not waste more time. My! But the Devil was entering her. Shut out those thoughts, she told herself firmly, and rolling over, hoped that soon she'd fall asleep.

* * *

"Wake up, Poppa."

James felt a nudge and opened his eyes. There was Hannah, on her knees before him. Where was he? Downstairs. He looked around. By the deadened fire. He'd fallen asleep in the night.

"It's over. The blizzard is passed. Sun's out. I'm putting

on wood, and I don't want ye to get burnt." She stooped and placed some dry twigs on the embers, coaxed them into flame, added a log or two. "Are you all right?"

"All right? Of course I'm all right." James reached up for a hand and Hannah helped him up. "I'll get me things on and I'll be right out."

"No Poppa, Momma said you're not to come. I can do it all myself. I'm used to it. Don't you trouble."

"What you mean, not go out?" Something stuck in James's craw. "I'll do what I bloody well please!" he shouted. He stood firm on his two stockinged feet and looked after his daughter who had gone into the back kitchen where they stored the firewood. Woodshed in winter, kitchen in summer. In hot July days, so much handier to make a fire back there, cook the meals, heat gruel for the pigs, even do the baking when they didn't want to fire up the outdoor oven.

Hannah came back in with more wood and looked at him in alarm.

"If I want to feed the animals, then feed the animals I shall." His voice carried upstairs and he heard Catherine call down, "James! Are you all right?" He heard movement on the rough boards above.

"Damn right I'm all right," he shouted. "I'm going to feed the animals with Hannah."

"No James, it's too dangerous."

He knew his eyes were flashing. He looked to Hannah for encouragement.

"The storm's over, Momma," she called. "I think it's all right. If Poppa wants to come with me, let him come. I'll be beside him."

Not often Hannah stood up to her mother, James

knew, but he could see that she was alarmed. As his anger subsided, he motioned. "Let's go."

Hannah threw her wood down beside the fire and followed as he went to the back door and struggled into his heavy coat and tuque.

The dazzling snowdrifts swooped over his farm in contours, reaching up against the hill behind, looped and whorled around the barn, lying in drifts about the stable doors and at the woodshed. James turned. The house itself was banked high, in some places over the windows. Hannah moved ahead, beating a way on snowshoes to the stable. They had been careful, some years ago, to build partitions on each side of the stable door to shield it from the snow so that it could open, and to place a peg for a shovel in case it didn't. But the partitions now, after this heavy blizzard, were of little use.

James watched Hannah shovelling, and stooped to fasten on his snowshoes. Not as easy as when he hunted back in the caribou highlands with the Micmacs. How he resented his aging frame not responding. But be thankful, he reminded himself, give praise to God that you are still alive and have everything you want.

He looked up and saw high, high above, the delicate streaks of cirrus wafting across the crisp blue sky, delicate whorls crafted by the Almighty, spreading out as if to extend a winter welcome. He was beginning to feel better: the worst had passed. He even felt guilty for his earlier outbreak. But how else could he have come outside, strapped on these snowshoes, and stood in his own farmyard in all its cloaked glory to behold yet again another winter?

Once in the loft with his two-pronged wooden fork pitching straw down onto the thrashing floor below, James felt cheerful. The motions of his arms, the rustle of straw, the barn smells of old hay and fresh manure, the occasional bleat of a penned sheep, all spoke to the notion that he'd go on for many more years. Comforting.

"I bet Jim is missing all this," Hannah called up. "I bet he feels pretty lonely in that there big city."

"I bet he does too, Hannah." Yes, how easy it had been for Jim to just take up and leave. His daughters, they could never do such a thing. They were dependent upon marriage, upon husbands, some of whom could even read and write. And why should that be? What about all his neighbours, who had not been schooled, as he, in the Old Country? Mind you, he'd run errands for the elderly scholar who tutored the children of the Earl so that he might learn from him. And learn he did. How much James had loved those sessions.

And then, the thought struck him: why not put yourself into a new project, one that indeed might live on? A school! Yes, build a school, right here in the centre of Shegouac. It could be used for church services, too, instead of way down in Port Daniel. What an idea!

Would that not encourage his son's return? The community would have its own school, and produce children proud of their learning everywhere.

Yes, he decided, set about building a school.

Chapter Five

At long last, Jim reached Lévis, opposite the capital city of Quebec. Below him lay the great Saint Lawrence River, heaving with all manner of ice pans, jagged, topsy-turvy, some an acre across, heaped with the remnants of many collisions on their way down from Three Rivers and Montreal. Below him on the flat shore lay three or four trunks of hollowed pine. A couple of horses waited at a hitching rail where a scattering of travellers had tramped the snow flat.

Jim then looked up at his first sight of Quebec City. A clutter of houses lay on the slope below great cliffs that held the rest of the town. These were the very ramparts that brave General Wolfe had scaled with his British troops less than a hundred years ago when he defeated the French General, Montcalm. Jim had learned something of that battle from a military man who had given him a ride with his entourage the last fifty miles. A decisive battle, although that Seven Years War had not really ended until 1763, when the *Treaty of Paris* ceded Canada to the British.

History was not something his father had focussed on in his tutoring. Jim knew about the Revolutionary War of 1776 that brought his maternal grandfather, William Garrett, and other United Empire Loyalists up to the

Gaspé Coast in 1784, where they had founded the settlement of New Carlisle. But most of the events of the past were hidden from him, because after all, when had any farmer time to indulge such fancies? Reading, writing, and arithmetic were what he learned, and that was quite enough.

Earlier on during the trip, he had watched the far shore seep into view across the mighty river. As that distant bank drew closer, he grew accustomed to the dark, fearsome waters between. He had walked, and hitched rides, two hundred or so miles along this south shore, but now he was finally staring the great river barrier in the face.

Several burly, heavily dressed men in hip-length boots sat on the edges of the great dugouts, for these now appeared to be canoes, twenty-five to thirty feet long, hollowed out of specially selected trunks. Did these men intend to manoeuvre them across that violent river? The black roiling surface would vanish and reappear as floes of all shapes, jagged and alarming, slammed against each other and then separated as the current crowded them together and swung them apart.

Terrifying images of the time he and his brother Joey had been out fishing through the ice near shore and an argument had developed. He had fallen and then broken through the ice crust. Down Jim went, the shock of the bitter cold water expelling all his breath — he choked and gulped a lung full. Frantically, he had clawed upward through the water, beat his fists on the jagged underside of the ice, found the opening, but almost immediately began losing consciousness.

His brother clutched him, grappled his coat, hoisted him up and out, then began to pump his lungs to expel the water. And there it was again before him, all that icy, black water. How on earth would anyone dare cross that?

His three other travelling companions began walking down and Jim found himself following. The burly canoe-men, or *canotiers* as they were called, rushed forward to solicit business: *"Allons-y,* let's go, *n'ayez pas peur!"* The other travellers standing around appeared rightfully hesitant, and looked to these newcomers for guidance. That wide and fearsome river flowing between this shore and the desired Quebec City did look dismaying in the extreme. A terrible grinding and roaring issued from the floes crashing into each other, heaving up others like giant white turtles in a love-fest, backing off, bumping into others. He stared at the open, black wastes of water that kept closing into glistening plains.

Much as he wanted to get to Montreal, fear blocked all progress and brought him to a halt. I'll never try that, Jim said to himself. Why not just keep to this side of the Saint Lawrence? I might bushwhack my way, though the only road lay along the north shore. But then, he remembered that Montreal lay on an island. The north coast probably offered a better crossing; so he realized, nothing for it but to try and cross here with the others.

As he reached the flat, his fear grew. But it would worsen the longer he waited so he decided quickly. "Let's go."

He asked how much fare they wanted, and seeing it was reasonable for the danger undertaken, he divested himself of his heavy pack. The biggest *canotier* grabbed it and threw it in the centre of his own shaped log, or canoe. At once, a half-dozen *canotiers* rushed to the other voyagers and grabbed their packs, whether they liked it or not. Soon, a good eight people had come to sit down in the hollowed trunk. Unstable on the flat ice, it rocked as each entered. They brought a horse rapidly forward, with growing excitement all around. When the last person, a woman, quite well dressed, got in near the bow, they hooked the single tree into the chain at the front of the log and the *canotiers,* two on each side, ran along as the horse dragged them towards the threatening black current, eddying and boiling a scarce fifty feet ahead. Jim scrunched his eyes shut, but the jolting ride made them fly open. No escape now.

Once the horse had got them up to speed, the lead *canotier,* "*Je m'appelle Pierre,*" unsnapped the harness with amazing dexterity and the *canotiers* on each side used the momentum to race the canoe toward the swirling water. Everyone tensed, not knowing what to expect as the black edge loomed closer; the well-dressed woman screamed. Not a lot of help to Jim, for sure.

Ahead, that threatening lip of ice might break under them at any second; Jim had an urge to leap out, and his gorge rose. Don't vomit, he told himself, as Pierre shouted, "*Venez monter!*" and the two *canotiers* leapt in at the last second.

They were off, paddling furiously; Jim had never seen such energy. The canoe gathered speed through the black water, and Jim began to relax slightly, until he saw a large ice floe coming at them. It would tip them into the river. He couldn't swim. He gripped the rough edges of the log — what now?

The great flat ice-pan struck the bow, but then simply turned the canoe downstream. A second time Jim's fear rose. A cheerful order from Pierre urged his men to back-paddle, and after Herculean strokes, they managed to swing the prow upstream and now aimed for a spot above Quebec City.

Paddling against the current, they dodged the ice floes in their unwieldy craft, but each minor crisis brought on new torture. Jim had never dreamed he'd find himself in a situation so fraught with terror. Heading upstream, the craft lost ground as dangerous chunks of ice swept past, but it managed to edge ever closer to the opposite shore. Clearly, the *canotiers* found it exhilarating, although the other passengers were just as terrified as Jim, gripping the rough edges in white-faced anxiety.

As they were paddling furiously around a large pan, Jim pointed. Another flat floe, forty or fifty feet across, headed downstream directly for them. Would it not crush them? Pierre shouted loud exhortations in French. Jim grabbed up the extra paddle again and threw himself into stroking, for even the *canotiers* showed apprehension. Jim could well imagine what would happen when the ice-pan jammed them against the other one.

And so it did, with a great grinding crash, striking their craft with immense force so that Jim was sure the trunk would break in two, dropping them into the icy depths. But he stifled the urge to cry out. The *canotiers* on the right leapt onto that floe and tried to haul their massive canoe out onto it. But no, it was jammed solid, and cracking. They would all be done for.

James said a prayer: at least he'd have died trying to fulfill his dream of getting to the big city — a worthy end. Pierre leapt out on the upstream floe, and also tried to lift the canoe out. No luck.

"*Débarquez tout le monde!*" he cried.

Everyone out? How? Onto the lip of this ice? Was Pierre crazy? It would crack. "We'll all drown!" someone yelled.

"Non, non — vite, vite!" came the reply.

Better do as he was told! Gritting his teeth, Jim clambered out with another *canotier* and three passengers. Right away, the shelf cracked.

Yelling, they all grabbed at their craft and dove back into the hollowed pine, which so far was holding up. One elderly man didn't make it and fell backwards. Jim froze, heart beating. As the man was almost sucked under by the current, two *canotiers* leapt across and grabbed his coat at the last second, managed to haul him out, sopping with ice-laden water, and flopped him back into the canoe.

Now what, Jim thought? Stay in the boat while it splits apart?

"L'autre côté," Pierre prompted, and clenching his teeth, Jim lurched out. A portly peasant woman reached, arms out, and Jim pulled her across the gap, though in a moment she fell on the slippery ice. But the shelf held. He helped her up and one after another, the others struggled onto this firmer floe.

Then every *canotier* and a few of the passengers tried lifting and pulling the log amid exclamations of encouragement and delight from Pierre. Finally, they got the canoe beached up onto this ice floe, itself moving inexorably downstream.

"Allez!" Pierre called, and the *canotiers* managed to pull the canoe toward the next ominous patch of black water, the passengers trudging behind, faster this time, with the woman who fetched up last hurrying as best she could, slipping and falling on the bare patches of ice.

One more black stretch left.

How would they handle that? The canoe had surely sprung leaks. Once they all got back in, would it sink? And dunk them into the black below as food for fish? But a few feet from the edge, Pierre commanded them back in, except Jim who he needed for help. Jim, caught up in the furor, could do nothing but obey, and stood ready to push the canoe out into the black water, though he felt sure it would mean the end of everyone. Being last, he'd wait to see if it were seaworthy. Other passengers were thoroughly panicked.

With a great shove, the *canotiers* heaved the canoe forward over the edge of the ice floe, which of course broke under its weight. Nothing for it but to leap in, each man for himself, scrambling for space, just in time.

The dugout sprouted water but held.

"Paddle for your lives," Pierre shouted in French and paddle they did, for down that current came another frightening fleet of jagged bergs, any one of which would definitely finish them off.

After a time of furious exertion, all panting desperately, the canoe drew close to the shelf ice on the opposite shore. A horse and two men were racing down toward them on the opposite bank. One man threw a line to Pierre, who quickly fastened it through the prow's ring. The man swivelled his horse which dug in its hooves and heaved the canoe with everyone aboard onto the cracking ice shelf at the shore.

So they had arrived. Safe.

Jim took a few minutes to collect himself. He'd never faced anything like that before. As his panting subsided, he began to feel almost proud of himself for what he had achieved, in the face, yes, he now admitted it, of almost continuing panic. But he knew that two hundred long and potentially more dangerous miles lay ahead on his route to the gleaming town of Montreal.

Chapter Six

Jim strode jauntily down the ravine made by steep-sided buildings whose square windows stared blankly out. Without snowshoes, his legs felt ten times lighter. He had arrived in Montreal after another arduous weeklong journey, trekking, hitching rides, sleeping in the occasional hostelry, bug-ridden but cheap. He had not stopped long in Quebec because he wanted to get straight to Montreal, a city burgeoning with all sorts of trades he might take up and factories to work in and buildings being constructed, schools for children, even a hospital. And now, here he was.

He'd never forget the first sight of the city across the black waters that stretched beyond the shore ice: a great cluster of buildings below the low rise of Mount Royal. So many more than in Quebec, some tall, the tallest being twin spires of some basilica, bigger than anything he'd ever seen.

After crossing the ice over the channel to the east of the island, he'd caught a ride, and though it was late, managed to find board and lodging in an attic with three other workers; Widow McMannus rented a house in a poor area known as Griffintown. One of her lodgers had just passed away and that floor space was now vacant, though not large and inclined to be chilly. Irish, probably in her late twenties, Winnie was snappy about getting her rent, that's for sure, thought Jim, as she introduced him to her son Mikey, ten, who also worked. All the next day Jim had lain upstairs, resting, hardly able to move, letting the month-long journey seep out of his bones.

And now today, although everything about the city fascinated him, he had first to post this letter to his parents. Winnie mentioned that along St. Paul Street, which led out from "the Griff," a new post office had been built. He'd see about the letter there, and then look for that marvellous edifice whose twin towers he had seen from afar. Meanwhile, he enjoyed walking down St. Paul with its tall, narrow, stone buildings, behind whose square windows hid countless men likely earning good livings, as soon he would, too. But he also saw a lot of burned-out shells, vacant lots draped in snowdrifts. A fire had passed through a couple of years ago, as he'd heard on the Coast: twelve hundred buildings destroyed, nine thousand homeless. He shook his head.

What a lot of passers-by this grey, windy morning! The occasional proud prancing coach-horse pulling a *caleche* caught his interest, the coachman shouting to clear the way. Yes indeed, so much lay ahead, so many experiences inaccessible to the lads back on farms in Shegouac. Girls? Lots, he had been told, and not all as upright as the ones at home. But then, how did one find a good wife? Perhaps he'd look for one smart enough to know her way around, able to avoid the tricksters apparently lurking at every corner. His daydreams were interrupted by a sign at the corner of St. François Xavier: POST OFFICE.

He went in to join the line of three people: one woman emaciated and drawn under her shawl, another man looking equally poorly and a third rather well dressed and in good spirits. As he came next to him, Jim tugged off his farm cap. "Good day to you, sir."

The man looked at him in astonishment, then nodded and turned back to face the counter. The others appeared to Jim too downtrodden to offer any help. He waited.

Getting to the wicket, he held up his folded parchment. "I've got this here letter I need to send to my parents."

The clerk, a pasty-faced man with thin wispy hair, nodded and opened a drawer. "And where might they live, young man?"

"Shegouac."

"Where's that at?"

"Near New Carlisle."

"New Carlisle?"

"Down on the Gaspé Coast. But we don't have a post office there yet."

The clerk shook his head. "Don't think we send letters down there. Halifax for sure." He frowned. "Gaspé itself maybe, and Percé. Wait here." He turned and went through an inside door.

Jim waited. A man in line behind him spoke up. "They told us in the summer they send letters to Ireland. Sure and that must be a good bit further than Gaspé."

The Irishman had a pleasant, flat face, pinched though, as was his wife, neither looking as if they had been fed on the fat of the land. She seemed shy, holding her husband's arm tightly.

"You're from Ireland?"

The Irishman nodded. "Came six year ago."

"What made you leave home?"

"Haven't you heard? Big famine. Forty-seven. I don't

know how we lived through it. We lost two children on the voyage, one in the sheds."

Jim frowned. "Sheds?"

The man gripped the hand of his wife, who was holding him close. "On the dock. No one's ever seen the like. Thousands dying, no one got through. We did. Ship Fever. Bodies piled on top of each other, the smell, we nearly died of the smell, it was a real hell." His wife nodded vigorously. "Then some sisters came, bless 'em, and they sorted it out..."

"The Grey Nuns," the wife murmured.

"The Mother Superior," the man kept on, "Mother McMullen, she saw us. From what they told us after, she went right back to them other nuns and told them, 'Now that plague is contagious, and it's terrible, just terrible. You might all be going to yer deaths,' she said to them other nuns, 'so I won't ask any of yez t'come wit' me. I leave it all up to you.' And you know, all forty come to help!"

"Saved us they did," the wife went on. "Them alone. Them's the angels what did it. The only ones, mind."

"The mayor of Montreal," the man broke in, "Mr. Mills, he came, and you know, he died, too. Aye, and of them forty nuns, thirty was lost. We wouldn't be here now, eh luv, without 'em, I swear to God."

"Come on now, Seamus, he's heard enough, that's enough."

"I gotta keep telling it, Shelagh, otherwise it'll all be forgotten. And you would too," Seamus stared at Jim with haunted eyes, "if you'd been through what we've been through. It's a miracle, that's what, a miracle we're alive. And you know what, more sisters came—"

"The Sisters of Providence," his wife threw in.

"Yessir, they came and replaced the others. Must've killed a pile o' them, too."

"Every so often it comes over him," the wife said apologetically, tugging at his arm.

"You not heard tell of the sheds?" he went on. "Twenty-two of them, right down on the dock. You new here? I'll show you where they was, after. My dreams is still full of it."

Jim nodded. "Thanks, but first, I've got to get me a job."

"They wouldn't let us into the city. Kep' us there to die. Don't know how Shelagh and me made it."

"The Holy Mother," Shelagh said.

"But she watched over the rest, too, mostly Irish, thousands died, I think it was five thousand."

"Six," said Shelagh.

"But now, so long after, no man knows, I got me a job. That's why I can send a letter home."

"A job? Where?"

The Irishman glanced around as though he did not want to be heard, then leaned closer. "Redpath Sugar. On the canal. Big bugger of a building. Only took a few, mind. Stone masons. I was one of the last to get in."

Jim turned as the clerk came in from the back room. "We can take the letter. Threepence."

"All the way to New Carlisle? Do you know when it'll arrive?"

"No telling. Not many mail couriers goes that way of a winter. Maybe to Carleton, Douglastown, places like that. You want to take your chance?"

Jim nodded, and found in his pocket the required three pennies which he dropped on the counter. The man handed him a stamp, which Jim studied. "You lick this here, and you put it on your letter, see, top right."

"That's all I have to do?"

The man nodded and gestured to the Irish couple waiting in line. As they took his place at the counter, Jim leaned his head towards the Irishman. "You couldn't tell me where I might try for a job, too? I'd be mighty obliged. I don't know a soul here."

"Neither did we. But you just keep trying. Keep trying."

Shelagh nodded vigorously.

Jim went outside into the cold air, put on his hat, and thought: Keep trying, yes, what else?

He walked along St. Paul and turned up St. Sulpice into Place d'Armes, a square centred by the statue of de Maisonneuve, the *seigneur* who defended the early city against the Iroquois. There to Jim's left rose the twin spires of that imposing basilica he'd seen. He walked up to stare at its ornate façade, and then came to mount the steps, tugged open a small door in the larger portal, and went inside the great Cathedral of Notre Dame.

He'd never been in a Catholic church before. In fact, some of his neighbours called it a place of devil worship. But he knew better: his Catholic friends were every bit as upstanding as the rest of Shegouac. For himself, he saw no difference, though the prejudice was that thick on the Gaspé you could cut it with a knife: Catholic to Protestant, Protestant to Catholic. And after all, wasn't it a good Catholic widow who let him sleep on her attic floor?

What ornamentation! In fact, what amazing decoration, all carved entirely out of wood, with dozens of niches in its curved chancel. Neither Hopetown nor Port Daniel boasted even a simple church, and in Shegouac not even one small school to use for Anglican services, as they did in the other communities. The only churches he'd been in were St. Andrew's in New Carlisle and St. Peter's in Paspébiac — and neither bore any relationship to this bizarre edifice with its statues of saints and angels, its spectacular stained glass, its bright, almost gaudy paintings, its huge, high altar patterned after St. Peter's in Rome, its tall golden cross — and those black-robed priests moving about their arcane duties in the chancel. Jim shook his head. Well, progress, he supposed.

In the vast golden silence, he wondered if the Good Lord — whom his father worshipped daily — would preside as easily here as He did in the bare Port Daniel schoolhouse where they worshipped each Sunday. For himself, he had seen no great evidence of a deity anywhere and wasn't about to absorb that curious idea of a heaven and a hell, much as it were bruited about in some quarters. But if God did exist, he used to think it wise to spend an hour each Sunday listening to the Reverend Mr. Milne, who so often preached about the glories of heaven and the torments of hell.

After a time, he thought, I've done enough sightseeing for the day — I'd better get job hunting quick. Buy something to eat and maybe bring some milk home for Mikey and his widowed mother Winnie. The father, Thomas McMannus, had died before Mikey was born. The two of them concerned Jim; they did need attention. For himself, he was not unduly worried: a job would surely be found quick.

Chapter Seven

So now, where to look?

Well, Jim figured, from the amount of beer drunk everywhere, the best place would be Molson's Brewery. They'd have the best jobs. So having asked directions, he set off east down Notre Dame Street towards St. Mary's current.

He kept revelling in the sight of all these tall buildings, some four and even five stories, and certainly no shortage of people passing — what a difference from the Gaspé! Countless sleighs and feet had packed down the snow so the streets were easily traversed. He finally turned down Voltigeurs Street and saw, across the road, the large grey stone–fronted brewery with other buildings behind. Fingers crossed, he walked along St. Mary's Street and turned in at a sign indicating employment.

It took him no time at all to find out that no position was open: this would be of course the first place called at by every immigrant. And a great many there were: thousands coming every summer. Montreal was known as the most thriving city in the East.

From the brewery he headed north and threaded his way through more gaunt, fire-damaged ruins. The great fire of Montreal had passed through a couple of years before, especially ravaging St. Mary's. The blackened spars and rafters, now edged with white snow, seemed to emanate silence, reflection, the impermanence of all things. His father had often spoken about a forest fire that had nearly taken his life at Jim's age.

He wondered how many people had died here. Death seemed to stalk everywhere, especially on those immigrant ships. Neither was the Gaspé Coast immune: he suddenly wondered when his father might succumb. Not too soon, he hoped. His grandmother, Eleanor, did last through everything, knitting furiously for her grandchildren. He treasured the scarf she had given him — today not so snugly wrapped; his brisk walk kept him warm. He loved winter and had no reason to fear its wrath, as in some of those stories his father told of the dangers of freezing, when he'd first arrived on the Coast.

Off he headed towards Griffintown and the industrial Lachine Canal that cut through. He kept near the docks, checking also for work there. He'd heard that last summer the first screw-driven freighter had arrived, with something called a propeller that actually drove it through the waves. The channel being too shallow, larger ships were usually pulled up through St. Mary's current by shore-based teams of oxen and so came to anchor nearby, serviced by many small craft he saw coming and going.

Why not try his hand at whatever establishment on the docks seemed open? But from the lingering groups of men forlornly waiting for a day's work unloading, he decided to press on. He came upon a small shoemaker's shop. No luck there either. Then on to a nail and spike factory (no blacksmiths needed here, for sure), a cooperage (he'd rather enjoy the barrel-making trade, he decided, but again, no luck), and a small iron foundry. None of them wanted a man of his age — they were all looking for apprentices, eight to twelve years old, to whom they need pay only a pittance.

Walking along the waterfront, he came to the Place Jacques Cartier and decided to cut up the broad avenue topped by a tall column on which stood a tiny figure. Who commanded such an honour?

He circled the base to see if anything was inscribed: Lord Nelson! The very Admiral under whom his own father had served.

IN MEMORY OF
THE RIGHT HONOURABLE
ADMIRAL LORD VISCOUNT NELSON
DUKE OF BRONTE
WHO TERMINATED HIS CAREER
OF NAVAL GLORY
IN THE MEMORABLE BATTLE OF TRAFALGAR
ON THE 21 OF OCT 1805
AFTER INCULCATING BY SIGNAL
A MAXIM THAT CAN NEVER BE FORGOTTEN
BY HIS COUNTRY
"ENGLAND EXPECTS EVERY MAN WILL DO HIS DUTY"
THIS MONUMENTAL PILLAR
WAS ERECTED BY A SUBSCRIPTION
OF THE INHABITANTS OF
MONTREAL
IN THE YEAR 1808

Well well well! His father had only mentioned Trafalgar a few times, and never with these details. Imagine what he must have gone through! He moved around to the east.

ON THE 2 OF AUGUST 1798, REAR ADMIRAL SIR HORATIO
NELSON WITH A BRITISH FLEET OF 12 SAIL OF THE LINE AND
A SHIP OF 50 GUNS DEFEATED IN ABOUKIR BAY A FRENCH
FLEET OF 13 SAIL OF THE LINE AND 4 FRIGATE UNDER
ADMIRAL BRUEYS AND DESTROYED THE WHOLE EXCEPT 2
SAIL OF THE LINE AND 2 FRIGATES WITHOUT THE LOSS OF
A BRITISH SHIP.

His father's first big naval engagement. Too bad Jim
had not pressed him for a more vivid description of what
happened. It must have been quite a victory.

He moved around, and on the west, he read:

ON THE 21 OF OCTOBER 1805, THE BRITISH FLEET OF 27 SAIL
OF THE LINE COMMANDED BY THE RIGHT HONOURABLE
LORD VISCOUNT NELSON, DUKE OF BRONTE, ATTACKED
OFF TRAFALGAR THE COMBINED FLEET OF FRANCE AND
SPAIN OF 38 SAIL OF THE LINE COMMANDED BY THE
ADMIRALS VILLENEUVE AND CARAVINA WHEN THE LATTER
WERE DEFEATED WITH THE LOSS OF 19 SAIL OF THE LINE
CAPTURED AND DESTROYED IN THIS MEMORABLE ACTION.
HIS COUNTRY HAS TO LAMENT THE LOSS OF HER GREATEST
NAVAL HERO BUT NOT A SINGLE SHIP.

So that was the great Battle of Trafalgar that saved the
British Isles from Napoleon's invasion. No wonder Nelson
was a hero. And his own father served under him. He felt
such a surge of pride. How different the old farmer in his
beat-up work clothes seemed from that brave young sea-
man manning the *Bellerophon*. Jim paused for a time to
ponder the meaning of it all: age and youth, the glories of
battle against the fruitfulness of farming.

He stepped back to look up once again at the great man atop his pedestal to whom no one passer-by gave a thought. At least his father would leave behind the farm and many offspring to grace his afterlife. But no pedestal, that's for sure. And he himself, what did he want indeed? A pedestal? A farm? No, he had left that behind. Money? Well, it might help. Offspring? What good would that do in this city teeming with thousands?

A tug at his elbow turned him, and he saw an elderly priest, stooped, arms folded together in a white robe, a face lined and somewhat flaccid, jowls drooping, evidence of good food and too little exercise. But kindly grey eyes.

"You like this monument, my friend?" the old priest asked in a decided French accent.

Jim nodded. "My father fought under Lord Nelson in the British Navy." He wondered how many other men here could say that.

"You know how we build dat here?" asked the priest. Without waiting for a reply, he went on, "I was just enter the order, me, after I become priest. I watch it build."

Jim frowned. "Who did you say built it?"

"L'Ordre de St. Sulpice. She be first monument to Nelson in all British empire. We give money." He laughed. "Oh yes oh yes oh yes, L'Ordre de St. Sulpice, we build in 1809. Me, I was twenty. I am nearly seventy. Yes, I am sure that surprise you."

Not in the least, thought Jim: what about my father? But he smiled politely.

"What many men, she get my age?" The old priest went on. "Maybe some priests, yes, we have one, eighty-two. But too hard here for people, they die soon."

True. But nonetheless astonishing: the French had

been beaten by Nelson — why would a French order of priests want to erect a monument to the victor? Jim voiced his doubts.

"Ah, *m'sieur*, you see, we try make big arrangement to get some land. This statue make us show our loyalty, how much we love this country here. It is our nation now. So," he spread his hands in an apologetic gesture, "we give monument. *C'est comme ça!*"

The first monument to Nelson in the empire. His father should know of this. Good reason, perhaps, to come visit his son after Jim had established himself with a wife and children and a proper house. Oh yes, that would be a subject of this next letter, no doubt. A monument to Nelson. Here in Montreal. How pleased his father would be!

Bidding the priest adieu, he continued his search, walking toward the Lachine canal where he had heard there were factories with good opportunities.

He walked along Notre Dame Street and passed again into Place D'Armes, where he saw three or four workers gossiping outside Dillon's coffeehouse and hotel. He stopped to listen, and then got up his courage to ask, "Good day to you, sirs, are you... waiting for someone?"

"Inside there, Thomas Molson," one of them said. "Saw him go in. Black overcoat, fine-looking old man for his age, sixty-two, I believe."

Well, thought Jim, a famous figure indeed. Perhaps he'd also wait around for a few minutes. But he asked, "Been waiting long?"

"I seen him going in ten minutes ago, so me friend David here, we decided to wait a spell. You know, them Molsons run steamers in the summers from Quebec to Montreal, there's talk of them opening a bank, lots of influence, so a job with them would be steady. We're gonna ask him, when he comes out."

Jim looked at him and frowned. Had he gone mad? The great man, with all his enterprises, would surely not be the person to accost here: it might just anger him. "Which is him in there?" Jim asked.

"Down at the back. Ye'll just have to wait till he comes out."

No time right now, Jim thought to himself, gotta make sure I get a good job to rise up in the world, so maybe one day, I'll be sitting in there, talking with him over a pint. "Thanks anyway." Off he went.

It was noon and he decided to find a brew and a snack. He wondered just how many lunches he could afford to buy with the few shillings his grandmother had given him; perhaps he should wait until he went back to the widow's where he'd eat some dried fish. He turned and walked down Mountain, past Gallery Square, and found himself by the banks of the Lachine Canal, now frozen solid.

The great Redpath Sugar building, already half built, looked a good prospect, especially as his post office ac-quaintance worked there. Surely they'd need someone strong and healthy. The wandering wrecks he'd seen look-ing for work seemed all underfed, often with frail wives dragging snivelling children. How far would they get when asking for work?

At the Redpath Sugar Refinery, the answer was no again. He might as well learn, he thought: building estab-lishments usually had their complements. And who might be hiring now, around Christmastime? Not a soul. Well, he owed it to himself to keep trying.

He walked a good way down the canal, crossed a lock or two, and stopped on the way home at each establishment: Gould's flour mill, and the bigger installation of Ogilvy's, Ostell's Sash and Door Works, a soap and candle-maker, a tinsmith, and other smaller places. Finally, late in the afternoon, admitting to being a bit depressed, he reached the Widow McMannus. So far, not a job in sight.

* * *

Jim had been finishing up the dried fish and boiled potatoes that the Widow McMannus had set before him when the door flung open revealing a lad, perhaps ten or twelve, small for his age surely, pale, drawn, shaken. Blood ran down one side of his head and onto his neck, staining his threadbare shirt. He let fall his light coat, hardly warm enough to protect him this cold night. Jim stood up in alarm.

Winnie crossed quickly to the lad. "Mikey, for the love o' God, what happened?" She tried to grab the boy in her arms but he pushed her roughly away.

Mikey stood frozen, looking about with large blue eyes set wide in a cramped face. Winnie opened her arms again, and this time he went into them. She hugged him and walked him over to the washbasin, where she pulled off his tattered undershirt and dropped it in a wash basket. She examined him, wiping his head and neck with a rag. Still the boy did not speak. Jim sat down to finish his potatoes; he knew better than to interfere. But he wondered what had happened.

"There now, it's not bad, it will heal. However did you do it?"

Mikey began shivering. She wrapped him in a blanket and then went to the only rocking chair in the sparse room, near the stove. She sat and gathered him into her arms.

Jim watched them. Lit by golden light from the lamp, she began to take on a new quality. Long, mousey brown hair formed a bun, but wisps and curls framed her drawn face with its large eyes like her son's. Her prominent nose protruded above thin lips, none of which betokened beauty. Approaching the end of her twenties, and a hard twenties it must have been, she had a frail look and a slight though voluptuous frame, but this image of the caring mother began to work on Jim, making her appear a deal more attractive.

The boy began to cry, silently at first. She rocked him, but then the sobbing grew into an angry grief. "Hush now, Mikey, it will be all right, it will heal soon."

"I don't care about the hurt," Mikey wailed in fury, "it's me shilling! They stole it offa me. Me whole day's work. Gone. I hate 'em, I hate 'em!"

"They stole your shilling?" Winnie closed her eyes and a flash of pain creased her worn features. "Now what'll we do?" She clenched her teeth, then looked down at the form scrunched in her lap. "I didn't mean that Mikey, don't worry, I'll get money, it won't be a problem. Love, now never you mind."

Jim lifted his head. "I got a shilling," he said. "I'll give it over." Winnie looked at him in astonishment. Jim shrugged, "You can put it against my next rent."

"You see, Mikey, there's always a friend to help. The Good Lord himself provides. He has all these years, and he will again tomorrow." She looked at Jim. "Thank you, sir."

"My name is Jim. I'd be obliged if you'd call me that, ma'am, because now I'm here, I'd like to be treated as someone you might count on."

Mikey had stopped his wailing, seemingly comforted, though Jim noticed his little hand still curled in an angry fist. "When I get bigger, I'll bash their heads like they bashed mine."

"Who did it?" Jim asked, surprised at his own vehemence.

"The bullies. They was waiting: three of them. I had no chance. They held me down. They beat me. They grabbed my shilling. They laughed at me." With that, he started to whimper once again.

"Now Mikey, it's over and done with. Just forget it now. Why don't I tell you a story, like I used to? About our heroes, in the days of old Ireland."

"No! I want to hear about me da again."

She glanced at Jim. "He always likes that story. He could never get enough of it," she said, by way of excusing what was to follow.

"I'd like to hear too, ma'am."

"I'm Winnie, you call me that, too." She began to rock. "Your father, Mikey, was a brave man, one of the bravest ever to come out of Ireland." She spoke almost by rote. "Before you was born, he had a job digging, working fifteen hours a day, six days a week, on that Lachine Canal, down Beauharnois way."

Mikey snuggled in and his thumb went into his mouth. Lying in his mother's arms, he let out a long sigh as if the anguish of the past would soon be forgotten. Jim could see that Winnie knew the pattern. She was definitely growing on him, the little lad in her arms, soon to be asleep behind a somewhat ragged curtain. So many travails both must have gone through.

"Well, Mikey, your father saved every cent, and I was working too. I served men after their work. Lord only knows how much beer they all drank! On the job too, I fear." She glanced at Jim. "They was almost always drunk when they came into the bar. But that's how I got to know the full story. Your father was too brave, he'd have never told.

"Well, the owners, they dropped the worker's wage from three shillings to two a day. Of course everyone grumbled. Those big, rich buggers, how they got away with it — downright scandalous! But so it went, and like as not to drop even more again. Oh Mikey, your father got so angry. But the men was all afraid, the job meant so much to them, and too many others trying to take it for themselves. Mighty poor job at that. Picks and shovels in the heat of the summer, all day long, from first light to last light, I never knew how they stood it. A lot of them gave up, some even borne home by their friends, sick to the death, but the stronger ones went on.

"One day, your father went up and spoke up for all the men, no one else would. And he got the owners to promise. They said they would put the money back up to three shillings if the men kept working. So on they worked. And then, devils that they were, they kept no promises at all. So your father called another meetin' and be the Lord Jesus, he took them awalkin', all of them, off the job. No work without proper pay — if you could call three shillings a day proper."

"So my father was the bravest of them all?"

"Your father was the bravest, yes Mikey, he led them all

out. There must've been two hundred of them, and they marched into the city."

"And that's when my father showed his mettle?" Mikey repeated, seeming to know the story.

"He certainly did, he stood up to all them owners, demanding workers their rightful pay." She paused, and Jim saw tears start into her eyes. She sighed.

"And then, Mama? Go on..." Mikey mumbled.

Winnie sighed. "And then... well, then the troops came, the Seventy-Fourth, and the Queen's Light Dragoons. They opened fire. Eight killed, and fifty wounded, they say, but they was many more. And the first one to die was your da, the Irish hero, Thomas McMannus. He was the hero of that strike. They all knew. Thomas McMannus. Why they didn't build a monument to him! Instead of to them buggers what built that canal." She looked down at the huddled form. He was peaceful, almost asleep.

Jim wondered at the lad's fortitude, and at the strength — and beauty, yes — of this little mother who cradled him. He'd heard nothing down on the Coast of such terrible goings on. But with no job nor prospects, the few precious shillings given by his grandmother soon finished, he had to find work, because now, he felt for the little lad, he felt for her, and with his desire growing — so grew his determination to stay and make a go of it all here in the big city.

Chapter Eight

"I'm sorry, James, nothing'll get me to agree to no school." Old George Robinson downed his piggin and wiped the last drops of beer from his bristly moustache and beard. "We already done a lot here in Shegouac. But there's more to do. We got our farms to think of. Ploughing and harrowing, what school teaches that? Time in class? Better spent learning how to cure a sick pig, I'd say, or when to plant. Lots o' time later for a school, but not right now." He rose to his feet with an effort. "Well, I'd best be off. Thanks a pile, Mrs. Alford."

Catherine smiled a reply, as James rose to see him out.

James could not believe it: all evening, he'd presented every notion he had prepared. Catherine had baked for two days for this supposedly impromptu meeting. But all he'd faced was stiff opposition.

Vid Smith, a tall, fine-looking sixty year old with a high forehead and chiselled features, swallowed his last morsel of scone and got up too. "I gotta say the same, James. I want no new expenses to be worrying about when I've got them twelve acres still to clear back behind. Look at Mrs. Alford here, she don't know her readin' and writin', but have you ever seen a finer mess of cakes and cookies and pies? By the holy gee whizz, how did she do that if schooling is so important? Beg pardon, ma'am, but this was a terble fine feast you and young Hannah put on today. It's too bad none of us agree with James, but maybe like Ol' George here said, the time's just not right."

Catherine acknowledged his compliments with a graceful smile. "Thank you, Vid," she said. "But just think, if you'd all agreed, you might have been treated to this every month!" As they chuckled, James nodded. "And," she added, "wouldn't it be lovely if your children could read the Bible on their own?"

Silence greeted that. "Well, Mr. Alford," Sam Allen, the youngest of the three, though not by much, with black hair and heavy features, leaned back in his chair, "that sure gives us something more to think about!" He looked at the others. "Maybe at the very least, we can think over what James proposed." He glanced at his host. "I know you and my poppa was the best of friends. He came here a year after you did — I was just a baby — and you helped him. So it hurts me to say no today. But you can count on me to do some thinking, and maybe even some talking, too."

James and Catherine helped the three men into their coats. He had never dreamed of such a response — even marked the calendar as being a red letter day when the trustees launched the school. Heavens! Imagine them saying: what's good enough for our fathers is good enough for our children. He knew they couldn't read or write themselves, so perhaps he'd been overly optimistic. He'd always had a love of learning himself, ever since he'd started doing those chores for the children's tutor while an underfootman at Raby Castle so that he could learn something himself. He had thought the desire for education was part of everyone's nature.

James saw them out into the starry darkness with a light wind blowing and a crescent moon showing them the way home over the snow. He paused in the open doorway, then closed it, came back through the outer kitchen and stood, shaking his head.

Catherine and Hannah were putting away the remains of the food. James could see they were pleased at how much had been eaten: a fine evening all around. And he also was pleased he had provided beer, over Catherine's objections. No one had gotten drunk, and the warm drink had helped them display their feelings openly. Much better that than hidden complaints voiced later.

His son-in-law Thomas Byers sat sipping the last of his tea and thinking. "But why did we ask Old George? And Vid? Why not the Nelsons? Sam is a great friend of yours."

James walked heavily forward and sat beside him. "You know they're Catholic. They have their own school."

"None here in Shegouac. If you're gonna build one, wouldn't they go for it?"

"Not how the system works on the Coast, Thomas, you know that. Protestants and the Catholics, they have to go to different schools."

Thomas shook his head, and rose. "Well," he said, "looks like maybe we lost the battle." He walked over to put on his heavy coat. "I'm sorry. But you know, I'll try talking to Old George's son, James, I know he'll be of mind to persuade his father. Specially with that there Bible idea. And Vid Smith's son, young Henry, he's got kids coming along, he might be in favour. We just have a lot o' work to do."

James nodded. But he was dejected and it showed. "Thank you, Tom, thanks a whole lot. I never expected all this, I dunno why. I guess the subject of a school never was thought of before. I mean, apart from church meetings, where nothing ever happens." He turned his head. "Catherine, you just did wonders, you and Hannah, you were both the best."

"I'm sorry, Poppa," Hannah said, "but as I told you, for me it wasn't that unexpected."

So now, James had neither his school, nor his son. What remained?

* * *

James found it hard to sleep. His mind kept going over the meeting: had he really done all he could? If he'd handled it differently, would it have changed things? No, probably not. New ideas, he'd seen how they'd been received in the Navy, and also in the Old Country. The status quo always prevailed.

He turned on his side and tried willing himself to sleep. But what was going on? For what reason had he been put on this good earth? He had done most things properly in life, and lived according to certain principles. Never had he lied or cheated anyone, so far as he knew, always relying on the Lord to provide the best judgement in any situation. So why was he now, with no heir, destined to leave behind only a farm headed for ruin, and children who would remember him, of course, but what else? Shouldn't that be enough? No, in his heart of hearts, he knew it was not. So how to make this failure — to provide his community with something lasting — tally with the image of a kind and responsive God?

And then in one awful flash, a thought struck him: What if God did not care?

Radical thought. And not unheard of, either. Several neighbours brought news of others in faraway climes who even questioned His existence. So what if, when he finally departed this world into the comforting arms of a Saviour, no arms were there? "What if he's not there?" he proclaimed out loud.

Beside him, Catherine stirred, reached out, touched him, and then moved closer. "Who's not there, my dear?" She laid a comforting arm across his chest. "Try and get some sleep."

"I have! What else have I been doing, the last hour?" Why had he snapped his response? But he was enwrapped in his own agony. It did not allow him to be gentle.

Catherine rolled over. "All right, James, better tell me what is troubling you."

"What if..." James just could not bring himself to mouth the terrible words.

"What if what, James?"

He struggled with his conscience. Would speaking the words make them come true? Or would it ease his mind? At any rate, he found himself saying, "What if God doesn't care? What if he's not even there?"

Catherine did not respond, at first. The sentence seemed to move through the inky darkness, threading among those dust motes that danced in the moonbeam slanting from the window onto their hooked rug. What response could there be?

"I'm sure he does, my dear." Catherine reached out to feel for his hand under the covers. "You've just got the soul sickness. That's all. Everything looks black. That is when the devil comes to take us. We must resist." She paused. James lay, hoping for more to console him. "When morning comes, you will feel better. This is always the hour now for dreadful thoughts. When the sun floods into our room tomorrow, they will all be gone. You'll be yourself again."

Myself again, James thought. Yes. Perhaps that was what was happening. But some instinct told him that once he had broached the unholy question, it would dog him. No, he had to reach a satisfactory conclusion. On the morrow, he would take up the Bible and read passages about doubt. That might do him good. At least, it was a start. He rolled over and clutched Catherine close. She turned on her side, and pushed herself into the crook of his body. With his arms around her, he soon fell into a deep, and now untroubled, sleep.

* * *

On the morrow, with the cow milked, eggs collected, cattle and oxen fed, the few sheep nestling down to chew their cuds in their pen, James sat reading his large Bible by the open fire. Catherine and Hannah were preparing dinner. A knock came at the door.

A visitor. So rare. James rose and went across to the back porch and opened the door. A letter.

He thanked the courier and invited him in for a meal as was the traditional courtesy. The man, tall and thin even under his bulky clothes, thanked them but had a good way to go, so he left.

James closed the door and announced, "Catherine, Hannah, Momma, we have a letter. From Jim!"

Excitement such as this should not to be taken lightly. They decided to have their dinners first. And then, over cups of tea, they gathered around while James sat by the fire and gingerly opened the manuscript.

"Dear Momma and Poppa,

So I got here. So much to tell. First, I met a doctor in Restigouche who told me about England. Medical things. A fellow could now go to McGill University and get a degree in medicine. Imagine that! I bet it's not too long before we all have doctors up and down the Coast. Though you'll have your doubts."

Catherine gave a laugh. "I have my doubts too, Jim." She smiled. Eleanor and Hannah kept their full attention on James. He went on to describe the medical developments the letter spoke of, and the amazing introduction of "ether" that put patients to sleep.

James paused and shook his head. "If only they'd had that in the Navy, how much suffering it would'a saved," he said. Then he read on, pausing to savour the paragraph about Nelson's monument, which pleased the others, too.

"That Kempt Road is really long, and empty. I only passed two or three coming past. I snowshoed the whole way, Poppa, you'd be proud of me. There are four places along the Kempt Road, the oldest up beyond Salmon Lake at its head called Pierre Trochu, at this end it's his son Marcel. But my best visit was Mr. Noble, at the Forks, halfway along. I was freezing, and I'd say he almost saved me.

"I made it to the Saint Lawrence. You know, that coast on the opposite shore is right out of sight. It's even wider than Chaleur Bay. Sometimes I got lucky with a ride in a sleigh. After a bit, I could see across to little white houses, and then, we crossed from Lévis to Quebec City, because the only road to Montreal is on the north shore, through Three Rivers."

James read them Jim's short account of the *canotiers*, which excited them all.

"Land sakes," Eleanor said, "the dear child, what has he been through?"

"Go on Poppa, go on," Hannah urged. "I want to know what happens."

"*At Montreal you have to cross the river again. It's over half a mile, I'd say, and you wait in a kind of building for the sleighs to take you. This part of the river, she ices up earlier than Quebec, and sleighs had already been crossing. Well, off we went, two sleighs, maybe half a dozen in each, with good fast horses.*

"*I got the sleigh with a smart driver. The other fella, I guess he didn't know too much. I reckon the two of them were having a race. But our fella, with a big, black beard, he'd been doing it a good while. The other fella got ahead, but when we reached the middle, our fella pulled up his team, and yelled at the younger driver. He looked back but paid no attention: he kept going straight across, like he was winning. Our fella, he turned us off the track and headed downstream.*

"*Well byes, first thing we knew, we heard cries and the other sleigh, she started down through the ice! Poppa, Momma, it was terrible. The woman and them were tumbling out of the sleigh, but that shelf of ice there, it just sank, and the whole lot of them, they just disappeared, pulled under, horses and all.*

"*In our sleigh we were standing up, me and another Englishman, we yelled at our driver, stop! We got to help.*

"*But our guy just held out his arms, shook his head, and kept going. At the time, we were angry but now I see he did the right thing. Nothing on earth could save those poor souls from under that ice. They was all gone. All the walk into town, I couldn't get the sight out of my mind. But here I am,*

I found this bit of attic, with a nice friendly widow, and I reckon I'll stay for a bit, and try my hand. I'll let you know how things go.

"*I miss the farm, and you both, and Hannah, even grandmother with her knitting. Tell her I wore her scarf the whole way and I was real glad of it. Bye for now. Your son, Jim.*"

James folded the letter and looked at the three of them. "The Lord be praised," he shook his head, "our son is safe."

All four sat without moving while they contemplated the picture Jim had drawn for them. "Well," Hannah started to get up, "we'd best be getting about our chores. No use worrying about people lost weeks ago."

"You're right, my dear." Her mother joined her in clearing the dishes, while Eleanor sat quite still in her chair. Then she looked across at James and spoke. "In the midst of life, we're in the midst of death."

"Never a truer word, Mother." Get over your black feelings, James thought to himself, they're drowning you, just like that sleighful. Jim'll fight his own battles. Time to fight your own.

Chapter Nine: Winter 1854

Jim climbed the ladder with what must have been the hundredth bag of gravel on his back. The others carried it on one shoulder, but he, having learned the trick from his father, used a tumpline, a loop of canvas around his forehead so that the weight was evenly distributed. And with each step to the top to dump the bag, the thought grew: what am I doing here?

Odd work in midwinter, but the only work available — and lucky to get it. After a full week waiting at the gates of this huge enterprise, trying to divine how the overseer picked his men, he had managed to convey his strength and ability. When a worker was carried out, overcome with cold and fatigue, Jim had seized his chance and now, here he was, two months later, earning a living. But what a pittance! These immigrants, having left Ireland with no great build up of strength, had been so beaten down by their Atlantic journey, their brushes with cholera and typhoid, and their ongoing struggle to survive, they had very little stomach for jobs as hard as this.

With every footstep ascending the ladder as if climbing into some higher awareness, the realization had grown stronger. Three and sixpence a day? Up and down, up and down. A donkey engine was said to be coming with the steam power to haul buckets up, but not until spring broke, when work on the bridge would begin in earnest. Eleven other men, four ladders, six pairs climbing up and down, enlarging a pit already bigger than a house for this first foundation of the bridge. On the deepening bottom below the frost line, other workers with picks loosened the earth and shovelled it into the canvas sacks. Hard work for all of them indeed: toward the end of every day they got progressively weaker, climbing slower, groaning more. Jim's legs felt like rubber. Apparently, the construction company, Peto, Brassey and Betts, had wanted to get a good start before the spring. And why not? All this labour begging to be put to work: weak, undernourished, but thirsting for money. What with his rent and food, at the end of a week Jim had little left over. But now, toward the end of February, he had accumulated a small stash. Indeed, more money than he ever saw at home. But then, at home, did they not work for themselves? And did they not trade their eggs for nails, flour for any item they couldn't make themselves? Always, they had enough to eat and comfortable beds in a pleasant house warmed by a happy fire.

Which is more than he could say here. He slept on a straw pallet in an icy attic with three other men: they sectioned the tiny space, no headroom to stand up. Yes, for breakfast, he ate a mess of porridge with molasses — and milk when he brought some home. Of course, he enjoyed staying in the home of a full-bosomed Irish lass to whom he had grown close over the last two months. That first vision of Winnie holding Mikey in her lap and soothing him to sleep had driven her charms into Jim's consciousness. Nowadays, he thought of little else.

Down the ladder he went to have his sack filled while he stood a moment to catch his breath. The wind on the surface was something fierce, the cold stung their noses and lashed their cheeks, but down here, the pit seemed oddly warmer. How much deeper did they expect to go? Well, the beginning buttress for a big bridge, he imagined they'd dig a long way down. The target was to have this pit finished by the end of April. And then, in warm weather, they would build the abutment with great blocks quarried at Pointe Claire.

Yes indeed, a good question, why *was* he doing all this? He hoisted the heavy sack of gravel onto his back and once again climbed the ladder, pausing for the climber above. The man seemed to be having difficulty; all day long, he had been pale and sweating. He had arrived from Ireland at the end of summer, and not worked until he had managed to land this job where workers were always giving up and being replaced. Jim hoped, as he got halfway up, pausing on each step for the man to go higher, the man would not fall on him.

By no means as easy to find a trade as he had expected. Did he really want to work in a foundry? Mikey worked in one, and had introduced him. But Jim demurred when he saw the conditions: a cavern from hell, flames, soot, grime, scorching heat, even in the middle of winter, white hot ingots dropped in vats of water. No sir, not how Jim would spend the rest of his life. And thus, his dream of excitement in a big new city was rapidly disappearing. Now, just try and hang on until he found out Winnie's intentions.

He saw her in the mornings at her most innocent, having just gotten out of bed and serving her son and the four boarders their porridge, bread, and molasses, for which, of course, they paid extra. His eyes followed her as she moved back and forth from her stove, a simple iron contraption much safer than those open fires back home. Stoves like that had become common in Montreal: it was the first thing Winnie told him she'd arranged with her barmaid's earnings.

Barmaids must make a good wage, he thought, enough to support her family of two. Why else did she disappear each evening so beautifully washed and fresh-faced and dressed in a blouse cut so low? In the mornings, when she placed Jim's porridge at his place, did she bend lower to him than toward the others, in what seemed an almost practised reach? That glimpse of her bosom portended such pleasure, should he ever be given the opportunity. But she was a good Catholic girl. No way of bridging that great divide.

He dumped the bag, paused, and went down the adjacent ladder. Four ladders, one brigade going up, another down, merciless work. By the end of each day, he felt no good for anything ever again, but after a night's sleep, often disturbed, he would once more face the fray. And today, was it not Saturday? The end of the week. Some of the other workers looked as though they might not even make it through till sunset. And this weekend was special: Winnie had agreed to let him come with her to the church she attended so faithfully. "I have to confess, Jim," she would say, "and I'm bringing Mikey along."

"Surely Mikey has nothing to confess."

"No, but we're preparing him for his first communion. Aren't we, Mikey?"

Mikey had looked up at her with his big, round eyes and nodded. Jim was not sure he approved of that whole process.

Down the ladder Jim went yet again. If there was no

future for him in Montreal, what about his attachment to Winnie, and her possible regard for him? What could he divine from her lilting laughter, her shy looks across the table, her relying on him more than the other boarders? The three workers came and went morning and night without paying her much attention.

As his bag was filled again, he asked himself for the umpteenth time, why can't she give me a signal that she cares? A practical signal. Something he could hang onto. Some affirmation that would leave no doubt. He hated being in this shadowy world where she would allow their hands to touch, she would laugh happily when he told stories, but hardly react when he brushed her shoulder or massaged her back, rarely looking up at him with any expression of real caring.

* * *

When the bell sounded, the men around him were groaning like lifeless shades in some curious manmade hell as they crossed to the paymaster to collect their shillings. Meek, dumb, too exhausted even to talk, they lined up in the frosty air, dreaming of green hills back in Ireland. But Jim knew also that, with coins in their pocket, hot soup in their stomachs, and having washed, they'd set the evening about its ears. Fights would break out: oh yes, Protestant and Catholic at it again, or perhaps neighbour against neighbour, worker against worker in some perceived grudge. Smashing each other with whatever was to hand. He wanted none of that. The other three attic boarders would not be home for their soup tonight: they usually returned late Saturdays, very late, even toward morning, often without the money for their rent, having spent it on spirits or on girls prepared to sell their skimpy charms for a shilling or two. Winnie was wise, he thought, to get their week's rent in advance.

This Saturday night he had Winnie all to himself. Mikey, at the end of a hard week, was too tired to do anything but sleep. During the long walk from work, Jim kept daydreaming about her as usual. Finally he reached the Griff, turned up Seminaire, then right along Ottawa Street past workers' shanties, turned up Murray to the patched wooden fence of their tiny yard with its outhouse. He banged on the door.

She opened it. She had changed early tonight and looked to Jim even more bewitching: hair done up in its bun, the curls falling in little ringlets to frame her face, the shapes of her ample bosom clear beneath the low, revealing blouse. She helped him out of his coat while Mikey sat at the table finishing the last spoonful of soup. Jim held his breath at her closeness but she moved quickly on to her fire.

"I'll just wash up." Jim went to the corner basin. She didn't reply.

"Can I have some more of me soup?" Mikey asked.

"Not now, Mikey, time for bed. I'm making you a big surprise breakfast in the morning. Go get some sleep now."

Obediently, Mikey went into the water closet under the steep attic steps and shut the door. The slop pail got emptied every night and morning in the outhouse. Jim proceeded to wash himself, more thoroughly than usual. He wanted to look nice when he sat down alone with Winnie for supper. The other evenings, the three boarders were there, slurping their soups, shovelling in their potatoes, bread, and molasses, and sometimes if lucky, chunks of meat. She seemed careful not to show any favouritism, so that none would get jealous. Or did she think of Jim no differently: another mouth to feed, another rent-giver, just like the others? He longed to know her true feelings.

Mikey stumbled out of the water closet, crossed the room and fell into his cot behind a curtained partition. He'd be asleep in no time, Jim knew. He glanced from his wash basin to Winnie, who was slicing some meat which she dropped into a frying pan. He could hear it sizzle. He worked all week to absolutely no purpose save for Saturday nights when he could look forward to this quiet hour with Winnie. He felt he could stay forever, not even eating, just looking across the table at her. But then she'd leave for work, sometimes staying away long into the night. He marvelled at her stamina.

After he dried himself, he climbed into the attic, crawled on his hands and knees across to his straw pallet and put on the clean shirt he'd washed the weekend before. Taking out a comb, he worked at his tousled hair to look his best when he went down.

Descending the ladder, he saw Winnie standing at her stove, seemingly tense. Was something up? He stood hesitantly at the foot of the ladder.

She turned. "I got to talk to you."

What did this herald? She had not talked this way before. He nodded, watched her as she crossed to her table and sat.

Suddenly she burst into tears. Oh Lord, he thought, whatever has happened? He had never seen her like this before: so out of character. He crossed hurriedly, bent down awkwardly to cradle her weeping form. But she gave no response.

"Dearest Winnie," he said as he came around to sit facing, "whatever is the matter?"

She wiped away her tears and looked up with those large, expressive eyes. "They're throwing me out."

Jim sat back, stunned. "But why? Whatever happened?"

She shook her head, and more tears came.

"What is it Winnie? Please tell me," he said in a voice that almost broke. He reached out to take her tiny hands in his rough fingers.

She cleared her throat. "The last while, they raised me taxes. So I put off paying. Finally, they came and said, I got to pay Monday morning or next week we're all outta here. I don't have enough saved." She looked up. "I got nowheres to go."

Jim sat silently, wondering. What could he do? It hurt so much to see her cry. "How much do you need?"

"If I give them two pounds, that'll do. Then in two weeks, I can give them the rest. But they won't wait. They said, it's two pounds Monday, or out."

Thoughts churned in his head. That was more or less what he had saved over the last two months. For his trip back on the steamer — or perhaps, for both their tickets, come spring. He'd been hoping that, once he got up the courage to broach the subject, she might join him.

"Don't worry, Winnie, I got something. I don't know how much. But you can have it all. We can't get you thrown out, now can we? That would mean," he added lamely, so that it wouldn't look too pointed, "I'd have to go too, wouldn't I?" He rose. "You just wait here."

She watched as he crossed to get his coat and cap and went out into the night, which had begun to snow, lazy flurries. He walked along the side of the house, opened the rickety back gate hung high enough so that it cleared the snow. He crossed to the outhouse and going inside, felt inside the hole onto a ledge where he kept his small purse. He'd been smart enough not to keep it upstairs in the attic, not after he'd noticed his sack had been rearranged, as if someone had been reaching inside.

He pulled out the small cowskin pouch, took out the money in the darkness, and then put back the empty purse. How long would it take to fill that again?

He came out, closing the outhouse door, three steps across the yard, out the gate, down the squared-beam walls of the shack, and in the door again. Winnie sat at the table as if she had not moved.

He sat across from her and reached out his hand. The coins he placed on the table.

She looked at them and then up to him, her eyes still wet. She reached out to clasp the coins in one little hand. As he looked into those big blue eyes, he found himself asking the question he had long been wanting to voice: "Do you love me, Winnie?" he blurted out.

She looked up at him. "With all my heart!"

She said it with such feeling that his head reeled. The answer — he had it now. And even more eloquently than he could ever have imagined. No doubt about it, no matter what, he would remain at her side.

Chapter Ten

Jim walked in, took off his coat, hung it on a peg and turned. Winnie had changed and looked just gorgeous. "I heard you was fired."

Jim nodded. "How did ye know?"

"It's all over town. They stopped work on the bridge for the spring. Did you bring your rent?"

"I did." He paused. "But Winnie, I was wondering..."

"Your rent, that's all I need."

He looked at her. No word of consolation? No sympathy? Probably she's too tense, he decided. But all the same, he felt himself oddly reverting to his former self before this obsession had overwhelmed him. "Winnie, I've been thinking..."

"Not a good thing, Jim. Never think too much, not good for you." He could see a certain hurt starting in her eyes. "Best not to, ever, I always sez. Otherwise..."

"I'm not sure I can stay in Montreal, Winnie."

"You got to! Them others, they're going to be out the door, too. I can't lose all me lodgers all at once. What'll I do? You've got to stay!" Her lip quivered. Was she going to cry again? "Please, Jim."

He reached out to her, and she came forward with a rush of emotion, but then stopped.

Maybe, like last time, he thought, if she sees my

money, it'll calm her. If she knows I've got enough to get us home. Somehow, Jim knew that today was the day of resolution. The Good Lord had thrown him a challenge. Now, he must respond. "Wait here a minute." He started to go to the door and get his coat.

"Wait! Where are you going?"

"I'm not going anywhere, Winnie. I'm just going outside for a second."

"Jim, just stay awhile, I made ya dinner. Why don't we sit and eat together." She smiled bewitchingly.

Jim looked at her. Was there a note of hysteria in her eagerness? Well, he had decided: calm her down, show her his money, it worked last time. He shook his head, threw on his cap, and quickly went out. Straight down to the yard, in at the gate, over to the outhouse. Reaching into the hole, he found his purse, drew it out. So light? In the darkness, he opened it. Nothing.

His money had been stolen.

He leaned back against the door. How would he get back home now? How could he bring her with him if he had not a cent? How could they manage? Did it mean he'd have to go look for more work? He felt his chest heaving — such a shock. He'd have to think.

Walk a bit first. Yes, that would give him time. The words of his father came back again, "Trust in the Lord." So he did. He went out the rickety gate, turned down the street in the opposite direction to the house. A ten-minute walk, that would clear his mind.

Who on earth had taken it? One of the lodgers? You never knew who you could trust. He'd find the fella and give him such a beating. But none of them had seen him put his money in there, or go get it. He had always hidden it "when nature called." Except once. Yes, when he had gotten it for Winnie. He stopped, heart thumping even louder. His Winnie the thief? Impossible. But who else? He turned and headed back.

When he came in, she was busy at her stove. She didn't turn. "Jim, I've got you a real nice dinner. Come now and sit. And we can talk."

Jim stood looking at her. "My money's gone."

Winnie turned with the steaming plate and came across to put it down. "Well, Jim, I've a lot of faith in you, you'll find it and get another job, don't worry. You're a strong man, honest, too, I know it won't be long." She put his plate down on the table, revealing more of her white body than ever before, and reached out. "Just give me your week's earnings for the rent, and we'll sit together, side by side, and have a nice chat."

"Chat about what? Where my money is?"

"What money?"

"The money. I saved it so we could both leave together. I'm still making that offer." He stepped forward to take her hands. "Come with me, Winnie."

She backed away, shaking her head. "But this is my home, Jim. You can't ask me to leave my home. "

"You may have to leave it, if I go, if all your lodgers go. No more rent. How will you feed Mikey? And pay me the two pounds I gave—" He stopped himself. "Down on the Coast, we've got a good house, big enough for all of us, and lots of food. Momma and Poppa would surely welcome you. Come with me. Please, Winnie."

She stared at him. She seemed about to accept. Then she spoke. "We've already talked about that, Jim — it's not what I want. Now just give me the rent, and we'll say no more."

The rent, well, yes, she did need it, if the others were leaving. They'd not be so stupid as to give her rent when that wouldn't leave anything for food next week. So maybe he should just give her the two weeks. It was actually all he had, these last wages.

Winnie looked at him, as if she knew he was softening. "That's it, Jim. You stay with me here, we'll let the others go, we'll be alone, it'll be so nice — I'll make it nice, you'll see." She reached out her hand again. "Come along, hand over the rent."

Jim reached in his pocket and took out the money. She did need it. He looked into her wide, blue eyes. They were pleading. But behind them, he sensed a rare steeliness.

He put his hand back. "If you go steal my money, why would I give you more?"

"Oh Jim," she cried, "you don't believe that?" And then, as easily as before, she sat at the table and dissolved in tears.

Jim stood without moving. Just how she had done it before. Well, this time, he told himself, be strong. Just wait.

She allowed herself to sob broken-heartedly, and then, oddly enough, rose and quickly wiped her eyes.

"All right, if you're so smart, keep your rent money. I don't care, I'll find someone else, you just watch." With that, she turned, put on her heavy shawl, and went out into the night.

Jim looked down at his plate. He was hungry. But now, he wanted to know where she was going. Why not follow and find out where she worked?

He grabbed his hat and tore out the door. At the end of Murray Street he saw her hurrying form. He strode after her, buttoning up his coat and winding his grandmother's scarf around his neck. Winnie turned right, toward the upper level where the better classes lived. He lost her for a while, then turned a corner, and yes, there she was on Mountain Street, still climbing. He followed her across St. Jacques and then St. Antoine, up the hill, until she finally turned in at a drinking establishment.

Now what?

He waited in a doorway, hidden from the gas lighting, while he made up his mind what to do next. So that's where she worked as a barmaid. He moved off, to keep walking, keep thinking. He did want to see her, just once more, before heading back to the Gaspé. For that's where his path must now lead. After some anguish, he made himself turn and approach the pub again. He plunged in.

Winnie was nowhere in sight. The pub was crowded with drinking men, mostly well dressed, so he felt decidedly out of place. He pushed through to the bar and ordered an ale. The barmaid looked at him askance, but seeing his coin, pulled him a draft of Molson's.

He made himself wait while he listened to the mostly military men discussing their sleigh rides. "You know Hugh, poor fellow? He and his muffin ended up in a snowdrift last night..." Their laughter surrounded him. "First time out with a muffin and thought he knew it all. They gave him rather too snappy a horse, I presume."

As they chatted on, he discovered that "muffins" were girls whom they brought out on sleigh rides for the devilry, mostly travelling over Mount Royal at high speeds.

A flight of stairs at the back caught his eye: a man and another "barmaid" were heading up. He kept watch, and soon another military man came down, buttoning a jacket.

What could it all mean? His mind tormented him. A few
seconds later another "barmaid" followed — his Winnie,
arranging her hair. The man turned back to smile his satisfaction at her.

Jim put down his half-finished tankard and tore out the
door. *So* obvious, what they had been up to. So much, he
thought, for the city and its delights, where a woman who
tells you she loves you "with all her heart" turns out to be
a common trollop.

*　*　*

His troubles had only begun. He packed hurriedly, head
spinning, put on his heavy coat, loaded his pack onto his
back and out he went. He should have eaten the meal
left sitting on the table and allowed himself a good night's
sleep but he couldn't wait, couldn't think of anything but
escape. How could he have been so gullible? But then,
had he ever known anything like that in Shegouac? Of
course not. So don't be too harsh on yourself, he argued.
At any rate, with addled mind and unplanned speed, he
set off homeward through the soon-to-be melting snows.
Don't think, just keep going, he told himself, but he felt so
jangled inside, so disorganized, his whole balance needed
readjusting.

The island of Montreal, some twenty miles across and
sixty miles long, sat in the middle of the great St. Lawrence,
which had to be crossed at Bout de l'Ile — the way for travellers to Quebec City and points east. Jim left the city ramparts and headed along the well-travelled road. All through
the agonizing night he trudged, with no sleighs passing for
a ride. His recent revelation kept paining — love always

dies hard, he consoled himself, but then, had it really been love? More an infatuation, perhaps, compounded by the unfamiliar way of life. And based, he now decided, on nothing more than glimpses of lovely breasts and flashes of a bare knee as Winnie had laced up her boots of a morning.

Sometime before dawn he arrived at the terminus, an aged wood building with a simple veranda and hitching rail. Already, a young man and wife were waiting there with their two year old, the three huddled against the rough logs. From here, they could dimly see north across the icebound river. Safety in numbers, Jim hoped.

The man looked up at Jim with mournful, pleading eyes.

Jim asked, "What time does the first sleigh go across?"

The man shook his head. "Whatever time, unless someone lends us a couple of pennies, we can't be on it, we'll have to walk. Soon as it gets light enough."

If it's only a couple of pennies, thought Jim, why not? He knew what it felt like to be penniless. "I might be able to help."

The man glanced up briefly, then sunk back and closed his eyes. All three were exhausted, Jim could see.

Soon, an older and sick-looking man joined them. He came, sat on the bench and gave a long sigh. Then he broke out in a racking cough.

"Think it'll be a long wait?" Jim asked, when his eruption subsided. "My name's Jim, by the way."

The emaciated man shook his head. "Maurice." He held out his hand, and Jim shook it. "They start early. *Trop chaud pendant la journée.* Too hot when the sun, she rise. *La débâcle*, she come any day."

"The breakup?" Jim asked. "This sheet of ice is soon going to break?"

The dawn was already rising downriver to their right, as the man nodded. *Pas franchissable pendant des semaines.* For weeks, maybe, no boat for cross here. *Non, m'sieur!*"

Oh no, Jim thought. He couldn't wait. His week's salary and modest bonus would not cover that and still be enough for the six or seven hundred miles of slushy roads, buying bread and cheese and the occasional bed. He just had to cross today.

He settled himself for the wait, and soon a clerk turned up who unlocked the door and motioned for them to enter. Once in from the icy night, the group felt better. They sat on rough benches to await the sleigh's arrival, while the sun made its appearance.

The wait seemed interminable. The older man grew more and more agitated. He glanced at Jim.

"The longer we wait," Jim muttered, "the warmer it'll get."

Maurice nodded, and got up to speak to the surly clerk, who shrugged and then talked rapidly in French.

Maurice turned. "He say, must be too dangerous. No sleigh."

Jim frowned. "Why didn't he tell us that when he got here?"

"Qu'est-ce que tu fais, toi?"

"Me? I sure can't wait around; I've just got enough for the trip home. Gaspé, it's a long way." He paused. "We'd better walk." But should they? He remembered the crossing with the *canotiers,* and how it had traumatized him, giving him bad dreams. Those black waters seemed to hold a special terror for him: could he overcome it now?

The young man rose quickly. "How safe will it be?" He bounced his child, who was just waking up.

"Well, if they've been using the sleigh until yesterday, surely the ice'll be strong enough to hold us today," Jim found himself saying. And yes, was this not true?

Maurice nodded, and broke out coughing. "But she be dangerous. *Très dangereux!*" The husband flinched.

Jim noticed. "Since you have that child, maybe you should stay and go back home." And he should himself, he thought, wavering.

"We got no home. My wife's cousin, they wrote us from Quebec, we can stay with them. If we don't go now..." He gestured. "Nothing left to eat, nowhere to sleep, we'll have to take our chances, too." Beside, his wife rose and clutched at him. Jim could see she was terrified.

Well, would he let this superstitious fear overwhelm his good sense? If she was going, why not he himself? "All right then, let's go." Jim started for the door, and they all followed him out, stopping to look across the melting ice, a clearer view with the sun climbing over the horizon. A long way to the other shore. Would they make it?

Jim felt frozen but made himself stoop to lace on his snowshoes. Then saw the trail ahead was packed hard. Quickly, he put them on his back, and set off on foot — just do not think about it, he told himself, and in twenty minutes you will be over and safe.

But after they had walked quickly along the trail for some minutes, an unmistakable rumble could be heard from upstream.

Maurice listened, shook his head. *"Dépêchons-nous!"* He half ran, half limped, with Jim following, the couple and child hurrying behind as best they could.

The rumbling faded. They made good time; the ice seemed firm underfoot. Jim took in the mountains of ice: great slabs, having crashed into others, rose on their sides, forming jagged contours across the whole surface. The track made by the sleighs wound among these great mis-shapen hillocks.

Jim avoided thinking about what would happen if the river actually broke. Such mayhem. Drowned for sure, all of them.

After about ten minutes, with the older man coughing furiously and the couple falling further behind, the distant roaring enveloped them. Jim looked upstream, but still saw nothing untoward. He glanced at the family: weak from not having eaten, they were all having trouble. Should he wait and give them a hand? They were now in the middle of the river. Beside them, Maurice scrambled up one of the higher slabs of ice to look upstream.

He pointed and then waved: "She start to break, way upstream."

Jim waved the lagging couple to hurry. They were not doing so well. Quickly he ran back, grabbed the frightened woman by the hand, lifted the child from her husband, and forged ahead. Without his child, the man made better time. Maurice stayed on his pinnacle, obviously wondering: cross? Or run back? As Jim and the couple passed, he pointed. "She come down behind!"

Oh Lord, thought Jim, and the woman gave a frightened cry.

"But maybe she okay ahead. We try!" Maurice skidded down the ice boulder on his rear end and set off at a fast clip.

"Don't worry, ma'am, don't worry, he knows the river,

we're all in this together, just keep going." Jim, with the child in his arms, dragged the woman as best he could and tore across the ice. "Faster, please!" Her husband also grabbed her and together they made better time.

Jim heard the roaring grow. He turned. Behind them, as if Armageddon had struck, a tremendous surge of black water broke over the ice, heaving the floes on top of each other, piling the shards higher, smashing others. The river was finally breaking through the ice, a powerful wall of black water swamping all before as if a dam had broken.

The opposite shore was still faraway. Behind them, the torrent tore downstream. How long would the ice ahead hold?

"Check again!" Jim called to Maurice as he paused with the child in his arms. Maurice scrambled up another crag. The ice began to shake under them.

"She open ahead," Maurice gasped. "We leave dis track. We head for downstream. Still good that way." He gestured to their right.

A tremendous jolt shuddered the giant floe and Maurice fell tumbling down the slab with a loud cry, and lay with his leg twisted under. Jim handed the child back to the husband. "Run with her!" He pushed the woman on as he crossed to Maurice, grabbed him, put his arm around his waist, lifted him, and helped him hop forward with an agility born from the impending crisis.

Sure enough, behind them another great surge of water threw jagged mounds of shelf ice across the former roadway. Ahead, too, the whole solid covering was breaking up — black water began to intervene between them and the opposite shore. The noise alone was enough to terrify anyone. Jim felt his panic rising, but he'd beaten the black current before and he'd do it again. His father's words came back: the only way to save yourself is to stay calm and think straight.

Jim yelled directions to the couple ahead and they veered off the sleigh track toward downstream. The floating ice floe seemed for the moment secure — not breaking up as they ran. Jim and Maurice overtook the couple. "Watch for cracks in the floe!" Jim shouted.

No sooner said than a giant slit in the ice sliced open behind them, right in front of the family.

The woman screamed, separated from her husband by a widening gap, now two feet. He reached out, she leapt, he caught her, then they both started to slip into the icy current as the lip of ice tipped. But the husband lurched back, tugging her over, through the water, regained his footing and pulled her on, as they slithered to safety.

"Give me the child!" Jim grabbed the kid so roughly it screamed. He didn't care. In his right arm he held the child, in his left he helped the injured Maurice as best he could. They dashed across their floe as it drifted downstream on the current. For the moment, the black water was on either side, but not rising to attack over the floe.

"How long will it hold?" the father cried out.

"Don't think. Just go fast. We're going to make it." But for the life of him, Jim did not see how. He had never floated on an ice floe in his life, and he had no great faith in its safety.

Then Jim saw their floating floe heading for a shelf of ice jutting out into the current from the far shore. "She gonna hit!" yelled Maurice. "She gonna hit for sure."

But that shelf ice was attached to the shore. After it smashed their floe, what then? Would their own ice-pan capsize? Or continue on downstream?

Smaller bergs jostled and collided with each other, all the while making a horrendous noise.

"When she hit, we jump! *Comprends?*"

"Damn right," said Jim. "Soon as she touches, leap across, no matter what. Get to the shore ice. It's our only chance."

The black water channel ahead narrowed. But floes kept crashing into this floe, tipping it and turning it aside, as the noise continued.

Just a few feet from the edge, the four stopped.

"Too thin?" Jim gasped.

"*Sais pas*. But we go. We go for sure." The black channel narrowed a bit. They all tensed for a run and a leap, not knowing if it would be to safety or death.

Then the floe struck, the jolt threw them flat. Their pan reared up over the shore ice. With the surface slanted steeply they picked themselves up somehow, the child screaming wildly, and on all fours scrambled up to the lip, a good six-feet above the shore shelf. Behind them, the black water surged upwards, trying to drag them down.

Jim managed to boost the older man up over the edge where he clung, looking down. Then Jim got the woman up, and finally the man with his kid. Just in time, for the whole floe shuddered, and began to slip backwards into the black current, taking them all with it.

Jim rolled over the edge and dropped. He reached up his arms. The father held out his child, let it fall onto Jim and then, because not holding on, tumbled backwards.

The wife screamed, "I can't. I can't jump."

"So stay and get drowned!" Jim yelled to shock her into action as he reached for Maurice.

The husband recovered somehow, and clambering up, fell heavily.

Maurice quickly turned on his stomach, hung down his legs and let go. He gave a wild scream of pain as his leg twisted under again.

Jim, the child still in his arms, grabbed Maurice and manhandled him away from the edge. Jim and Maurice kept heading for the bank as the husband pleaded, "Jump, Millie, jump! Please!" He lifted his arms as the floe slipped surely back into the frozen river.

Jim could not wait: he had the child and older man to think of. They kept slithering along as the ice grew firmer under their feet.

He turned to look back. Before jumping, Millie had lain down sideways — but too late, as her whole floe slid under the black water and the man screamed, reached out to her. He made as if to jump in.

"No!" Jim yelled. "Your boy, think of the boy."

The man covered his eyes to hide the sight of his disappearing wife, then turned toward them and, with an agonized cry, hobbled along to his own safety.

"*Regarde!*" Maurice pointed.

On the bank upstream, Jim saw figures running down toward them. Rescue was at hand. He slowed down, his panic controlled, and began to relax. For the second time he'd faced danger, and won.

But now five or six hundred miles lay between here and home. Would his luck hold out?

Chapter Eleven

"I just have a feeling," Catherine said, "that Jim will be along any time now. He won't like it there. I've always known it."

"I hope you're right." But James had his own doubts. He bent with his shovel to clear the makeshift drain that directed the runoff each spring, diverting the rush past the house and down their driveway toward the road, a snowy ridge packed hard by passing sleighs. Catherine worked with a smaller spade at the lower end.

Spring had brought its usual deluge, streaming down from the melting snowbanks drifted high against the hill behind the house. Patches of barren ground had appeared, soon to spring to life with fresh crocuses and a fresh crop of vegetables from seeds planted in their garden, eyes cut from potatoes, and peas, parsnips, and cabbage. Wheat sown in autumn fields would push up through the moist earth nourished by manure spread by James who stood tall upon its dark pungent mound in his oxcart to fork goodness across the acres that the plough would then turn and harrow flatten, in another rich and fruitful season on his beloved Gaspé Coast.

But for himself, the seasons might be drawing to an end. Even with a breeze from off the warming fields bearing messages of fruitfulness, his aged frame felt more in tune with the stiff trees showing no hint of buds on their cold black branches, although for them, summer was on its way.

And worse, what would happen to his farm? "The old homestead" as the children called it — after all, had it not been their vital centre for forty years? — would it fall into disuse? Nothing about it looked old. In fact, it seemed so young, newly cleared, even after so many seasons rolling past, freezing rain, tempest and storm, frost and thaw, the fences of stumps easily weathering any onslaught winter could throw at them, guarding the boundaries of his acres as they would for decades to come. Yesterday on his first spring tramp, he'd seen that he'd have to put up a new fence down in the Hollow between him and the Nelsons, but on the whole, the farm was ready for another bountiful year. Was it all going to waste?

They were interrupted by the appearance of his grand-daughter Jane who came hurrying over across the raised path beaten from the Byers next door. Catherine and he glanced at each other. What was up?

"Little Joey is sick," she called from afar.

Catherine thrust her spade in a snowbank. "What's wrong with him?" She quickly adopted what James saw as her professional manner. Known in these parts for her healing abilities, she had kept all but one of their children alive, a tribute to her powers, and to the medicine pouch, long since depleted but often replenished, that James had gotten from Magwés. All that Micmac wisdom had been passed on to Catherine. She had even come a couple of times with him to visit the band in Port Daniel and met again Full Moon, her brother, One Arm, and her son, Brightstar, now a handsome and accomplished fisherman and trapper, likely to inherit from his uncle the chieftainship of the band. Catherine had spent a lot of time with those Micmac healers and medicine women.

It had been hard for her, that first trip, James knew, for it brought back memories of the earlier pain on learning that James had married before. That secret would die with them both: no one would learn of John's ancestry, and Catherine had even told a little white lie at the office in New Carlisle, and to the census takers when they passed by. Officially, John was her second child.

"Me brother's terble hot and crying, and he even started to cough!"

James's heart sank. Not whooping cough! That disease had taken so many of the Shegouac children including, thirteen years ago, their own daughter Elizabeth. Catherine saw the alarm in her husband's face. "Now listen, you two, don't go jumping to any conclusions! Of course he coughs. He has a lot of mucus from the crying. We'll get him right as rain in a few hours. Go home, quick, and tell Mariah I'm coming with my bag." She smiled at the child, a warm and certainly calming look that had its desired effect.

"Oh thanks, Grandma. I'll run right off and tell them."

James marvelled at his wife as she hurried into the house. "Tell Hannah to give me a hand with the shovel," he called after her. Just a bit more work and he'd have this spring runoff under control.

* * *

James had just gotten into bed when he heard a knock at his bedroom door. "Come in."

Hannah entered. Earlier, to accommodate the growing children, they had added another modest side building accessible through the back wall of the house, and divided this room into four. He had been thinking about taking down one of the partitions now the children had left, to give them more space, but then decided against it: Jim and any wife might need that for themselves. Oh-oh, Jim again — if only he'd stay forgotten.

Hannah was looking particularly vulnerable. "Is anything wrong?" he asked.

"With Momma sleeping over at Mariah's, it must mean little Joe's in a bad way."

"Not at all. It just means someone should be looking after him during the night. You know, Mariah has to rest; we don't want her getting sick as well, do we? Far better your mother take over. You know how often she spends the night at others' homes."

"But that's my little cousin, Joe, he's only five months and so cute. What if he dies?" James could see she was about to cry.

James opened his arms and his daughter, even though now twenty-two, came over and lay for a moment, letting her tears flow as if she were a little girl again. Nothing like the good strong arms of a wise daddy when you're in trouble.

She soon calmed down. "Poppa, would you read me a story?"

James was put in mind how he'd gather the children around and read to them: the best way to get them interested in learning to read for themselves. "Of course, of course." But he realized, without a school, all his good intentions went for nought. What about his children's children, too? The thought made his ire rise — he just *had* to get that school built.

Hannah went to the books in one corner and brought over three or four. James glanced at the covers of *The Last of the Mohicans* and *Two Years before the Mast.*

"I can't read which one it is," Hannah said, "but I want Peter Parley."

"Peter Parley it will be." He handed the others back and picked out that one. "Now you come lie beside me and promise me you'll shut your eyes and try to drift off. You can go back to your own bed when you're ready to sleep."

Hannah dutifully climbed on the bed beside him, and curled up.

James began: *"When the winter had passed away, with its snow and its dreary winds, and the green grass was already springing up in the meadows, the two robins were always heard on their favourite tree. Early in the morning, one of them would ascend to the highest bough, where he would pour forth his lively little song, and at evening he would again take his lofty seat, and repeat the same strain, with almost endless variations."*

Hannah reached out and touched him, as if to stop the reading. "Poppa," she said, "I've changed my mind. I wish you had taught me to read when I was little. I think I would have enjoyed that. Your school is a very good idea." With that she shut her eyes again, and James continued his reading, pleased at her remark. If only the rest of Shegouac would be that easy.

* * *

Long after Hannah had gone back to her own bed and was sleeping soundly, James found himself tossing and turning, wrestling with doubts.

Going back over his life, he'd certainly had some escapes that were nothing short of miraculous. He'd been
attacked by a mother bear and Tongue had rescued
him. He'd thwarted a cougar attack and been healed by
Magwés: the scar still itched on occasion. And then, after
heading into certain capture and a grisly punishment on
the *Bellerophon*, his Captain had surprisingly given him
his freedom. So many times in the intervening years, he
had escaped danger and lived. But, on reflection, these
did not really provide the proof for a living God he needed.
The inescapable finality of the end was approaching so
rapidly...

As Catherine would say, had she been beside him:
you'll feel better in the morning. But then, was not the
night a time for questioning? Soon, he would be going into
the darkness forever. Or into the light. If only he could
arrive at some assurance of which it would be. Speak to
me, he asked, please Lord, speak.

In the vast darkness of his bedroom, James lay and
waited for the response.

But as he looked out into the void, it formed itself into
great jagged cliffs, icy chasms that were charcoal-black as
scorched logs, a vision of desolation. Nothing moved, not
even himself — as if the flames of hell had passed through
and left their charred remains. Such was a view of life
without God.

And what about that stranger he kept glimpsing in their
rumpled mirror? That lined face with its great drooping
moustache and its white mane and even tufts sticking out
from his ears, and that old floppy hat. Who on earth was
that? Where was the upright clean-shaven Midshipman?
Where had young James gone? He felt so much more akin

to that young sailor who had swum through paralyzing icy waters to safety and gone on to build his cabin by the brook.

A short trip at the best of times, as old Will Garrett use to say, sailing these seas of a paltry lifespan. Why should he be "Ol' Poppa"? Why not young Poppa? His brain was still sharp as a gibbin' knife. All right, so maybe the limbs didn't always do what he wanted. But whyever did the Good Lord invent this cruel joke called age? Surely, when you spend seven decades on earth, the wisdom you have acquired striding down endless corridors of weeks, passing along the vast roadways of year-laden decades, all this — was it accumulated only to be crammed into a rough pine box and consigned to the cemetery of St. Andrew's in New Carlisle? No church yet in Shegouac — but no! Don't start diverting your energies from getting that school.

And the same question applied to his farm. For what reason on earth had he worked so hard from dawn till dusk, just to let all this fall back into wild bushland from which those dense spruce forests would again spring?

There seemed no answer. Perhaps he should not worry. Perhaps he should let the Good Lord take care of the farm on his behalf. But did He even exist?

Get up, he ordered, you'll feel better. But last time, he had just ended up sleeping by the open fire downstairs. Best stay tossing and turning on the soft mattress Catherine had stuffed with her chicken feathers. Best stay under the woollen blanket she had woven from their sheep. Soon, they'd get shorn again, yes, he'd better ask young Henry Smith to come and help. Washing fleeces, what a dirty business! And he had no doubt that Edward Hayes would soon ask for Hannah's hand and off she'd go.

Why else would he be building a house? And then, the house would be truly empty. Just him and Catherine, for even the tough Eleanor would soon pass on. Yes, as always, he came back to the same dead end. No Jim. And no God. Spinning circles, leading nowhere. Unhealthy, even he could see that. But how to stop?

Only by finding a solution. So keep on the quest, because he knew the Holy Grail, if he ever found it, brought peace. He turned on his side, fluffed up his down pillow, and just as he began to fall sleep, he heard a banging on the front door downstairs.

He sat bolt upright. Another nightmare? The banging came again. He swung his legs out of bed, put on his slippers and hauled on his jacket — so cold in the house; the fire had gone out.

Who on the earth was it? Some family beset by an urgent illness, wanting Catherine's advice? Or much worse, his son-in-law Tom Byers with bad news? He padded across the hooked rug covering the upstairs planks and started down.

Another round of banging. Hannah called from her room, "Poppa, Poppa, someone's at the door!"

He crossed into the back porch, lifted the bolt and flung the door open.

There, beard encrusted with ice, eyebrows white from hoarfrost, gaunt, looking half starved, stood his youngest son, Jim.

A wild whoop of welcome burst out of him. In a gesture so unlike him he flung open his arms, wrapped them round Jim, hugging him with all his might. Who cared if the wind blew through the open door and froze the house. The Prodigal had returned.

Chapter Twelve: Spring 1854

"So, Uncle Jim, how's it feel to be back here, away from all them pretty girls in the city?" John Alford, now fifteen, was driving a picket into the ground with a heavy mallet. "You miss all that?"

Old James was bent over, sharpening another picket with his axe while his son Jim and their neighbour's son, Sam Nelson, carried a heavy rail over to the next panel. All around them in the damp cedar woods this hot spring day, snow was dripping. Sam and Jim had hung their coats on cut-off branches nearby while they slogged through the deep slush, working about ten feet back from the still frozen brook. They were running this fence along the boundary line between James and the Nelsons', using rails floated down the brook last spring when it flooded. Below, the brook ran a couple of hundred yards down to the great pond formed by Manderson's dam. Their own cattle and Nelsons' would drink down there.

"Well, John, m'boy," Jim said, "powerful pile of girls to be had up there. But if I was you, I wouldn't want any one of them."

His father looked up. The first hint — rejected love, just what Catherine had guessed. Jim and Sam dropped the rail onto its slot between two pickets to complete a panel. The old man felt gratified to have them all working together as a family once again. Much earlier, Janey's baby brother, Joey, had been cured, of course, like others Catherine had seen to. Jim's arrival had given James such a surge of elation and helped ease his pain over the continued failure of the school. He and Catherine even made love two nights in a row, a thing they had not done for years. Jim's first day back, Catherine had made sure her son did nothing but rest after his trek home. They all needed a rest actually, for that first night, James had broken out the rum, a thing he rarely did, though he kept a stash in readiness.

"But lots of work to be had up there?" Sam Nelson asked. In his early thirties, brawny, he stood panting for a moment before going for another heavy rail to place at the bottom of the next panel. "We'll need all o'yez on this one, I guess. Bring the peavey, John."

James put down his axe and crossed to help with the next rail. The four heaved up the great log, well over a foot thick.

"Well Sam, I could say the same about jobs," panted Jim. "Lots of jobs, but none you'd be happy doing." They dropped the log in place. John grabbed a picket and Jim hammered it into the ground.

"There must've been something ye liked about the big city," John asked his uncle, holding the picket straight.

"Best thing I liked was the leaving of it."

Good to hear, thought James. No worry now about the farm going on. Maybe now, he could focus on getting that school built.

"That's good," John said. "Never had no hankering to go myself, so I'm glad I won't be missing out." He stood back and surveyed the fence as Jim slogged through drifts to the next rail. "Terble pile o' snow fell this winter."

"How so?" Jim said. "Never seen much in Montreal."

"Oh no? Here she came down all winter. Must be a lot different so far inland."

"Yes, byes," Sam countered, "gonna be a terble rush o' water when this here brook goes."

"Did ya get any logs cut this winter, Poppa? We gonna be floating some down when she breaks?"

James shook his head. Back cutting, James confessed he wasn't as agile around the stumps and brushwood as before. In fact, he'd taken a couple of nasty falls, without letting on he'd been hurt. Next winter, he said he'd leave the logging to the others.

"These damn rails are sure heavy in the spring," Sam grunted. "Maybe we should'a left them dry till midsummer."

"Maybe," James said, "but you'll be pasturing your cattle here soon as they're outta the barn in the next weeks, and mine too." Great for grazing, the lush ground of the Hollow produced excellent grasses and hay, and of course all the water the cattle needed.

"Your father's been doing some persuasive talking while you was gone, Jim." Sam picked up the next heavy rail with the others.

"Just leave it lie!" James didn't want to spoil the fun of them all working together.

"Don't let it lie—I want to know what my father's been up to."

"Foolish ideas, if you ask me," Sam blurted out. "Everyone's talking. Seems he wants to build some damn fool school — excuse me, Mr. Alford — but you Protestants are getting yer dander up, I heard. Most everyone is against it, anyway."

"I heard the talk too," John put in. "Most farmers, they

don't see the need. Me, I'm even in two minds myself."

"You're what!" Jim went for another rail while James stayed sharpening a picket.

"Well, my grandfather here taught me all I need to know," John replied, "and fun it was, most of the time. He learned me arithmetic, and reading and writing, and I don't see no reason for a lot more."

"What about children that don't have parents to teach them?" Jim asked, eyeing Sam and John. "Lots of farmers don't even know how to read or write themselves."

"Well that's true, for sure," Sam said. "My poppa don't."

"And look how many children around Shegouac need schooling," Jim went on. "My sister Mariah, she's got three would go, sister Ann's got two, Mary Jane two. And Sam, what about your sister-in-law, Sarah Nelson, over there?" He pointed. "She's got five."

"They're Catholic," James repeated grimly.

"Catholics," John echoed, "they're against it, too."

"Catholics don't go to Protestant schools on the Coast." The old man wished the subject would go away. "They count on their own system."

"Poppa, once you got that there school built, just watch them all come."

"All the parents, they say, what's good enough for us is good enough for the kids." Sam stooped to take a drink of water. "What about how to grow wheat? What about how to birth a cow, what if the young pigs are born too early? A fella's got so much to learn about farming — who's got time for rubbish like reading old books? That never did no one no good."

Jim was stooping to pick up another rail, but he stopped and stood up, hands on hips. "All right, you fellas, listen.

You know, I worked on building some bloody great bridge across that St. Lawrence, a sonofabitch of a river, must've been over a mile wide from where we started. And every day, from morning till night, I worked —"

"And what d'ya think we do here?" snapped Sam.

"I know that, Sam," Jim replied calmly. "But we're working for ourselves, here. And our own work is different each day. There, I just carried buckets o' gravel up and down ladders, up and down, I don't wish that on the worst ox in Creation. And let me tell you, one day some fellow came and told us all we'd have to stop for the spring thaw. Clean-shaven he was, big bushy sideburns, all dressed nice in a black suit. If you'd have checked his hands, they be smooth like a woman's. Now of course, he'd have his own problems — different sorts, I've no doubt. But no carrying buckets up and down ladders for him, no sir. And you know what made the difference?"

James watched. His son, having been to the big city, had gotten a real authority, holding forth like a man twice his age. Amazing what one trip could do to a person.

"Easy to see," John said. "He was rich, and you're poor."

"Right you are, John. But why was he rich, and why was I poor? He didn't start out rich. Probably started like me, but what made the difference? Education. He got to a big university, that's what. And how? Some good school first. And he got himself a piece of paper that said he was an engineer. Or whatever it said, I don't care. But he stood up there on the lip of the pit, talking down to us, very nice too. And we stood and listened beside our buckets of gravel, before we came up to get our last pay. That convinced me."

James thought: better said than even I could've spoken. Quite a son!

Sam shook his head and sighed. "Well, Jim, I guess, maybe, you made a point! Yes sir."

"And maybe," John added, "maybe I'd be for a school now, too, though it don't matter what I think."

"Oh yes it does," Jim said. "We all got to talk, we all got to help Poppa get his school."

James broke into a grin. What a clear-headed and strong-willed advocate he now had! But how could one young nineteen year old, with city learning or no, ever change these toughened settlers firmly planted on their soil of Shegouac?

Chapter Thirteen

A few days later, Jim watched his father sit back, satisfied. "Damn fine potatoes, don't know how they weathered this winter with all that snow." James rose and clumped over to his seat by the window to look out at the spring storm shaking trees and lashing the window with ferocious rain. "But I'll be glad to see the end of this salt pork and eat some good fresh cod."

"They'll be putting the boats out any day now, I s'pect," Jim said. "Though I don't know how those fellas go out so early. You'd never catch me being a fisherman. Specially with these spring storms."

"Those potatoes, Poppa," Hannah said, "they're all thanks to Jim, you know."

"How so?"

"Well, when we finally got you to enlarge that root cellar last summer, Jim made sure he put in those wide shelves off the ground. Made all the difference, eh Momma?"

"Yes dear," Catherine replied, "our Jim's very clever, but we must be careful not to overdo it. Might get a swelled head, specially since he's been to the big city!"

"Aw Momma, you know I'd —" Jim was interrupted by the back door bursting open.

Ann's husband, Will Young, came rushing in, breathless and wet from the rain. "Byes, we was at the top of the brook hill and we saw this here great rush of water coming down, took away the bridge!"

"They're gonna be cut off!" Hannah cried. "Port Daniel's cut off."

"There's three kids on the bridge! It's hangin' by a thread, they can't get off."

Jim leapt up, followed by his father. Without saying a word, they threw on coats and tore out, followed by the womenfolk. "Grab a couple of axes," James hollered, "and a coil o' rope."

Jim detoured, grabbed the implements his father wanted, and tore down the hill in the downpour, James following as fast as his old legs could travel.

What a sight greeted them: the brook ice had indeed broken, high up above the Manderson dam — might even have taken the dam with it, Jim thought. The patchwork bridge had swung downstream, just held on one side. Three forms — they looked like girls — were hanging on for dear life, with no way to leap across that violent river, or make it back to the other side. Jim had never seen the brook in such flood before.

Slipping on the ice patches, he and Will ran as fast as they could, but before they arrived, the bridge broke off and started to lurch down over the shelves of rocks the fifty or more feet as the current bore it into the stormy sea. Jim's heart froze as he saw one form swept into the water — "It's a Skene girl," Will yelled. They raced to reach the turbulent current where now the floating fragment had passed them and then tumbled out onto the waves, half floating, half submerged.

The girl, whom now Jim could see was Christy, maybe nine, bobbed to the surface where the immense thrust of the current met the sea, the wind churning the waves.

Right away, Will plunged into the surf, wading out as fast as he could, while Jim kept his eyes upon the broken part of the bridge with its two occupants. One form he now saw was Margie Skene, hanging onto her smaller sister, Agnes, about seven. "What'll we do?" he yelled over the uproar of the ferocious storm that only the spring could bring to the Gaspé.

Panting, James gasped to Jim, "Get this rope onto it, and we'll haul her back."

"But it's sinking out there!"

"Might hold. What's Will doing — he can't swim neither."

Jim saw Will was up to his chest in waves which knocked him about, but he still headed for Christy only a few feet beyond. From her thrashing, Jim could see she was just managing to keep herself afloat. But with those heavy clothes, she'd soon go under.

Beyond Christy, the broken flooring of the bridge and its railing looked as if it were sinking. "Poppa, it's too deep out that far." Then Jim spotted a floating log roiling with the flotsam and jetsam brought down by the flood. If he could just get on it. "I'll grab me that log." No time for doubts, no time for anything but action.

His father was fastening the rope round his waist. "Watch she don't roll, me son. Hang on tight."

The fragment of bridge was drifting further out on the brook's surge. Quickly, rope round his waist, Jim strode into the waves. The shock of its icy wrath struck him like a club, and he almost crumpled. Lord, was it cold! He kept wading deeper. Soon up to his waist, he could hardly feel his feet, slipping and tripping on the rocky bottom.

Get out of that coat, he realized, it'll pull you down. He threw it off, kept going, waves striking his face, washing over him, driving that childhood fear of drowning into his very bones.

Slow going through the deep water, and he saw the log drifting away. Freezing, he put aside his fear and launched himself out into the waves as he'd seen swimmers do, kicking his legs hard, sweeping his arms forward so that somehow he reached the log. But now, get onto it? Every time his icy hands grabbed a stub of limb, the log rolled.

"Hurry up," he heard Margie shriek. He looked. The fragment of bridge was slowly going under. The two girls would drown for sure.

Kicking, he managed to get both his arms over the log, and with that purchase, swung the log so that he could drive it out to them by the thrust of his legs. But the wind and rain in his face slowed him so that he made little headway.

Fatigue set in. Through the rain he saw the girls up to their waists in the freezing bay. That bridge was going down. What should he do? He couldn't swim...

Or could he? He'd gotten to the log — so try! But through these waves, heavy boots, no strength left and ten feet to go — he'd drown for sure. He pushed off from the log, gasping and choking, forcing himself to try and swim to the floating fragment.

On shore, James watched in horror. Behind him, down the hill came Hannah with some blankets, and a sleigh with two more neighbours. Out of the corner of his eye, James saw that Will had grabbed the thrashing Christy and was half floating, half struggling back to shore with her. Looked like he would make it. But his son — was he actually trying to swim? In a sea that brooked no swimming? The waves, though not exceptionally high, were choppy, breaking over him: Jim would drown, too.

Unaccountably, James felt at one with him, felt that same ice, that same numbness overcoming him, as many years before, he had struggled to get to shore with a rope round his waist too, tugging a crucial survival bag.

How ironic to have made it himself, and then to have his son and heir succumb to the same waves that he himself had beaten. He roared in anguish as he saw Jim go down, and stay down. James felt himself out there with him in the depths, trying to unloose his survival bag, snagged on some rock along the bottom. He had been numb with cold, worn out, as only those icy waters can make you in just a few seconds and — more frightening still — how they took away any will to survive. Jim, he prayed, don't give up the fight Jim, only a few more feet!

Then his son popped up. "Swim, Jim, swim," James cried hoarsely; others yelled their encouragement through the drenching rain.

"Will's made it. He's made it!" Thomas Byers cried as he left his sleigh to wrap Will and the half-drowned Christy in blankets that Hannah had ready. "I'll be taking them right up to Catherine," he shouted, "you stay for Jim and the girls. Look, James Travers got here, he'll take care o' you fellas — I'm off."

James was hardly aware of anything: not Hannah helping the bundled forms into the sleigh, nor Hannah calling out as Jim closed in on the girls. "He's going to make it, Poppa. He's swimming!"

But a good way from shore, Jim had no idea that he would make it. Numb from head to toe, buried in waves, gulping air whenever he got the chance, he reached out and grabbed onto a spar of pine, floating between him and the girls. "Jim, we're going down!" Margie shrieked.

And going down they were, water up to their necks. Mostly submerged, the waterlogged bridge was sinking. In seconds they'd both be gone.

Margie's cry made Jim fight even harder, but he just had no more strength left, paralyzed by the frigid water. He kicked, hefted, got to the spar, swung it toward the girls.

He tried to yell, "use the float," but couldn't, he was choking, he couldn't breathe — just trust that they would know, and yes, as a wave broke over him, he just saw Margie lunge and grab her kid sister, hauling her into the sea as she groped for the spar. They somehow made it and hung on. Jim got his arm around one of them and then felt a tug at his waist — the rope, the others were pulling. Margie, with youthful strength and tenacity, had locked herself round the spar. "Pull," she shrieked out, "pull hard!"

As the rope tugged him shoreward, Jim felt his hands slipping off, so numb. Choking, he gasped, "Wait! Don't!"

"No, no, pull," Margie yelled. With waning strength Jim wrestled for a better hold. But the waves and the current were winning. Agnes was slipping out of his grasp. In a panic, she flailed her arms and legs, unaware she was drowning them both.

The team on shore kept pulling hard, Jim couldn't yell again, and down he went with Agnes. Into the black waters, finished.

No, no, he felt bottom, pushed himself up, gasped some air, and went under a second time, hit bottom, and again thrust himself up, this time with his last strength thrusting Agnes out to the spar which in terror she gripped, just before Jim went down for the third time.

Before losing consciousness, he gave himself to the waves, and then, in shallower water, willing hands pulled him and the girls ashore. Quickly bundled into James Travers' sleigh, all four sped up the hill to the welcoming fire of the Old Homestead, and safety.

Chapter Fourteen

"What's that, for pity's sake, Poppa?"

James saw his son eyeing his contraption in the middle of the threshing floor. This Sunday, Jim was hitching Keen in the oxcart to take them to the church service in Port Daniel school. The bridge incident was long forgotten.

"You're the one as told me about it, you should know," James replied. "Montreal stores was full of them, you said, big sellers."

"A churn?"

"Sure is." James eyed it proudly. "Robins had this one on display, and I got it for Catherine and Hannah. Walter Ross brought it here last week. I kept it hidden to surprise the women."

"Well," his son said uneasily, "it means Momma and Hannah won't have to wear their arms to the bone every week on that old dash churn?" He scratched his eyebrows.

"Thought you'd be pleased." James eyed his son.

Jim nodded, shrugged. "I am, I am, I guess."

"You don't sound pleased." Not often James found himself at odds with Jim. He couldn't understand his reticence.

"I know I sound like I don't care but..." Jim stood up and faced him. "You see, Poppa, I been planning all along, since I got home, on getting us a horse."

"We can still get us a horse." James raised his voice; he didn't like his children getting "lippy" as he called it. "You should —"

"Should what, Poppa?" Jim cut in. "I mean, I come all the way home, I work to cut them extra logs late this spring to make us some money, and you spend it all on a churn when I'd been counting on getting a horse."

"Jim, that's no way to talk. There'll be lots of time for a horse."

"I told you, I like us getting a churn, but right now we need a horse more. A lot more."

"We can do without a horse! A horse is a waste of money!" James shouted, though he didn't really believe that: his son had just gotten under his skin.

"Yes, we keep on bumping to church in an oxcart. Well, I can tell you, that is the last time I go down to Port Daniel to hear Reverend Milne, until we get our horse!"

"You don't mean..." James found himself roaring, "... you're taking this out on the Good Lord above?"

"Missing that awful, never-ending oxcart ride is not taking it out on the Lord, Poppa! And darn right, I'll miss church. What's the good anyway? How many people in Montreal go? Only half, if that, and the rest don't see any need, at all, at all!"

"They what?"

"No sir. And matter of fact, I don't either. Who's proved there is a God? No one I know. Old Reverend Milne going on about the joys of heaven — what about the joys here below? What about travelling in a horse and buggy? To hell with church. No need, no point, I'm just not going!"

James stood as if struck.

* * *

"But Momma," Hannah was saying, "I could never do that!"

"My child, I'm not saying you have to go to any lengths. All you have to do is just bring some of your scones to Ned while he's at work. Jim will go with you as chaperone."

They were taking turns working with the dash churn, up and down, up and down their arms went. Tiring work, pumping that darned handle. The conical barrel, smaller at the top, had a hole through which a round stick, with a crosspiece at the bottom, could be lifted and dropped to beat the cream into butter. They'd take turns every twenty minutes or so and, in about an hour and a half, depending on the temperature of the cream, they had butter. Once a week they did it, but of course, it was well known in Shegouac that if you wanted good, quick butter, you only churned when the tide was rising.

"In fact, I have a better idea," Catherine went on. "Say you're on the way to your sister, Mary Jane, and Dan; they only live a ways beyond. But dress up, mind. You could tell him the scones were for their children."

"Well, I don't see as how there'd be anything wrong exactly."

"And then, maybe, you go a second time. And a third."

"Momma! That would be terrible! He'd suspect something."

"My dear child, you have no idea how stupid men are. They never suspect anything. I've lived a long while, and I can tell you, every word I say is true."

This very rainy July afternoon, with water bucketing down, Jim was at work repairing the kitchen door. And because the tide was rising, his mother and sister were churning.

Jim had often wondered how they would know what time of day to churn on the second range, a good mile inland. One day, he had asked old Mrs. Nelson. She told him, "Oh no dear, we don't have to walk out to the front to check the tide. No siree. We just pick up a cat and look at its eyes."

"But Momma, if Jim's with me, Ned will never say a word — he'll just talk to Jim."

"That's just because he's shy, dear. Some men are like that. They're especially shy around anyone they've taken a liking to. And I tell you, at that threshing bee, and then the thickening bee, he couldn't take his eyes off you. Why else do you think he's building that house?"

"Because he doesn't like his stepmother, the whole country knows that, and he wants a place on his own."

"You mark my words, no man alive wants to live on his own. They build a house so's they can put a wife in it. Of course, some of them, they're so shy, it takes them a few months."

"Months, Momma, I can wait months. But years, that's what I'm afraid of."

"So you just listen to me. I know the way things work."

Just then, old James came in with a strange object.

"Me and Jim, we wanted you to have this!" James announced.

Catherine looked up at him. "What is it?"

James shook the rain from his coat. "Newest invention! Jim found out all about them in Montreal. Walter Ross brought it down from Robin's."

Jim could hardly believe that his father, the old rascal,

was bringing him into the gift. Though he had to admit, the new-fangled churn was one thing he had raved about after getting back.

"We kept it hidden so's me and Jim could surprise you."

Catherine stood, astonished, and then rushed over to give her son a powerful hug. James beamed as Hannah rushed to kiss him too, and then switched with her mother, as they both hugged and kissed the men in great delight. Jim saw the present was a huge hit, and of course began to soften.

"Show them how it works, Jim," James said. "You're the one who brought back the idea from the big city."

Jim came to sit on his mother's chair and moved the handle back-and-forth. Effortlessly, the barrel spun round and round. "See? Simple."

"We'd better send young Jim to Montreal more often, seeing all the ideas he comes up with!" Catherine exclaimed.

The two women set about exploring the churn, undoing the top that was ratcheted on, peering inside, looking at the gears that transferred the back-and-forth thrust to the cogs that turned the churn. It whirled so easily!

"Jim, Poppa," Hannah cried "you're the best!"

* * *

The first sunny day, Jim set off down the road with Hannah dressed in her best. Edward Hayes, known to everyone as Ned, was building his new house about two and a half miles toward Port Daniel. Their older sister, Mary Jane, lived another half a mile beyond.

Full of anticipation, Jim allowed that he loved

subterfuges, but was a little hurt his mother had not let him in on their plan. He was waiting, from his overheard conversation, for Hannah to suggest they take a look at Ned's house.

Heavy banks of clouds were folded like eiderdowns over the landscape: blue grey, and soft, but heralding no downpour. Their dense, almost velvet covering crept across the sky. A herring gull screamed over the expanse, leaving no mark to say where it came from or where it was going.

Hannah pulled Jim out of his reverie by shyly saying, "I've heard the Hayes family is building a new house. I wonder how she's gettin' on?"

"It's not the Hayes family, Hannah. It's Ned." He was determined to make this hard for her, as part of the fun.

"Oh," she said, and lapsed into silence.

"All the country knows that," Jim said.

"Oh," said Hannah again.

"I wonder why he's building it?"

Hannah shrugged. Jim noticed she was a bit breathless. From the pace of their walk? Or the thought of seeing Ned again.

After another silence, Hannah said, "I've heard he doesn't get on so well with this new stepmother, that's why. Nor that stepsister Johanna. But, I don't know."

"If you don't, no one does," Jim said with devilry. Then he grinned.

She slapped at him. "You're mean."

After what seemed to Jim an unbearable silence, they heard hammering across the fields. When Hannah kept silent, he said, "Shall we take a look?"

Hannah nodded.

Now if he and Hannah went in together, Ned would

not take so much as a look at her. So as they were turning up the path, Jim suggested, "I've changed my mind, Hannah, I'll go straight on. Here, you take the scones."

"No-no-no!" she pleaded. "I won't go alone. Please Jim. Please..."

"But you told Momma when you were churning, he wouldn't talk to you if I was there." He couldn't stop his grin.

"Oh you! You listened! You heard us talk!"

"Of course I heard yez talk. I like the whole idea. All right, if I come in, then Hannah, you offer him them scones you baked. Everyone knows you make the best. That way, you'll be sure to catch him."

Hanna blushed in spite of herself. But what else could she do?

Ned had gotten the house frame up and was kneeling, pegging rough floor boards to the joists. He stood up when he saw them coming.

Jim smothered a grin as he saw Ned's embarrassment; why else did he keep looking down at his feet? "Hello there, Jim."

"Hello, Ned. Look who I brought: my sister Hannah. We're on our way to see Mary Jane, and Dan Bisson. We wanted to see how that house of yours is coming." He knew that Hannah would be pleased at him taking the lead.

"I'm glad ye came, Jim, come, take a look-see." He still had not cast one glance at Jim's sister, a sure sign. He'd tell Hannah later.

So while he and Ned talked, Hannah pretended to be interested in the structure, all the while casting glances at Ned. Clean-shaven, slight but wiry and strong, he was not a large man. A good carpenter, Jim observed. He was older than Jim, and had been brought by his parents at the age of two across the bay from Miramichi after the great fire in October 1825, when the whole area had been destroyed. His parents were Catholics from Ireland, but Jim's parents had discussed that and resolved it, once Catherine had spotted Ned's attraction.

"I bet you run that sister of yours ragged, eh Ned, bringing you lunches from your home farm," Jim remarked innocently.

"Oh no, I don't know why, but she never comes."

Jim thought, better and better. "So how do you get your lunches?"

"I bring them m'self."

His mind moved fast. "Look now, Hannah brought some scones for Mary Jane's children. And some other cookies, and stuff. I reckon as how she wouldn't mind parting with a few, would you, Hannah?"

Hannah blushed and shook her head. Jim opened his bag and took some out. Hannah quickly pre-empted him, laying a little towel on the rough planks and placing the cookies and scones neatly, with a little mug that Jim was surprised she had brought. In it, she poured a glass of ale from a flagon she had also hidden away. Then she glanced at Jim.

He stepped into the breach. "Hot day like this..." He covered up his surprise, understanding why the bag he'd been carrying was so heavy, "we thought you might welcome a mug of beer."

Ned seemed to relax. "Byes, you don't know how good that'll be. Thank you kindly, Jim." And then, at long last, he looked at Hannah, smoothing his napkin. Jim saw in his eyes a look of such appreciation that again he stifled a smile.

And then, the devil took hold of him. "Well, you know, Ned, Hannah here agreed to take care of the kids while Mary Jane's off looking after Dan's mother down in Port Daniel." Would Hannah know enough to play along? A sidelong glance told him she'd turned her back. "So when she comes past every day, I could get her to drop in, bring you some stuff she cooked."

"Thank you kindly!" Ned exclaimed, not even trying to hide his delight. Hannah whirled and looked at Jim. He looked right back.

She turned away. "We'd best be going, Jim," she said clearly, her first words spoken. "Charley, Dannie, and John, they'll be waiting."

The two of them set off. Jim was delighted with this first encounter, though he wondered how pleased Hannah would be. And as it turned out, she ended up being mighty pleased as well.

Chapter Fifteen: Winter 1855

"No no no no no!" John Travers, rather distinguished with a beard and prosperous bearing, slapped the table. The Traverses were leading figures in the community, having settled up by a road back to the Second, known as Travers Lane.

"Could you make that a bit clearer?" asked James, and they all laughed. This snowy midwinter evening, the prospective school trustees had not been able to agree on anything, in spite of James doing his best. Even the school idea itself was still far from being approved. James had picked January for this meeting because summers the settlers worked from dawn to dusk, no energy left for anything but pure survival on this harsh but fruitful coast of the Gaspé. Although Jim had been working hard to support his father among the community since coming home last spring, only the older members of the community spoke at such gatherings, and Jim had to sit, inwardly seething but silent.

"Well gentlemen, next item: how much shall we charge each student?" asked James. "Always supposing we do decide to build. I gather from Mr. Travers's reaction that we don't favour mandatory allotments of men and materials." He glanced around. "Perhaps that's only right, we should let everyone give whatever they feel like. But fees for students, well, we will have to charge."

They looked at one another. "How much do they charge up in Paspébiac?" asked John Travers.

"I heard it was a shilling." Andrew Young, related to the Alfords through his brother William's wife Ann, Jim's sister, had become a fence sitter about the school. In contrast Thomas Byers, sitting next to him, was known to be in favour. "A shilling a month?"

"Nearer two shillings, I heard." Somewhat prim but well organized, Edward Legallais had been asked to be secretary treasurer, if the school motion passed. "Seems we'd better wait a bit."

"Wait a bit?" broke in Andrew. "You know how fellas is. If we tell everyone we're not gonna charge, and after, we ask for fees, it'll be too late. Tell 'em right away. I can order the stovepipes you need, but my suppliers won't wait too long to be paid." Andrew was thinking about setting up a store. So far, if you wanted molasses, or salt, farmers here had to take a sleigh across the Nouvelle River up to Hope or down to Port Daniel.

"Well," said Thomas, "why don't you give stovepipes instead of fees? You'll have three children coming."

"I already offered yez pencils and paper, and maybe a few books. That's about as far as I'm willing to go till I know what is happening. We won't be having this school anyway, I'm damned sure."

"How can we set a fee?" asked Edward. "Or even think of building, until we know if we're getting that fifty pounds from the superintendent of education?"

James grinned: perfect time to produce the letter. "Gentlemen, I've already written, and the superintendent says we'll get the same grant as others in Hopetown, or down in Port Daniel." He held it out.

That did set a silence about the table, while Thomas Byers thumped it happily and downed his piggin of beer. "Best news yet!"

"Hold on now," Mr. Travers broke in, "will us trustees have to give more, even though we don't have no children at the school?"

"Fair enough question." James could see a real argument coming up. Donations had been discussed, and so far, he presumed that families would end up giving their time, and perhaps modest donations of wood, shingles, nails, pegs, even barking as insulation. So he headed this one off. "Why don't we stick to the question of fees?" The others nodded.

"We can always come down in fees," Andrew proposed, "but sure is hard to get them back up after. This first year, I say we pass a resolution now setting it at two shillings."

"I second that," said Edward.

"All in favour?" James asked.

They all nodded. "So ordered." James motioned to the secretary, Edward, who made a note. Well, that was one agreement. Perhaps now he should try and bring up that burning question, the one key to it all: "So are we far enough ahead now that we can get a resolution voted to say go ahead with this here school?"

"Far enough?" John Travers let out a snort. "We just got a start on saying it's not gonna work, that's as far as we got! No further."

"I second that," said Edward. "I agreed to join this here discussion committee, and before I knew it, I was a trustee, and then secretary! I don't know how you work, James, but yer as cute as a fox, and from my point of view —"

"Oh he's cute all right," Andrew agreed, which they

knew meant clever, "but there was nothing wrong in us discussing it, for sure. If we end up with no school, everyone will see we did our best, we went over everything, that's what's important."

"No sir," James burst out, "what is important is a firm decision —" he stopped as he heard a sleigh draw up outside. He shook his head: more trouble arriving.

Just then Catherine and Hannah came in from the back kitchen with plates of cakes, cookies, scones, and pies. "Not as much here as for your last meeting, I'm afraid," Catherine said, in response to the happy reaction, "but we've done our best." Janey Byers came behind with a large pot of tea and mugs.

"Yes, by jeez," Jim said, "be a lot more if you all agreed with Poppa!"

They laughed and muttered assorted exclamations of delight. "Be the holy gee whiz, Mrs. Alford, what have you been up to?"

Someone banged on the door.

James went into the back kitchen and opened the door. There stood Big Bill Sullivan, a barrel-chested man with the strength of a giant, even more imposing in his heavy winter garments, dusted with snow. Beside him, Alexander Mann, bearded, also snow-covered, looked equally threatening. He was smaller, dark, never a sunny individual. James remembered when his father, Isaac Mann, had arrived soon after he and Catherine had begun on their house — not much grace there either. But later, most of the Manns went back to Mann's Landing at Restigouche where they had substantial holdings.

"Come in, come in, gentleman." James motioned and they shed hats and outer garments, stamping their feet before entering the main room. "We're in the middle of a meeting, but if you've got any —"

"It's the meeting we come about!" Bill looked grim.

Edward Legallais took off his spectacles and rose in alarm. John Travers stood up like the patrician he was; Thomas Byers brought down their last chair from upstairs. "Just what we need, new ideas, might wake us all up."

Alexander gave his hat and mitts to Catherine to put by the fire. "You fellas is Protestant, and us is Catholic." The two of them stood in their heavy jackets. "Two separate systems. But we came to tell yez, we got no money to build one fer ourselves." He looked at the nominal trustees. "So is you fellas thinkin' about including us?"

"Yep, you plan on letting us Catholics in?" Big Bill looked dour. "Lot of us around, like the Vautiers, and..." He was about to go on, but everyone knew who the Catholics were.

"Well now, you're welcome to have a cup of tea," James said genially, though he felt anything but. "Catherine, pour these fine fellas a tea, and gentlemen, take your fill of cakes — don't be shy."

"Right at this moment," Mr. Travers broke in, "you fellas got nothin' to worry about. There's not going to be any school."

James looked up, flushed and frustrated — not the time to betray that view.

Andrew Young, gregarious, tall and full of good cheer: he could melt a snowball on bay ice, got up from his seat. "Ye know, we were just discussing the question of Catholics and Protestants. We all reckon that this here school, if it gets built, she'll never work if we exclude half the country." He smiled appealingly. "Maybe up the bay, they divide us — them priests don't want us Protestants teaching their pure little darlings the Devil's works!" He gave off a laugh, and the others joined in. James watched the visitors: would they take offence?

Shoulders unwound and they grinned, too. "So you think it's gonna be for all of us here? Thank you, ma'am." Bill took his tea and helped himself to the largest piece of cake on the plate.

"Right now," John Travers went on, "this here meetin's to decide if we're going to have a school at all. James here, voted in as chairman, hasn't called the vote, but I reckon it's going to be a pretty firm no."

Again James felt his stomach churn. All this effort going down the drain, and likely for the last time. He glanced at his son Jim, watching with a frown. Catherine pretended to occupy herself with pouring tea, making sure everyone was happy.

"Well, first of all," said Bill Sullivan, "what are you fellas thinkin' about fees? Us fellas with the half our land not cleared are working terble hard just to keep going. Last winter was real bad — Ned's father, old Will Hayes, had to kill their last chickens to keep his mother alive, and they all nearly starved to death. Well, there's no money around, you fellas all know that. So how d'you think we'll pay for other's children?"

James did not like his manner one bit. He was about to hammer out a retort when Andrew stepped into the breach again. "Well," he said, "we've been thinking about that very thing. Give us your ideas, so that we can all talk a bit, and you fellas can go away satisfied. We won't do anything the majority don't agree with."

"No sir, and for a start," Thomas Byers broke in, "that

superintendent of education promised us good money from Quebec City."

Big Bill straightened. "That solves one problem, right there." He turned to Alexander Mann as Catherine was handing him his tea. The Manns were known to be troublemakers. James saw Alexander eyeing them cautiously.

Andrew went on, "We'll have to charge students, because those educated fellas teachin' has gotta be paid. But this meeting is not going to impose burdens on our community. We're all hard-working, you said it, with only small farms, too. Right here, we're just trying to do our best by everyone." He smiled. "And it's a thankless task, let me tell you."

Alexander nodded. "Yes sir, I agree, a thankless task."

Was he mollified? James wondered. So he voiced the challenge. "Specially as it looks like we aren't going to have any damned school anyways."

"Won't have a school?" Bill raised his eyebrows. "Then what the hell're ya meetin fer?"

"Well," James went on stoutly, "I called this to see if maybe, once we got some plans agreed, there might be more of a willingness. But it's plain," he went on with undisguised sarcasm, "we seem to want Shegouac children to forget about the outside world, forget about reading their own parents' wills, get them read by them shysters in New Carlisle, and why ever would we want the schooling so's we could check them bills up in French Paspébiac —"

"Hol' on a minute!" Bill turned to Alexander. "We never came here to stop a school, did we?"

His friend shook his head. "No sir. We just wanted to make sure our kids would be educated along with your'n. That's why we came."

"So you fellas," James put out innocently, "you Catholics, you're all for a school? I mean, if the costs are fair and worked out fine?"

The two nodded. "Damn right! We had a meetin' last night, and all of us agreed. Us, we speak for the rest."

James turned to the other trustees, noticing a sparkle of glee in Tom Byers' eyes. "So what do we think, now? If the Catholics are solidly with us?"

John Travers led off: "If they're so keen, why not have them build themselves a Catholic school, and our children can go there?"

Edward Legallais nodded. "Good idea. Our kids won't mind."

Bill looked taken aback.

But old James leapt to his feet. "Just look at us! No finer men exist anywhere — and what do we do together? Nothing. Take that bridge in the Hollow. It joins the whole coast together, and what did we do? Talked it over — and over, to get a good big one built, and nothing ever happened. Same thing as now!" He felt his voice rising. "Last spring, you all know what happened. When it went out, my son Jim here nearly drowned saving them Skene kids." Overtaken by emotion, James waved his arms. "And all because we couldn't damn well work together to build one bloody bridge."

He was panting, and he saw out of his eye that Catherine seemed concerned. Was he going to be taken with a bad heart? The other men were looking down at their feet. "So no — doing nothing won't work for me, I tell ya."

With that, James sat down, and was silent.

No one spoke.

"Now gentlemen, I made all these cakes," Catherine

volunteered brightly, "and I hope you'll make the most of them!"

"Thank you, ma'am," said Bill. Taking another large piece, he turned. "I reckon James is right. Let's get together, let's build us a school, Protestants, Catholics, let's just all get together this once, get our kids educated, give 'em a fair chance at life."

Surprisingly, James heard them begin to agree. But he was beyond caring. He took out his handkerchief and wiped his face. He'd done all he could.

"Thank you, Mrs. Alford." The treasurer took another piece of cake. "I vote we start by assessing everyone." He got up and started to put on his coat.

Alexander slurped the last of his tea and wiped his mouth with his hand. "Mighty nice of you, Mrs. Alford, I sure didn't expect such a fine piece of cake. But yes, and the sooner the better, I say."

"Now Bill, you know you're always welcome at our house," Catherine said, watching James.

At the door, the visitors turned. "Well, looks like we're on the right track," Alexander said. "I want to thank you, James, and your missus."

"Me too," said Bill. He glanced around. "But I'll sure be anxious to see what you fellas will cook up in the end." With that, he put on his hat and followed Alexander out the door.

"So now, James," John Travers put on his coat, "how do ya think we'll find a good teacher?"

"Send a dollar up to that there paper in Montreal, what's it called?" Edward Legallais asked.

"*The Gazette?*" Jim threw in.

"Post notices around the Coast too," Andrew said,

dressing up like the rest, a decision made, at least in his mind. "None of us gets that paper down here. We got to be sure everyone gets a chance."

Thomas Byers clapped James on the shoulder, as he prepared to leave. "No fox like an old fox," he mumbled as he went out the door. So far so good, James thought. And now, amazingly, his school might get built, yes, and maybe they would all co-operate. And maybe they wouldn't...

Before long, he intended to hand it all over to John Travers and Ed Legallais; he was too old for these arguments. More especially, he wanted to avoid placing more responsibility on Catherine. He had told her not to prepare anything for tonight, but she wouldn't hear of it. Then he began to grin. And he saw his son smiling, too. Catherine herself sat, and slowly broke off a piece of her own cake. She seemed very pleased.

Chapter Sixteen: Spring 1855

"What can I do for you, Thomas?" James asked as he sat eating his breakfast.

His son-in-law, Thomas Byers, stood uncertainly. "I maybe got some bad news."

James rose from his bowl of porridge.

"I was back early to the head field," Thomas recounted. "Wanted to get a load of seaweed spread afore breakfast. Partway back, I heard Buster barking. Then John Young's dog came tearing past, and the both of them set up a terble ruckus. When I came over that hill o' your'n by the stony bridge, I saw a big black shape run off into the woods. I reckon the dogs scared it off."

"A bear? Spring, sure, that's the time."

"Well, them oxen, your two, they was back there..."

Yes, enjoying the fresh spring pasture beyond the stony bridge, but surely no bear would attack them? But then, springtime, a mother bear, with cubs, and nothing to eat...

"Well, I'd best be off, they're waiting breakfast on me." Thomas sighed and left.

James found himself sitting down again. Neither he nor Catherine spoke for a moment.

"Jim can deal with it when he gets here."

James nodded. "But who knows, maybe that bear'll come back. Bears can make short work of a cow, or an ox, if they've a mind." But his own fears multiplied. "I'll just take a look." He put on his jacket, and then went for his musket.

Catherine frowned. "Now James, you're not going after that bear!"

James shook his head. "No no, don't you worry. I'm only going for a look-see."

"James, I'll not have you going off after a bear at your age."

"Send Jim back, then, when he's in from Saint Godfrey. Anyways, I'll just sit by the oxen a bit, keep watch."

And with that, he was up the hill with his musket. After all, had he not hunted moose, shot bears, tracked wolves? He'd be quite all right.

At the top, having forced his pace, he had to stop and lean against the trunk of an old birch. Feel that old heart working! No doubt about it, he was short of breath. What old age did to a man, eh? But he still was quite spry enough to face any bear.

He headed out over the spring-moist fields. Dark spruce, highlighted by white birch, seemed motionless as if in stoic disapproval. High above, herring gulls happily mewed and wheeled in their open playgrounds, beneath malevolent clouds.

He opened the gate onto the track back around the Hollow, trying to build up his pace, but the easy stride of yesteryear had disappeared. What would happen if a bear came at him? Well, of course he'd be ready. He glanced down into the Hollow at that cedar rail fence by the brook that he and Jim and Nelson had put up last summer. It would last his lifetime, and probably Jim's, too. If only Jim would get a wife, and have some offspring, it might outlast them, too. If he didn't, what then? All this overgrown and returned to wasteland? He shook his head at the thought...

Had he been wrong to pasture Keen and Smudge back down in the gully by the stony bridge? Bears did roam in springtime. Last year, Ed Legallais had a couple of sheep taken. Twelve years ago a wild cat, probably a cougar, had actually gotten a cow back on Joe Young's across the brook. He himself had gone to check on the half-eaten animal and saw the tracks. Thinking of that, the scar on his shoulder from that cougar attack at his cabin his first year here began to itch.

Musket loaded, he strode on. You needed a steady aim to kill a charging bear, that was for sure. Well, his aim had always been steady, in the past. Was it still?

Nothing could be more glorious, James thought, than walking among these stubbled shoots of wheat in the hot sun, which now this fine spring day beamed down, coaxing up a fullness that would encourage the kernels to ripen, and later, be ground into loaves of thick, rich bread, yes, all hidden now in the thrusting stalks. How James enjoyed his land and the cultivation thereof, hard though it had been. He reached the long field before it dipped into the gully, gripping the musket even tighter. Better be ready. He swung the musket up to his shoulder, sighted, but the darned barrel kept wavering. Oh well, no bear was around, he was sure. The explosion itself would be enough to frighten any fool animal. Unless it got enraged...

When Keen had been born, James laid him across his knees and held him up to get a good suck at his mother's teats. He had been worried that something was amiss with the little calf. But no, soon as he got a good bit of nourishment, he could stand and suck like the others.

Frisky little fellow. Good breadth across the chest. Dark brown splotches against a white hide, playful. But then the difficult day came when he and Charlie Chedore had to neuter him. His first bull, Broad, he'd slit the bag at the bottom and squeezed out the balls, then cut them off and sewed up the bag. Big chance of infection. Nowadays, they never cut, just fixed a rig, two small boards screwed together tight enough so that the large drooping ovals below withered away. Keen wasn't so frisky after that, but still 'keen' and full of life, no doubt. Broad One, way back, his first ox, had been the making of this farm. How well he remembered that trip from Paspébiac with the little fella draped round his neck and those two ruffians after him.

Young Keen had not liked one bit being yoked to old Broad the Second. But after James had put him in a lightly loaded cart beside Broad, Keen had to fall in. Yes indeed, not long in getting the trick of hauling, in fact, he even enjoyed it, doing his best to out-pull the other fellow. The next year he put on weight, gained strength, and also, it seemed, intelligence. Soon, no finer ox on the Coast than Keen. James crested the rise before the stony bridge and stopped short.

Keen lay there, his back half torn off.

Smudge stood forlornly by. Seeing James, he began to bawl.

Slowly, the realization took hold and James's shoulders slumped. He began to run forward as best he could, but he knew it to be a lost cause.

"Yes yes, Smudge, coming," he called, but Keen needed water. He hurried down to the brook where he'd left a bucket and filled it.

When he brought it up to the fallen ox, Keen saw him

and did his best to rise. But with his skin clawed off, he could not rise. Back broken by the bear's weight.

The great ox looked up at him with huge eyes and lowed. James tipped the bucket so that Keen could take a couple of great gulps, spilling some.

He knelt beside his old working companion and stroked his nose. Then he bent and put his head against the temple of his old friend. So much had they shared over the years. Why is it, he thought, as his eyes grew moist, why is it we are born into the world, we have our day, so very short, and then, leave? Such a short sojourn.

How the fifteen years had sped by! Each time he'd said goodbye to a farm animal, no small pain ensued. But none stabbed with such anguish as this. He put his arm around and scratched the ox behind the ear, where he loved it.

He heaved a great sigh. "You and me, Keen, where does it all go, eh? So much happens that neither of us will ever understand. Just keep going, I guess, we all have to do that, no matter what."

James coughed, pulled himself together, and got to his feet. Can't spend all day. That new yearling will have to be castrated and trained. The farm has to go on. He turned to Smudge, and yelled for him to leave. Did he want him watching while he put an end to his friend? He went to smack him on the backside. Smudge looked around, surprised.

"Go on, Smudge! Go! Get! Skedaddle!" He whacked him again.

Smudge obediently trotted off, but then stopped and turned back to look. He set out to smack him again, and stopped. Smudge would just turn and walk back. Nothing for it but to get the deed done, no matter how difficult.

James knelt a final time, stroked the great ox along his strong broad neck, gave him a couple of slaps of affection, and then rose. Quickly as he could, he pointed the muzzle behind his ear, slanted it so that it would destroy the brain in one shot, and pulled the trigger.

Keen, his faithful worker, lay dead.

* * *

Jim came bursting into the room, sweat dripping. "Byes you know how much I paid for them nails we needed?" He stopped as he saw his mother upset. "Where's Poppa?"

Catherine glanced down. "Tom Byers came in. Said he saw a bear back by the oxen. Your father, stubborn old fool, took his musket, and off he went."

"What? Alone? Not after a bear?"

Concern showed in his mother's eyes. "I told him to wait, but he wouldn't listen."

"When?"

"Breakfast," Catherine seemed close to tears.

"Breakfast! That long ago?"

Catherine nodded.

"I'll take the other gun." And grabbing it, out he went.

Before long, Jim reached the long rise and looked down beyond the stony bridge. He stopped short.

What a grisly sight! Keen lay torn open, dead, in a pool of blood. Smudge again bawled when he saw Jim coming. But Ol' Poppa, where was he? Jim began to search the damp spring ground for tracks. Yes, bear prints, no doubt, a mother bear and one or two cubs. Danger for sure! His father would never be a match for the likes of them.

And there, yes, the flat-soled prints of his father's boots.

They went off in the same direction. Oh-oh! Should he go for help with the bear? Or track his father? He stood in the sloping field beside the great dark woods that stretched back for almost a hundred miles, broken only by the Second Range Road a mile back, and the beginnings of the Third, another mile, and then nothing but wilderness, wolves, caribou, moose — and bears.

Silence filled his ears as he pondered his decision. He lifted the musket and began to load it. Sure looked like his father was heading after the bears. In search of revenge? Fearful, Jim traced those footsteps to the bridge over the brook, and then into the pasture. Now where? Should he keep following? Or go back, get others to come beat the woods, spread out, send calls. He tipped his head back, and shouted his father's name.

Silence. He shook his head. This time, he was really afraid. He knew in his bones what had happened. His father crashing through woods would have attracted that mother bear. Sensing a decent dinner, with her stomach raging, she must have come upon him. Old Poppa, he'd have gotten off a shot with his wavering aim and weak eyesight and then, trying to run, had tripped, and right then and there been torn to pieces.

Gripping his musket, heart beating, trusty Rusty at his heels, Jim went forward to seek out the worst.

* * *

Leaving the fallen ox, James had turned his attention for badly needed solace to the June woods. This glorious invigorating wind that blew in across the fields carried its aromas of manure, seaweed fertilizer, cattle out on new grass. If only it could always be spring.

So now he'd better head home along the Hollow trail, and get Jim Wylie the butcher. Keen would supply them and his friends with many a good feed of beef this summer. He threaded his way among the trunks of huge cedar, as he had done as a young man with the Micmac. But hard going! He used to swing through the woods at a fine trot, heavens, all the way from Port Daniel; now, he found it hard even walking.

The relentless march of time.... Again, he tried to grapple with this mysterious pattern laid down by the Almighty. What does life prepare you for? Only to leave this world and move on into the next? If there were a next. And he knew, having asked Milne as well, that the clergy seemed only to offer pat, obvious, scriptural answers. No vivid illumination. Maybe he'd have to find that himself?

He stood next to a giant pine, his hand resting on the rough trunk. So silent. But was it? No, something moving through the woods! But where? Behind? Thank heaven his hearing had not diminished. Yes, an animal, but not stealthy, no sir. He gripped his musket hard. "Well, Mrs. Bear, I'm ready," he whispered. "I'll just wait till you get closer, otherwise I might miss." Adrenalin poured through him.

And then he heard a shout. The Nelson boys, crossing the brook. Well, why not? What an old fool to worry. They faded off.

Did it seem, in the impressive stillness, that all was proceeding according to some Divine Providence, God or no God? The call of a crow, almost beautiful, as was the song of the 'oh happiness bird' in a spruce. The brook's gurgling nourished these songbirds; all around, small animals going about finding food, making nests for imminent broods, muskrat and mink playing in the icy waters. Further up this very brook, two beavers had made a dam to submerge their new house. And the bears, yes, on the prowl no doubt. Keep alert, he reminded himself.

He passed by shreds of birchbark on a narrow trunk reaching fifty feet up to catch sunlight. On another, intricate lace of blue green moss ascended, draped in odd patterns. He could smell so many surging plants and delighted in perky wild flowers in patches of sunlight. But there, an aged tree had not made it, withered into sticks.

Quietly in the heavy farm boots McRae had fashioned from hides of his own cattle, James made his way past turns of the brook and found them familiar. Then, by some happy intuition, he turned left and stopped. There, what remained of his cabin, still standing! Well, walls of logs and roof fallen in. Fifty years old. He sighed.

The door lay aside, rotting, but he went forward and sat on the sturdy bench he had made. Here, he had begun a good life. Never dreaming his family would begin a new community, now so grown. He leaned back and took a deep breath.

How long he sat there, he didn't know. Had he been asleep? He heard a definite crashing through the woods. That mother bear — had he forgotten her? He stood, he'd show them all, he'd show his mettle, an old man but a sure shot still, he'd prove that by finishing off the damned killer bear, no doubt. He lifted his musket, aimed at the sounds, heart thumping.

"Poppa, Poppa."

He shook his head. What could be wrong? He cupped

his hands and hollered back, "Here, at my cabin. Come see."

Jim ran up, frantic.

James frowned. "Something wrong back at the house?"

"Nothing's wrong, Poppa. I...I was just worried. You know what time it is?"

James looked up to check the sun, hidden by leaves. It did seem past noon. "Must be soon time for dinner?"

Jim threw his head back in a relieved laugh. "Dinnertime? That was an hour ago. You missed it." He grinned again. "But don't worry Poppa, they're holding you a plate."

James clapped his hand on his son's shoulder, and they set off. Father and son. To mourn their loss together.

Chapter Seventeen: 1855

"Just because she's getting married, there's no reason for Hannah to act like that, Poppa!" This first year after coming back, Jim was hauling timbers up the Brook Hill to build the new school. "I try to help, and she snaps — she's like a chicken with her head cut off. One day she wants one thing, the next it's another. Never seen anything like it."

"Remember how your sister Ann was?" panted his father, lagging behind with his staff: that Brook Hill was steep. "Usually so mild, but didn't she turn porcupine two weeks before the wedding? Women are just like that."

"We didn't have to whitewash our house before *her* wedding."

"The house needs it now."

"And the red ochre? That wasn't needed."

"But that trim — we splashed whitewash on it. Looks bad."

Jim laughed. "Nothing I hate more than whitewash. Stings the hands, gets in the eyes..."

"Anyhow, try to be nicer to Hannah, she's terble nervous."

"All she does all day is bake, find new recipes, think up special cakes when she should be helping Momma — we're gonna be feeding the whole of the Coast next week, the way she behaves! If I'd a known all this, I'd never have brought them scones to Edward Hayes with her last year."

Smudge and his new partner put shoulders to the yoke and sped up over the brow, Jim hurrying beside. "Everyone sure got together and did a fine job on the new bridge over the brook down there. You must be proud."

His father, panting behind with his staff, shook his head. "All of us, working together, we did it." It did look good, built well above any future spring rush. "I just wonder how you'll behave before your own wedding."

"Not you too, Poppa!" Jim shouted at the team. "Momma's always after me to find some girl. But I'll never find one like Momma, I can tell ya that much."

"If you think you're going to end up with your mother looking after you..." James set off with his son along the dirt road to Nelson's Lane below which Will Skene had sold his lower field for the school. "You watch how quiet the place will be in another week. Just Eleanor and me and your mother. But without Hannah.... Dunno how we'll manage."

Jim turned to give his father a look, and James changed the subject.

"Now Jim, you know last winter how we were complaining about not enough room for all our hay?"

"Yes sir, nearly lost a pile outside."

"Well, I been thinking.... Maybe we should get ourselves a new barn."

Jim let out a whoop. "That's just about the best news ever!" So good, also, that his father seemed to be claiming it as his own idea, and not his son's who'd been pushing for it before he'd left — indeed, one of the reasons he'd gone off to Montreal.

"Gee! Gee, boys, gee!" Jim yelled the command to turn

the oxen right, down into Skenes' lower field. Jim had spent the winter cutting this load of logs with his nephew, John. At the building, Jim undid the rope and they tumbled off in a heap.

His father stood taking it all in. Was he moved, Jim wondered. After all, the school was becoming reality. By the bank, they had dug a saw pit, and luckily, the Maugers, or Majors as they were known hereabouts, agreed to help build the actual structure, once the boards were pit-sawn.

"So Mr. Alford, how do you like your new school?" asked Fred Nelson, youngest son of James Nelson, who had arrived back the brook soon after James.

"Just fine, thank you Frederick." James nodded at his oxen. "I'll just take the team back — water them on the way."

Jim checked the large foundation stones which marked the eighteen-foot-square perimeter: an achievement, no doubt. Big Henry Smith, Vid's younger brother, Jim's age, was setting the last one with Jimmie Robinson, a real devil, always messing about. Each family had agreed to put in time and had been apportioned jobs.

"Come on now, Jimmie, time to get to work." Jim stood astride a beam and began swinging the broadaxe between his legs, shearing off the rounded edge of a log for the foundation.

"We just gonna put that there beam onto the foundation stones?" Jimmie asked. "What about mortar to hold it?"

"My dad's been burning lime fer it," Fred replied, "but he sez he don't think we need it. With these jeesly great stones Henry's father brought, nawthin's ever gonna shift them, mortar or no."

"That was the idea," Big Henry said as he sighted along the square edge of the boulder he'd placed. The Smiths were powerful men.

Jim agreed. "Looks firm enough to me."

Fred Nelson fell to squaring another beam. "Gonna be a big party at your place next week, they say, Jim; it's the talk of Shegouac."

"Yep. Hadda make a trip to Paspébiac for more flour. Tom Byers and John, they've been brewing buckets and buckets of beer."

"And you're gonna be next, Jim! We all thought fer shore you was bringing a wife back from the city."

"Now, Fred, no one'll get me near a woman for a good while."

Fred grinned. "Me, I can't wait to haul that Isabella into the hay mow. Not gonna come, she says, till she gets me to an altar." The other two laughed. "She don't mean it at all, at all."

"You don't want to go to church with her, me son," Henry said. "We all know her type. Don't know how to cook, don't want no family —"

"You're right. She just wants fun..." Fred said, ruefully.

"So, have fun!" Jim interjected. "Let her climb into that there loft with yez."

"Sure hope you're right." He looked up, and Jim turned to see Margie Skene, the very girl he had rescued, come down from her house across the road with a tin pail. As she approached, Jim noticed her freckles on the straight nose, the shy brown eyes, and the curly hair done up in a bun under a bonnet. Pretty nice picture: she had filled out some in the last year too.

"Well well, Margie, thanks," Henry held out his cup as

she arrived. "I'm thirstier than a sinner in hell." The three watched as she passed, giving them each a cold drink. "Mighty good of your poppa to send ya, Margie. And t'give us this here land."

"Wish he'd given it sooner," Margie said. "I been wantin' to read and write fer a long time. We've all been at him, Christy and Agnes, and me brother Will." She gave Jim a special smile and then, blushing, headed back to the Skene house by the lane.

"You know why she came, o' course?" Jimmie Robinson asked. "She's took a shine to ya, Jim."

"Pshaw, she's still a kid." Jim gave a laugh.

"Maybe, but she sure looks ripe for a ride," Henry said, then stopped himself as he saw a look of annoyance cross Jim's face.

"She's a good girl," Jim said. "And I told you fellas, I'm not getting me no wife for a good while yet."

Fred and Jimmie exchanged looks. Jim realized they were in cahoots, probably cooking all this up during the morning. But he did think back to the concern his father had voiced: how would his aged mother cope with two men and an old mother to feed?

"You fellas know of some young girl might like to come help Momma for the next while? She'd eat fine, and she'd have a good soft bed."

"Fine bed fer sure, you lying between her shafts," Fred cracked.

"What?" Henry gave a raucous laugh. "You want us to go up and down Shegouac asking who wants to share a bed with Jim?"

"You dumb sonofabitch," growled Jim. "I ask for help and all I get is a bunch o' stupid jokes."

"We'll sure do some thinking," Fred broke in, trying to calm Jim. "What about that schoolteacher I heard they're gonna get? Someone from away."

"Yep," Henry said. "Jim's got his father to order up some young Montreal filly, so she'd stay at his place, and you kin bet fer what."

Jim dropped his broadaxe and strode over to Henry, eyes blazing, though Henry was six inches taller and could finish Jim with one arm tied behind.

"Jim, Jim, just calm down," Freddie said. "Henry and us, we're only kidding ya. Look, me and some of the fellas found a keg of rum up in the loft where Poppa kep' it hidden. Wanna come over tonight?"

Jim turned away. Whatever had possessed him to fly off the handle? Why not just laugh at these friendly jabs? "Sorry, fellas, but Hannah's been driving me crazy. Don't know whether she's comin' or goin'. I'll be sure glad to get her out of the house. So that's why we need a helper fer Momma."

"How come she's so nervous?" Fred asked. "I heard she was keen to get married. Trouble is, poor Ned, he's so shy, no idea how he came to poppin' the question."

"Oh," said Jim, "you want to know how that went?"

The others stopped their work — Jim usually told a good story.

"They're good Catholics, of course. So when Ned got around to it, he asked her, 'How'd you like to be buried over with my folk?'"

They all burst out laughing. "What a way to propose!"

"So Hannah, she says, 'Well, I might not be buried with them, but I wouldn't mind spending time in this here house you're building. Looks pretty fine. No better carpenter than you, Edward Hayes.'" Jim laughed. "I guess that did it."

They all fell to chuckling and gossiping. Jim thought, his sister, with all the sweat and the fuss she was causing, was still doing right. But where did that leave him?

Chapter Eighteen

"Matrimony was ordained for the hallowing of the Union twixt man and woman," the Rev. Mr. Milne intoned, *"for the procreation of children to be brought up in the fear and nurture of the Lord; and for the mutual society, help, and comfort, that one ought to have of the other, in both prosperity and adversity."*

He was standing before Hannah and Ned, reading the words from his large prayer book, although he pretty well knew them by heart.

James glanced around. Their relatives filled the room, while others waited outside to attend the reception. Standing behind him were Hannah's older sister Mary Jane and husband Daniel Bisson, her brother Joseph and his wife Margaret Jane, both couples having been married the same day up in St. Peter's church in Paspébiac. Rev. Mr. Milne had decided to conduct this ceremony privately here, which often happened when there was no church for miles. Hannah's other sister Ann and her husband Bill Young were there, and of course the relatives of Hannah's groom Ned Hayes: his father Will Hayes, born in Ireland, and his second wife. Too bad, thought James, my daughter Ellen couldn't have come down with Billy Robertson from Cascapédia. All the grandchildren did look their best — but concentrate on the service, James told himself. His mind was wandering more and more of late — what was Mr. Milne saying? He was heavyset, with wire glasses, bushy white eyebrows and smooth pale cheeks flanking large lips, some paunch indicating his work was not physical but of the heart and mind. Lucky to have a clergyman here at all, James reflected.

"Edward Hayes, wilt thou have this woman to be thy wedded wife, to live together after God's ordinance in the holy estate of Matrimony?" Lost in reverie, James found the words ringing in his head like the peal of distant church bells. What repercussions! Echoing his own ceremony with Catherine long ago.

"I will," Ned responded. The Rev. Milne turned to Hannah. *"Hannah Alford, wilt thou have this man to thy wedded husband, to live together..."* Oh yes, oh yes, magical words, but what was this wave of emotion coming at him? *"Wilt thou obey him, and serve him, love, honour, and keep him, in sickness and health; and forsaking all other, keep thee only unto him, so long as ye both shall live?"* James made an effort to pull himself together.

"I will." Hannah looked radiant, but dropped her eyes. She never liked being the centre of attention.

Keep only unto him, yes, what a heaven-sent thought! Bringing such opposites together in one flesh, a man such as he, with all his frailties and now his aging body, and that glorious wife next to whom he lay every night in darkness, thanking the Lord for his luck. Nothing like the touch of a woman's fingers on your cheek, the feel of her lips against your ear, those fluttering words she had whispered when they were first married. The long road of their life had been bumpy, but such glorious vistas along the way — a journey blessed by heaven, no doubt.

"Who giveth this woman to be married to this man?"

Proudly James passed Hannah forward, so that Edward took Hannah by her right hand, as he followed the Rev. Milne in saying...

"I Edward, take thee Hannah, to my wedded wife, to have and to hold from this day forward..." James found his eyes filling with tears. Such power those words had, even when haltingly repeated by Ned: *"...for richer for poorer, in sickness and in health, to love and to cherish..."* James blinked, straightened up in his black suit, coughed gruffly, adjusted his tie. *"I Hannah, take thee Edward, to my wedded husband, to have and to hold..."* Just what Catherine had said forty years ago. How those words moved him, but never more than now. Was it because he'd not hear them again? *"To love, cherish and to obey till death us do part..."* Hannah looked with love at Ned.

James's shoulders shook, and tears spilled out, running down into his beard. With his handkerchief he tried to wipe them away, lost, even broken. What had come over him? So lonely, all this. But the phrase: "Till death us do part..." Yes, foretold in the oath Catherine and he had sworn. Would they not soon part, perhaps not a parting, more like an interlude, before meeting once again in the great Hereafter? But then, who could tell what promises would be kept, for who indeed knew whether God did in fact care? Would the two of them really meet again? The leaden weight of that phrase hung upon him like a dark prophetic anchor, dragging him down.

Catherine motioned for her son Joseph to bring a chair for her husband. He sat, head in hands — how awful to cry at your daughter's wedding.

* * *

But as it turned out, his being overcome had been highly regarded by the multitude, who had eaten their fill and indeed drunk a goodly amount of beer. Then afterwards, the group had moseyed over to the barn where old Xavier, whom James had bargained for down in Port Daniel, was playing the fiddle, with Exoré, the best foot-beater on the Coast, sitting beside him, beating away to his heart's content.

On the walk over to the threshing floor, Catherine had been solicitous. But altogether, James felt in the best of spirits, now that his anxiety, despair, and yes, joyfulness, had been released in a bucket of tears. Well, he was old, they should excuse him. And excuse him they had, as it appeared.

On the way over, Hannah ran up, "Poppa, you're not sad I'm leaving?"

"Oh no, my love. I'm the happiest father in Creation. Those were tears of happiness. I'm sorry if I —"

"No Poppa, I was so pleased. Everyone was watching you instead o' me. So I got relaxed, and enjoyed myself." She gave a happy laugh. "And you know, I have to have my first dance with you."

Later with the party in full swing and an old-fashioned jig playing, Catherine motioned up the ladder. "James, better climb into that mow!"

"I just checked it."

"These youngsters," Catherine said, "they take every opportunity. Look what happened to Ellen at our last wedding."

"That was at no wedding, Catherine. Billy got her in the back of a sleigh! Remember that week? The pile of sleigh rides? That's when."

"I don't care whether it was a sleigh ride or a wedding, I don't want any families blaming us for another forced wedding."

In his heart of hearts, James blessed Ellen. She was a plain girl. Billy Robertson, from Cascapédia, well, he was the handsomest fella around. She'd been under his spell for a while, even though only eighteen. So if that's the way to nab the handsomest man on the Coast, good for her! Of course, he'd never dare say that to Catherine. The child was born five months later.

Now it was well known all over that, although a newborn usually took nine months to make, the first one, well, God often formed that one a lot faster.

Then he turned to Catherine. "Time for the latest joke?"

Catherine nodded.

"All right, you know Mr. Milne, he came to visit sick old Mrs. Hottot. He asked her, my dear, have you ever been bedridden before?"

Catherine looked worried. "Is she sick again?"

"No, I think she's all right. But you know what she replied?"

"No. What?"

"Bedridden? Hundreds of times. And twice in a buggy!" With that, James headed for the ladder, leaving Catherine convulsed in laughter but doing her best to hide it.

He climbed over the broad beam to find the mow in complete darkness. Now what?

James coughed. "Now I've been sent up here to say, any young girl better leave right now." James spoke loud enough to be heard by the parents below. "There's a ladder down the other side and you can come back through the stable. So take your time, but I'll be back here with a lantern in five minutes, and any girl I find, I'll be telling her parents!"

That should do it, he thought, praising the Lord for putting those words in his mouth at the last minute; he'd been in a panic about what to say.

He took his time coming down the ladder with a good few piggins of beer inside him. Fellas had brought a keg of rum from Carlisle, and a bunch of boys kept going into the stable and emerging, decidedly happy, if not cross-eyed. Thank heaven this was the last daughter. He sat down beside Catherine.

The fiddler struck up a tune. The couples started to form for a square dance. Catherine took his hand. "James, not many more times we'll dance together. Can you take me onto the dance floor?"

Imagine! This packed earth referred to as a dance floor. He rose and, with Old World courtesy, bowed. He placed his ever-present big floppy hat on a low beam and they began to dance, manoeuvring among the many young girls flushed with exertion, sparkling eyes smiling at James as the host, even batting them in a provocative manner. Was he still attractive? He doubted it, but sure appreciated the fact. He and Catherine bobbed and wove in and out under the caller's orders, and whirled each other round.

Oh yes, he felt just like after the birth of Mary Jane. They had gone to a grand wedding up in New Carlisle, with dancing and music. He saw his wife again with her blonde curls poking out under the bonnet, cheeks flushed, full lips grown somewhat thin of late, but looking still delicious. Youthful sparks filled her too: she laughed and frolicked and flirted with the young men as they sped around. On the next exchange, Jim was her partner and whirled his mother around while James spun his beloved Ann, who had done so much to help his school get started. Such a pretty thing, slight of frame, brown eyes, still serious even during the dance, although she did flash her father a warm smile as they parted for the next circuit.

This reel ended and he and Catherine went to sit before they wore themselves out. A young fellow, bit of an upstart, came up and said, "Mr. Alford, sir, you cut a fine figure. Tell me, will every young fella have to go to that there school of yours?"

James nodded. "Don't you want to go to the school, Will?"

"Depends if ya got a pretty teacher or not. I heard we was gettin' someone from away."

"Don't worry, you'll get all the reading and writing and arithmetic you need. Now run along."

After the next reel, James saw Jim head toward him, sweating, looking unusually pleased in his one good suit. He bent down. "Poppa, everyone's been telling me, this weddin's the best yet."

"Maybe you'll find yourself a wife!"

"You never know..."

"But now I reckon it's time for you to climb that ladder with a lantern, and see what's going on."

"Aw Poppa, you're not going to give me that job? What if I find two or three girls?"

"Shoo 'em out like chickens. Or come down and tell me, and I'll go straight to their parents." Jim winced. "Go ahead now. And good luck."

Yes, all in all, a good party. Now the next milestone: get Jim married. And then, help him construct a fine barn to last the rest of his and his children's lives.

Chapter Nineteen: Summer 1856

"Well now, byes, you really want three threshing floors?" Charles Mauger asked, pronouncing it "thrashing," as did everyone here.

James looked askance at his son. "No no, two is all we need. Two mows, one at each end, loft in the middle, two threshing floors in between, is fine."

"Poppa," Jim said, "that's not what I had in mind..."

James could see from his son's remark Jim had been holding himself in and might blow up at any minute. Well, better get the design of the barn right.

On the one hand, he had a grudging admiration for the boy: his ideas were so grand. I mean, why the biggest barn on the Gaspé? They did need a larger one, and the present heap was not worthy of the "Old Homestead." But would it not be too large to finish? "You'll never get it done."

"We will, Poppa, never you mind, now."

James could see Charles eyeing the both of them.

Jim went on quickly, "And each threshing floor long enough to take a team of oxen, with hay cart behind."

Well, James thought, yes, you should be able to drive right in, and pitch the hay off the load into the mow. Good idea, in fact. He'd not thought of that.

"Well sir, we make her two dozen feet," said Charles. The Maugers came from Jersey so they spoke both English and French. Charles had settled in Shegouac where everyone was English, but his was still not perfect.

"And alongside of the *three* threshing floors, we want three hay mows, sure, but at the end nearest the house, we want a loft only, you see Poppa, and under that, we'll put a woodshed for Momma to open this side nearest the house."

"What rubbish is that now?" James asked tartly. "What's wrong with the back kitchen. We always used that. Your momma —"

"My momma hates not having enough space to take off our outer clothes in winter when we stack all that dry wood in there. She's asked me over and over!" A vein or two bulged on his son's neck.

"All right, all right, I agree. But the barn is just getting too, too big!"

"She gonna be one real big barn," Charles agreed and shook his head.

"No point in building it if it's not big enough," Jim almost shouted. "Why go to all the trouble? I'm the one in charge." He stopped himself. "Well, I mean you will be, Charles, but I'm cutting all the wood next winter." He turned to his father. "I've got Joey to help, and we can get more, if there's any money after buying that churn..." he ended, rather scathingly.

"Money, we've got money," James snapped. "But what about the wood? You'll never cut enough beams in one winter."

"So I'll do it over two winters."

"Gonna take a pile of lumber," Charles threw in cautiously. James could see he didn't want to offend either of them, but was cautious as any carpenter should be.

"Poppa," Jim blurted, "didn't me and Joe cut all those beams for the new school foundations? We only had a couple of fellas from up Saint Godfrey helping, fine workers, okay, but I know what cutting wood is."

"This will be ten times that schoolhouse," James roared in spite of himself, and then looked down, feeling somewhat sheepish.

Charles nodded. "For sure, oh yes yes yes. Lots of good strong beams. Maybe even eighteen inches square."

"Well, there are still three stands of good cedar back by the Second," Jim argued. "No trouble to float them down, if that brook floods again like this year."

"And if it doesn't?"

Jim shrugged.

James noticed his son was almost beginning to give up. "Well, far as getting help goes," he admitted, "we do have something put away. Probably do more good in others' pockets. If ya can get them fellas down Gascons way, they're real good lumberjacks. Maybe we could find some extra pound notes."

"Or dollars, they're comin' in now," Charles added. "Canadian dollars. Like in America."

Jim turned to Charles. "My question is, Mr. Major, how long you want those beams, and how many?"

Charles grinned and sat down. He picked up a board, and started to jot figures with his keel, the black chalk used by lumberjacks to mark logs. Jim and his father waited patiently.

Charles looked up. "You know, much better to work with a pattern. You take thirty feet deep for the threshing floor, so the whole barn, that make her thirty foot wide."

Jim nodded, thinking. "Go on."

"Well by jeez, fifteen feet wide each threshing floor. Them mows, thirty feet, she make," he paused, scribbled, "one hundred five feet long overall, by thirty feet wide. Longest barn around, for sure."

"So, how many beams?" Jim asked.

"She's comin, she's comin. Sure and a big pile of thirty-one-foot beams, and another pile of beams maybe not so wide, as rafters for the roof.... I figure out more tonight, and tomorrow at church I give you measurements." Although the Maugers were French, they were also Protestant.

James shook his head. His son had won. He'd gotten his big barn. Would he finish it? Would he himself live to see it finished?

* * *

"Well my dear, the poor woman didn't want anyone to know she was pregnant. Now how do you hide that, I'd like to know?" snapped Eleanor Garrett.

Catherine shook her head. "Terrible thing, for sure." She was spinning while her mother rocked and knitted, having the afternoon gossips she loved.

"So all right then, hide the fact you're pregnant, perhaps give the baby away, but don't for heaven's sake throw the little mite to the pigs!" Eleanor stopped her needles clacking. "That killed it, you know Catherine."

Catherine did know. The story had gone up and down the Coast in a flash, like all bad news. Her mother began knitting furiously again. Catherine now found it hard to concentrate: she was feeding the raw wool she had carded, twisting it between her fingers while turning the spinning wheel with one foot.

"Who's ever heard of such a thing? Imagine! Where was the Good Lord?" Eleanor shook her head. "Little newborn, torn apart by pigs."

"Mother, I'm as shocked as you are, so let's not discuss it." One thing she had kept to herself: it was rumoured Widow Carlson had conceived the child from her own father — another reason why, perhaps, the little dear was better off in heaven.

"I don't blame you, my dear. I don't blame you one bit. I mean, every time I think of that little baby, did the mother offer up a prayer as she threw it into the pig pen, I wonder?"

"Mother! Don't think about it!" Catherine was sick at the thought.

"No, I shall put it right out of my mind. All they found, you know, was part of the head, and a little arm..."

"Mother! Isn't it time for your nap?"

"Yes dear, I believe it is." Her mother put her knitting down in her lap and turned to Catherine. "You know, dear, you're looking tired."

Mothers — why do they have such perceptive eyes? "I am, mother. Very tired these days. I don't know what's coming over me."

"I know what's coming over you, Catherine. It's old age. You're nearly seventy. And you're looking after a houseful. You know my dear," she paused, and took a breath, "I've done a lot of knitting in my time. I hate to say it, but sometimes, enough is enough. Perhaps we should both of us slow down?"

"How do you mean, Mother?"

Eleanor paused, then looking straight ahead pronounced loudly, "We should sell the sheep."

Catherine glanced up. Her mother herself seemed shocked at her own words. "There, I've said it. You, you've made enough blankets. And the carding, I watched you yesterday. You're plain worn out."

Catherine nodded. "I was, Mother, I confess. I don't know what to do."

"Sell the sheep, that's what. Tell James. If you don't, I will."

"Well, let me think about it. It could be time. We do need the money for Jim's new barn."

Breathless, Martha rushed in with a basket of eggs. "Look, Ol' Momma, look what I brought yez. I almost got me a dozen." She set them down. "One, two, four, five —"

"Now dear, what comes after two?" Her daughter Ann who lived up by Travers Lane was sending Martha over to help every afternoon. Nice gesture, though she was only seven.

"Two? Three!"

Catherine nodded. "Go on."

"Three, four, five, six, seven..." she paused, "Ten?"

"No dear, you remembered yesterday. Aren't you learning your numbers in school?"

"Yes, but we got no school in summer. I can't remember numbers, but I like spelling. C-A-T, D-O-G, listen, M-O-T-H-E-R."

Eleanor rose. "Well, I think I'll go upstairs. Now you look after your grandmother, Martha, like a good little girl." She walked to the corner staircase and before making her regal way up, she paused. "Well, one good thing — that dreadful war in the Crimea has ended. What a saint that Nightingale woman must be!"

"Yes, Mother, Reverend Milne had us say prayers for

her last Sunday. Now go on up for your nap. We can talk about it tomorrow."

Eleanor smiled, and disappeared, happy no doubt they would have another subject for their daily gossip tomorrow.

"I'm ready to wind this skein, Martha. You remember how we do that?"

"Oh yes, oh yes." Martha came forward and held out her two hands, just wide enough for Catherine to wind onto them the new ball of wool she had spun. But even this, for some reason, was wearing her out. And she still had the washing.

As they passed through the summer kitchen, Catherine paused at her wonderful new iron stove — the gleaming black box on which she now cooked their meals. So much easier than the open fire, for sure, but it had taken getting used to. She hoped they'd include a woodshed in the new barn. With some more barking to keep the place warm, this summer kitchen could serve as a winter kitchen too. Another room. What a joy!

Once outside, Catherine realized how pleased she was at the return of the sun. Martha handed up the clean, damp clothes from the basket and Catherine began to pin them on the line, when she had to sit. "I think..." she said to Martha, "I'll just rest awhile. Take that tub, put it upside-down, and you can stand on it and hang up the rest of the clothes all by yourself."

"Oh goody," cried Martha and did just as she was told.

The three men came round the end of the old barn, so higgledy-piggledy with its outhouses and attachments, a shelter built on for the sheep, somewhere else for the extra hay, and a chicken lean-to.

James came forward. "You all right, Catherine?"

"Quite all right, James, thank you," she said cheerily. "I'm just taking a little sit down." Then she sat up tall. "You know, James, my mother is getting too old to do much more knitting."

"I've been wondering the same thing," he replied, thinking she must be in her nineties, though no one took much notice of birthdays hereabouts. Birth dates were marked in the family Bible, and then forgotten.

"So perhaps," Catherine went on, "we could do with fewer sheep..."

"Get rid of them? Good idea, Momma!" Jim glanced at his father. "Those blasted sheep, always gettin' through any fence a man could build. We've got all the scarves and mittens we'll ever need, and so have the grandchildren."

"And enough blankets, James," Catherine added.

"Come on, Poppa? Whaddya think?"

James frowned. Catherine knew sheep had been a part of his life for years. James nodded slightly. "Let's sleep on it."

He would end up agreeing, of course. The end of an era, in a way. If only another one would begin with Jim getting a wife.

Chapter Twenty: 1857

"I see, I see," cried his grandchild, Martha Young. "The three stars for his belt, and three there, for his sword."

"Good, Martha," James replied to Will and Ann's eldest. "Now can everyone else see that?"

A chorus agreed. Late this autumn evening a year later, James was giving a class in the constellations outside the new one-room schoolhouse. Lanterns had been set up by the door. "All right now, for something more complicated, Orion's shoulders. They're called Betelgeuse and Bellatrix." As they crowded round, he pointed. "See up there, where his shoulders should be, those two bright stars?"

One after another, they voiced their agreement.

Before he went on, he noticed at the corner of the schoolhouse, the new teacher, watching. In the dark of the moon, James could not see his pasty face but recognized the gaunt frame. Oh-oh, trouble. He had never liked the young man, but he was the only one with a diploma to apply from Montreal. Earlier in the week James had approached him about teaching the stars to the students, but the pimply schoolmaster had objected. However, James was chairman of the trustees, so the twenty-two year old had to swallow it.

"And now, everyone, you're in for a surprise. Did you know that stars have different colours?"

A couple of the older boys scoffed. "Prove it to us," challenged his grandchild, Charlie Bisson. James's grandchildren outnumbered the others because his own children made sure to send their offspring after supper. The Smiths were there, too, with Sarah Nelson's children, Sam Allen's, and several others.

"Prove it? Look above Orion's belt, his left shoulder up there? That's called Betelgeuse. Now go the same distance down to his right knee, see that bright star? Named Rigel." Most of them nodded.

He felt the teacher's eyes boring into him. Pity the young man didn't want to learn. James's time in the Navy had taught him a good deal. Even the fishermen here who used stars didn't know their names.

"All right now, look back and forth. Notice a different colour in each star? What is the top colour?"

Several of the older boys, including Charles Bisson, called out, "Red, orange, pink."

"All right and what colour is the bottom one?"

They began to call, "Blue."

"There now, you see? Different colours!"

Out of the general surprise came a question from Charles again: "Why?"

"None of us know that yet. But just be aware there are different colours, and one day, you might get the answer."

He then went on to point out some of the easier constellations, such as Taurus, with the Hyades sprinkled around. He had picked a good star night, with no moon.

As he was explaining, his mind went back over the night he'd stared up into the heavens when his first child, Mariah, had been born. He always found such consolation in the age-old patterns, with their myths every naval officer knew. Imagine, four decades later, that little baby Mariah had children of her own, already grown up and learning about the stars themselves. How the years roll by!

"Now let's all have a little cup of hot soup before I show one more constellation, and then, it's home to bed!"

Jane handed out the soup that her mother Mariah had made, hot and watery. Margie, Will Skene's daughter, handed the old man a cup, casting her eyes down. James didn't notice and sat to relax, marvelling in this new building, finally finished this October. Twenty-seven students on a good day when they all came. Well, now he could retire from the trustees at Christmas. Better focus on the barn, which had to be perfect for Jim who was doing most of the work. It might inspire him to get married...

He glanced up to see the teacher still watching. He refilled his cup of soup and walked over. "Like some soup, Henry?"

Henry shook his head. "Sir, this is no time or place for lessons. The students have enough to do. I find it hard enough to get the Scriptures into them, without you diverting them every night."

"Not every night, Henry, once or twice in autumn, and maybe once or twice in spring, when the skies change." James wanted to bash the little whippersnapper, but reminded himself to behave.

"You may be chairman here, sir, but I'm complaining to the superintendent of schools." With that, Henry strode off.

James looked after him. Should have bashed the skinny fella after all — might have knocked some sense into him. Then Margie Skene shouted, "Mr. Alford, Mr. Alford, look!"

"It's on fire," another voice yelled.

James turned to the bay, and froze. There, just beyond the cliffs, he could see a schooner, three-masted no doubt, and on fire. What appeared to be sailors were climbing the burning rigging, others were running back and forth with pails, trying to douse the flames. No hope, James could see: it was still afloat, but going to sink for sure.

"Quickly," he roared, "down to the brook, oldest fellas first, maybe we can row out. How many rowboats we got down there?"

"Two this morning," a voice piped up, probably a Vautier, who used the brook beach as a landing.

"First ones down, jump in and row. I'll go in the second lot."

The children tore off, and James grabbed his staff and followed. What on earth had happened? It looked just like one of the privateers the *Bellerophon* had been chasing. He remembered all too well that once, when a ship had not heeded their flag signal to surrender, the Captain had issued the order to fire. Only a few shots, but they'd set the ship afire. Since it was only a privateer, the Navy crew felt badly. Lowering boats, they had rowed quickly across the intervening waves, but by the time they reached it, the schooner had sunk with all hands perishing.

He reached the Brook Hill and started down. The children raced on ahead. He saw them stop and bunch up where the road veered near the cliff. "Go on, go on," he cried.

"It's not there!" they called back.

James crossed to the road's edge and looked out over the bay.

Nothing.

But no boat would sink in that short a time! What was going on?

They gathered round, all talking at once. "I heard tell of that before," young Billy Skene said. "My dad, he told us about it. Him and two fellows was coming home one night from down Port Daniel way, and he seen the same thing, maybe the year afore I was born."

"My momma too," another one called out. "She told me she seen it three year ago. She was so scared she didn't tell no one, made us all promise. Same thing, ship on fire, three masts, sailors runnin', then she up an' disappears."

"Must be the ghost ship," an older boy called. "We seen the ghost ship!"

They turned and scattered home, all talking excitedly about what they had seen.

Well, the story would be all over Shegouac tomorrow, James knew. He trudged down to the new bridge with some of the children. Could it have been a vision? But they all saw it. He reached the opposite side of the Brook Hill, climbing it slowly, while the others ran on ahead.

Well, better not wake Catherine. In the morning they'd speak of burning ships and constellations. So he passed the house, deciding his addled mind needed time to sort it all out: this visitation, if that's what it was, his search for faith, and his son, Jim, still without a wife. The oxcart track ran diagonally up the side hill; he climbed it in silence. Not as easy as before. Would there ever come a time when he couldn't climb it at all? No sir, he'd stride up till he dropped. Three-quarters of the way, he saw Mariah's children scramble in their back door, agog with their sighting and all their grandfather had explained about the constellations. No going to bed for a good while yet, he guessed.

Panting hard, he reached the top, and looked up. The whole northern sky had come alive with the dancing shifting bands of the Northern Lights, made more vivid with no moon.

So long since he'd seen them — what a treat! The past summers he'd taken to going to bed with the sun and getting up when it rose. There they were, delicate, shifting curtains, all the happy spirits, dancing especially for him. He leaned back on his cedar rail fence, marvelling.

Right now, seeing these heavenly arrays, he asked himself: how could God not exist? Who else created such a celestial spectacle? He studied the purples, pale mauves, and then vermilion, with streaks of white flashing, the mythic heroes up to their hijinks that his old tutor at Raby Castle had spoken about. The man loved Greek myths and had explained a lot of them to young James.

He didn't feel the cold, though wind swept the frozen fields, rattling the barren branches on the crest.

As he stood, transfixed, in the distance, he heard a woman's voice.

From the heart of the gracefully waving colours, he heard, "I am here." The voice of Little Birch! "I am here, James."

She had told him: "I will always be here for you in the dancing lights." Yes, he remembered, oh so very long ago, her lithe sapling form, her strength as she held him in lovemaking, so powerful, the grasp of nature itself, of an original inhabitant, nurtured by the bay, by forests, salmon in streams and caribou on their interior highlands, all that first year. How could he ever forget his Magwés?

His eyes misted up. Damned old man: bent frame, wrinkled cheeks, worn-out heart. What a fool, crying at everything and anything: his daughter's wedding, the birth of his latest grandchild — old idiot, with far too much reason to rejoice. Just as the sky above gathered in its clouds, so his old mind gathered in to itself the milking of his cattle, scything his wheat, stooking sheaves, shovelling pathways through deep snow, seeding his barley over rolling acres, those walks on springtime fields and autumn trails, so many and such wonderful seasons, ever more quickly passing by for him and for his aging wife.

Indeed, how very lucky to have spent so much time at her side. If only he could make up words to say that, he thought, as he hauled out his big handkerchief to smear his face dry.

"So tell me, Magwés," he cried, "is He up there with you? The Great Creator, is he there? Can you tell me, once and for all?"

James forced his mind to fall silent, and to listen. The wind picked up, he could hear it soughing in the nearby pine; patiently he waited, waited for the words he needed to hear.

But after an endless time, still bathed in the magic of the heavenly curtains, drifting, wafting, caressing the black sky, no word came back.

Chapter Twenty-One: Winter 1858

"I'd love to go for a ride," Angel Dowd had said. "I didn't think you had such things as sleigh rides here on the Coast." Jim's parents had invited the new schoolteacher over for a bite of supper. The trustees had happily managed to replace that surly youth from the previous year.

"We don't usually," said his father. "But you know, Jim bought himself a new stallion. Very fast. I reckon he'd like an excuse to take him out on a sleigh ride."

Jim glanced at his father: were they setting him up? The pressure to get married. Would she really like settling down to wash clothes, clean house, bottle jams and preserves, work from dawn till dusk? Well, he'd find out.

He'd bought the stallion with part of the sheep money from the summer before, and trained Lively himself, with help from the Rosses who'd had horses all their lives. He'd pastured him back in a pasture in the Hollow he'd cleared the year before going to Montreal. Lively loved it there, although Jim's father had warned of possible bears. But none had turned up — he'd like to see the bear fast enough to catch Lively! And cougars, which he had heard about, even the one that attacked his father at his cabin by the brook. Well, they stayed further back nowadays, only rarely spotted in the fields the last ten or twenty years. Summer evenings he'd get Lively used to a halter and bridle, hitching him in the sulky, and even, sometimes, using him to haul cartloads of seaweed, or sand, though the oxen were much better at this. So now, he'd just have some fun. "I'd sure be awful glad if you'd like to come."

"Thank you kindly," Angel had replied with a smile. Jim had had the curious sensation she had been angling for just such an invitation. And so here they now were, together, bundled under the "buffalo," setting off on a crisp night's adventure.

Strange feeling, no doubt, snuggled up against a girl after such a long time. Jim was pretty pleased at his luck, though Angel was by no means greatly attractive. She had broad square features, large glasses that covered her grey eyes, and a petite, though athletic, frame. So she might be all right for hard work, if she had a mind for it. He'd picked her up back at the Nelsons' where she boarded, and now they were heading down Skenes' hill toward the main road. The full moon lit up the whole white, pristine countryside as if it were day. In front of the Skenes' house, Jim saw some youths in a snowball fight.

As the sleigh swished by, Margie Skene looked up to see him and froze into inactivity. A snowball caught her on the side of her head and sent a shrapnel of snow showering across her shoulders. What a look of alarm!

Jim wondered why. Of course, not often in Shegouac did one see couples on a sleigh ride.

"Who was that?" Angel asked.

"Oh, just a bunch of neighbours having fun."

"No, I mean the girl. She looked at us. What was wrong?"

"Her? Oh, that was Margie Skene. A fine girl. You're not teaching her?"

"No, she's too old for school. Old enough, I should think, to be looking for a man."

"Oh no, she's just a kid." Jim hauled on the reins to turn Lively left onto the main road, a packed track built up to snow level by many sleighs and marked by poles near areas of drifting. As they trotted briskly along, some farmhouse windows showed a low orange glow from their lamps still lit. But many of them were dark, the families having gone to bed with the sun.

Angel nestled against him. It was cold, not the bitter frost that bit your cheeks and hurt your eyes, but just enough to make one slide further down under the buffalo. "You like our 'buffalo'? That's what we call these here sheepskin blankets. When we butchered a couple of sheep last year I saved these."

"Mmm." She moved her head in its woollen tuque closer to his. "And I like the name of your horse, too. Lively."

Jim found his arm moving around her shoulders. She snuggled even tighter. "Ever been for a sleigh ride before?"

"Oh yes, lots," Angel said. "We would gallop over Montreal mountain, in parties with the officers. They called us muffins." She giggled. "Such fun. I was studying for my teaching diploma."

A muffin girl, oh yes, Jim remembered those military men in that pub. But what were they — surely, not whores? "Would you always go out with the same fella?"

"Did I have a boyfriend, is that what you mean? No, silly, I had no boyfriend. We all did it for fun. Several officers did want to get married, but that always ended in disaster. Myself, I knew better than to accept any proposal from an Army man. Besides, I have my own life. I don't want to be a wife. At least not yet."

"Good for you." Well, that put paid to Ol' Momma's and Poppa's idea.

Lively trotted along like a prince among horses, as full of life as his name implied, his hooves kicking up a bright flurry of loose snow. The runners made a lovely crisp sound as they coasted over bumps and ruts. Nothing like it! Jim felt light-headed with the pleasure of a lively horse, a girl in his arms, a full moon, a black night above, white glistening snow below, everything aglow with a magical light.

"So do you miss the big city?" Jim asked, by way of getting her to talk, though he soon found there was no problem there.

"A bit, yes. Always something going on. Last year I worked with the Abolitionists — they help slaves come up from the southern states. Lots in Canada West, but some in Montreal, too."

"Oh yes?" Jim wasn't really up on the subject. "Abolitionists?"

"None here yet? They are tryin' to abolish slavery south of the border. We've even found safe places for them up here."

"No, no one's been down, hereabouts."

"Well, they'll come. Methodist preachers, mostly. Wanting money for escaping slaves. Montreal is so advanced, I guess. You know, the Victoria Bridge is almost finished."

"That bridge across the St. Lawrence? I worked on that, you know."

"Did you now? Twenty-five spans, all iron, stretching almost two miles across. They say it's one of the wonders of the world. How they ever did it! No one dreamed it would get finished. Queen Victoria's coming to open it, next year."

"Well, that'll be pretty much of a celebration."

"Amazing how the world is changing. You can now take a steamer, and more or less count on being across the Atlantic in two weeks! Just imagine! My father knows a man who went over on business and came back the next month, no problem at all." She rattled on, "Yes, and you know, when the bridge opens, you'll be able to go by train from Montreal right through to Boston. They predict in twelve hours. How it's all changing! That's why I love the city. You never know what's going to happen next."

"Things are changing here, too. We bought my mother one of those iron stoves. When I was little, she always cooked on an open fire."

"Really. Stoves are new here?"

Jim nodded. "Two kids burned to death when I was young. Clothes caught on fire." Angel gasped. "Well, that's all we had. These new iron rigs are so much easier, Momma says."

He felt her hand slide round his waist. "All in the last twenty years. Montreal's got probably a hundred thousand people now," Angel went on. "Father can remember when there were fields all around Monkland, you know, the residence of the Governor General, and he's nowhere near as old as your father."

"Yes, I guess Poppa's seen a lot of changes. Never even heard of a screw-driven ship. But you know, he fought in the Navy against Napoleon."

"Did he? He must have been very brave." She snuggled closer.

The night was nothing if not romantic. "It's something I've always wanted, a sleigh. And of course, even better, a pretty girl beside me..."

He was surprised when in answer, she reached up and kissed him on the cheek. Before she slipped back into her warm corner she lifted her face expectantly. Of course, he turned and their lips met.

My! What an exciting sensation. So long in coming. Her tongue began to move over his lips, then she retired under her "buffalo" once again.

How easy that had been! Why was it so hard with all the others? Could it be that she liked him? "Is that part of being a muffin?" he asked, rather gauchely.

"Oh no. I like you. You're much smarter than the other fellows I've met around here. You're someone I can have fun with."

"But not marry?" His heart beat faster.

"No, I told you, I have a career." She moved away slightly.

They reached the crest of Port Daniel mountain. Jim had hardly noticed. As they broke over the top, they could both see before them the lovely curve of Port Daniel bay. Glorious in the moonlight: little white houses huddled in drifts with their pristine snow curled comfortably around, a dim light or two showing, the distant tinkle of sleigh bells as other horses whipped along below. Behind the town lay the great, flat pancake of Port Daniel lagoon, half a mile across, iced over, with a dark ripple of moonlight where the river flowed out from the black forest.

He pulled Lively to a stop. They were silent for a time, and then Angel said, "I suppose if I were a different person, I would love nothing more than to spend my life here." Was she changing her mind? "Though I suppose you get used to it."

"I guess you do," was all Jim could say. But could anyone ever get used to it?

He began to hunger for another kiss. He slapped the reins and off went Lively, careening down the hill at top speed. They both shrieked with delight — such an exciting ride. They hit the curve, and slowed down as Lively galloped past the small settlement: small houses, a blacksmith, and a general store at the foot of the dark hill opposite.

Jim pulled Lively to a walk.

"What's up ahead?" Angel asked.

"Gascons. The badlands first. No house for miles. Folks don't go, especially at night."

"Oh goody! Let's try." Angel looked up at Jim.

Jim frowned. Would it be wise? Would he be blamed if something happened? She cut short his thinking by reaching up and, holding his cheek close with her little mittened hand, kissed him firmly.

"All right, we'll give it a try."

Lively climbed into the dark pine and spruce forest. The track was still visible, no doubt, but not nearly as travelled as between Port Daniel and Shegouac. The horse began snorting, nostrils flaring. Not enjoying this, Jim saw.

And then, another magical happening, Angel kissed him on the mouth, and with her hands behind his head, clung to him as though she could never get enough.

He wrapped both his arms around her, leaving the horse to trot on its own. They both began to breathe more quickly, as though they had been running. He could almost feel her heart beating through their heavy clothes, and her cold lips, now getting warm for sure, pressing against his.

They went on for some minutes until Jim could stand no more. "It's wonderful, it's just so wonderful. But don't you see, it's driving me crazy."

"I know what to do," she whispered. With that, they disappeared under the buffalo.

What an amazing sensation — quite new for him. When at last they emerged, he opened his eyes, the stars were still above, sparkling in the harsh blue moonlight. A light wind moved out of the dark spruce woods across the rutted road.

He saw an indentation ahead, and turned Lively round.

Lively set off at an usually brisk pace, knowing he was en route to his warm stable once again. They loved the speed. And the glorious moonlight. They talked little, planning nothing, but happy at this unexpected encounter.

But with it all, the whole experience left Jim rather dissatisfied. These were the goings on of a big city, and not for him, no sir. But perhaps she might even stay another year or more? "You are going back to Montreal, Angel?"

"Yes Jim dearest, in June. But I will never forget our sleigh ride together."

A sure bet, neither would he.

Chapter Twenty-Two: 1859

Jim was not afraid of a fight. Oh no. But that last time they'd had a big scrap with the French down in Port Daniel, Little Arnold's big brother had busted his wrist, and it never healed well, so he had to do all his work with one hand. Now if you're a farmer, you could not risk that sort of thing. But he knew what happened when fellas got to drinking.

And to make matters worse, he'd heard rumblings last time he'd gone down to Port Daniel to have Lively shod. Dan Legallais had apparently got a French girl in trouble, and his family had refused to let him marry her, because she was Catholic. And so in spite of the girl's pleas and his own protestations, they did not marry. The Frenchies were all up in arms now, blaming the whole of Shegouac. Well, if they wanted a dust up, he'd be in the thick of it.

"Whoa." At the Smiths, he pulled Lively to a halt, pleased to see Henry waiting. "Jump in." He was bigger and stronger than anyone in Shegouac.

"She's gonna be some meetin'!" Henry vaulted in. "Bet the whole country will be there. You ever seen a black fella, Jim?"

Lively took off, trotting merrily for Port Daniel. Nephews and nieces from the Byers and Youngs were hanging on behind in Jim's new express wagon, a buggy seat with a space behind for hauling things. "Yep, saw a couple in Montreal. One black as charcoal." A Methodist minister, an Abolitionist, was bringing a former slave, a black fellow. The whole country was on its way to see what he looked like.

"Bound to be a pile of French fellas there," Henry ventured. "Hope there's not too much liquor."

The sun was sinking behind a low bank of clouds as they made good time through Shegouac. On the way they passed couples and families walking and Jim stopped to give them lifts until the express wagon bulged. Lively enjoyed a good pull, but Jim knew he found it hard going. They climbed Port Daniel mountain and, once over, arrived at the Port Daniel schoolhouse. Other horses were already tied up, with more coming. They dismounted and Henry tied the horse to the hitching rail as Jim stood to survey the scene. Yes sir, kegs of beer on the backs of carts, and flagons of rum were being passed around. A real celebration.

Jim spotted Margie Skene. When she caught sight of him, she turned away. Ever since that night in the sleigh with Angel, Jim had found her acting odd. He stared at her: she had filled out for sure. Well, he thought, if only she'd been born a bit earlier...

Jim decided to head into the crowded school to find Sam Nelson. Most of the seats were already taken, so he had to stand at the back, but there was Sam.

They greeted each other and chatted while they waited for the meeting to begin. In came Reverend Lyster, who had trained under the Reverend Mr. Milne and now was in charge of Port Daniel and with him was another gentleman in clerical garb, probably the Methodist. Following, the crowd gaped as they saw an imposing black man. He caused gasps and excited giggles from the assembling gathering as the three took their places in front.

Soon Reverend Lyster introduced his Methodist friend with a few words about the abolition of slavery. And now, here, they would all learn first-hand how on the Coast they could help this worthy cause.

Then the Methodist, Mr. Watkins, gave a short preamble, and went on, "Families down South, they actually own other humans! You don't pay a slave his wages, you just buy him. And if he escapes, like sheep over a fence — instead of acting like the Good Shepherd and bringing them back into the fold, you know what they do? They hang 'em!"

This caused a ripple of shock and disgust among the listeners.

"Oh yes, and listen to this, if you have women as slaves, you can do whatever you like with them."

This caused even more of a horrified reaction, and voices rose. Jim clenched his fists as his ire rose, when Sam, who had his head cocked to one side, said, "Something's going on outside. Come on!"

Jim was loath to leave, but followed. In the semi-darkness of dusk, Jim saw a brawl in progress. A few girls, safely out of harm's way, watched with wide eyes. Should he run in to alert Mr. Lyster? But then he spotted Henry Smith on the ground with four French fellows on him, pounding away. He tore down the steps and launched into the fray.

He hauled the smallest one off first and knocked him backwards. He grabbed off the next, threw him aside and fell on the third, slugging it out. The French fellow, short and built like a bull, gave Jim a mighty wallop that sent him flying, but when the man went to pounce on him, Henry had gotten up and came to the rescue.

Real mayhem. Both sides were piling on each other with full vigour. Freed from the heavy Frenchman, Jim grabbed another who was pounding a Shegouacer on the grass. He hauled him off and smacked him good, knocking him flat, but another jumped him from behind. As he spun round, another crashed into him and he fell. Struggling to get up, he got knocked down again. Two English fellas from Port Daniel rescued him, only to be attacked themselves by four others.

What a brawl! Though his jaw ached and his eyes stung from the blood, Jim was almost enjoying himself. In he went again, swinging wildly, landing a good few punches here and there, helping comrades, ducking blows, tackling others, being hauled off and getting himself pounded in this wild free-for-all! Shouts of *"Câlisse"* and *"Tabarnac,"* and *"You bastard"* raged back and forth over the grounds until at last the doors opened and the big, black ex-slave, Longuen by name, boomed out, "Brothers, brothers, stop all this!"

He grabbed the rope and hammered at the school bell hanging by the door so that it jangled loud and true. "Stop right now! Listen to me. Listen, aren't y'all brothers? Men your age down South are chained by their necks, starving, harnessed like horses to haul wagons, and here you are, free men — acting like fools!"

With the jangling of the bell and the funny accent of the black man, each side shook off the other and lay about in pain or exhaustion. "Listen to me, I still got relatives rattling their chains in Southern prison houses, and here you are, acting like chillun. Shame on you!"

"Damn right," a few English yelled, amid cries of *"Qu'est-ce qu'il dit?"* from the French. Mr. Lyster translated his message into French.

"C'est pas nous," one big thundering French tough yelled. "They start! They act bad to our girls. They no good!"

There was a chorus of agreement and disagreement, but at least, no more fighting. The meeting was brought to order.

"Brothers, brothers," Longuen boomed, "apologize right now for any insults to the ladies. Both sides!" This was met with silence, and odd looks. "Come on now, make your apologies. Be friends. I'll tell y'all stories ye'll never forget, but only if you calm down."

Others came out of the hall to stand on the stairs or lean against walls. The fighters began to unwind like obedient schoolchildren. Stories? Well, that made one sit up and listen. Nothing like a good story, everyone knew.

"When Sister Moon comes up, we'll all do our share of singing. Songs from the South. But for now, just listen."

Oh good, a singsong. Jim shook his head to clear it, tried to rise, but just fell over again. Damnation, he'd sure taken the bad end of that brawl. But then he saw, wending towards him... Margie Skene! What was she doing?

She knelt by him with a cup of water she had gotten from the school pump. She got out her handkerchief. "Jim, what *have* you done to yourself?"

He shrugged. "They musta knocked me about a bit. Lotsa fun, though." His face felt as if it had been kicked by a dozen Livelys. In Margie's big brown eyes, he saw concern mingled with determination. She began to smooth away the blood and to wash clean the cuts. "Jim, you mustn't do that sort of thing," she whispered in a motherly way. "You could get yourself hurt."

Those eyes, he hadn't looked closely into them before, so wide, brown, full of tenderness. Freckles on her nose, too, very pretty. And what a womanly touch in someone so young, as she cleaned up his blood.

She too seemed to be studying him. She put a cold folded hankie on his temple where a bruise was beginning to flower.

Meanwhile, Longuen was speaking in rich, deep tones, the voice of a true orator. Margie turned and sat beside Jim, so they could listen. No more fighting tonight, that seemed obvious. The man held them spellbound, with harrowing tales of what went on in those Southern states, and of the blood-curdling escapes that his compatriots had made, finding their way finally to Canada West.

"We don't know how lucky we are on the Coast, Margie."

"That's for sure, Jim," she said simply.

He had a great urge to turn and kiss her, but restrained himself. This was not the time nor the place, in front of everyone gathered in the moonlight in front of the old Port Daniel schoolhouse. But one thing for sure: Margie might be young, but she was someone worth waiting for. Oh yes, but would she wait for him?

Right now, he only squeezed her hand, and mumbled, "Thank you, Margie."

After a time, she broke the silence. "When I seen ya with that schoolteacher o' yourn, I swore to meself I'd never speak to you again. You'll never guess what that did to me, Jim Alford. For me, that was the finish."

"So, how come you're nice now?"

She shook her head. "No idea. When I seen you beaten around like that, I just went right to that pump and got me some water." She shrugged. "If a fella needs looking after, I guess I figured, that's my job."

Chapter Twenty-Three:
Autumn 1859

The service opened with the ancient reassuring summons: *Dearly beloved Brethren, the scripture moveth us in sundry places...* The one-room school was packed: quite a turnout for this first visit of Quebec's Bishop Mountain to Shegouac.

Nothing like joining this community in worship for a sense of stability and even, yes, permanence. If only, old James thought, he could just give himself up to the collective feelings, but doubt and disillusionment on whether God existed still plagued him. He missed Jim, too, for sure. Maybe once he took a wife he'd start coming again, but would that ever happen?

His mind inevitably went back to their dinner earlier. The Reverend Mr. Milne had brought the Bishop to the Alford house for their midday meal. "Such insidious new ideas," Mr. Milne had mentioned, "sweeping England! Questioning the very existence of God!" He went on to say that hundreds, if not thousands, of Anglicans might be lost to the church.

Heavens, thought James, others beginning to doubt, too? How could that be? "Survival of the fittest?" Mr.

Milne went on. "How so? I haven't read him myself. But he'll have us descending from monkeys next."

"Oh, he has." The bishop's words came back to James all too clearly.

"Dreadful business," Rev. Milne had said. "So you think it's affecting our believers?"

"Well, of course, not over here, but in the Old Country there's been a big hue and cry."

"Some even leaving the church?"

"Afraid so. I don't myself see the fuss. That Darwin fellow is a scientist, it seems. But you know, Lyell, the fellow who found those buried dinosaurs, he refuted the Genesis idea of creation some time ago. Though I'm not so sure the Old Testament is meant to be taken as literal, or really scientific, theory."

James could see the good sense in the survival of the fittest idea. Any farmer knew how to breed from the strongest animal. But if that meant that God did not exist, where else could he turn? Scientists claiming that Genesis was wrong! But how? And when? What did it all mean?

"Are many in the Old Country upset by all this?" Mr. Milne asked the bishop.

George Jehoshaphat Mountain hailed from England and had recently co-founded Bishop's University. "Not sure. No trouble hereabouts, though. I doubt anyone on the Coast has heard of Charles Darwin, nor read *On the Origin of Species*."

James thrust this conversation from his mind. How awful to hear, from the very mouths of the clergy, that so many others were now doubting the existence of God. Where else could he find faith?

Hear what comfortable words our Saviour Christ saith

unto all that truly turn to him: come unto me all that travail and are heavy laden and I will refresh you. So God loved the world... Yes, comfortable indeed. So often on so many occasions, summer and winter, they had not failed to give him serenity. But now...

Catherine leaned over and whispered: "James, you know, I'm so pleased Jim had the foresight to buy Lively two years ago, over your objections. There is nothing I enjoy more than being driven to church in a buggy."

James shook his head. "When that son of mine gets an idea into his head, there's no stopping him."

After repeating the General Confession and absorbing the main service, James and Catherine stayed behind for the communion. He wanted to kneel beside her at the altar rail and receive the body and blood of Christ from the very fingers of the Bishop of Quebec. As he knelt, he prayed for some absolute conviction to descend. In his cupped hands, he took the morsel of bread and swallowed. And then the chalice: *"The Blood of our Lord Jesus Christ, which was shed for thee, preserve thy body and soul unto everlasting life..."* But nothing. No great angel of faith touched him on the forehead, as the dove had descended so long ago on the Jordan River. How destitute he felt, never to be given the ultimate conviction of Someone greeting him as he marched forward into the Great Darkness.

He rose and returned to his seat along with Catherine, who seemed somehow stronger after she had received the Sacrament. Well, at least he could say in all truth, how glorious was this gift of his wife! Perhaps that in itself was a kind of proof of the goodness of the Divine. But plagued with his obsession and his quest, he sat down to wait out the rest of the service.

* * *

That autumn Jim knelt on the roof of the barn, nailing on his last few rows of shingles. He was only half concentrating. The surface of the blue bay was sparkling as a cool autumn wind ruffled its waves. Further out, the surface gleamed like the silver sheen on a chalice. To his left, a point of land would one day make a fine spot for a wharf. He might get families together to help construct it, instead of using the brook's mouth as a landing for their fishing boats. After all, he'd organized the school getting built.

His grandmother, Eleanor, was probably still sitting in her favourite chair looking out over the bay, too. The Rev. Milne came at least once a month to see her, ailing as she was, though still alert. What worried Jim mainly was his own mother, who seemed increasingly frail. I wonder if I'll ever get to be as old as my grandmother? Or Old Momma and Poppa. With all the accidents, disease, whooping cough, diphtheria, meningitis, will I live that long?

If only Jim could believe, too. He genuinely longed to, but frankly, there just seemed so little likelihood of a decent God when so many good people around were hauled off by that old fella with the scythe, and so many others maimed in accidents, and felled by disease.... Maybe he should keep asking in his heart how to develop a strong belief like his father.

Above the glimmering bay, the horizon shaded up into a pale blue with the low flecks of cumulus. Overhead, the clear azure heaven was crossed by herring gulls crying a lament for their land stolen by these settlers and, as Poppa so frequently said, from the original inhabitants, the Micmac. All in all, what better place to make a home:

water for the cattle "back the brook," lots of pastureland, enough acreage to feed all the cattle they'd ever need, and maybe sheep again, too?

The back door banged as someone came out. Time for supper? James slid six more shingles out of the pack and laid them on the plank he had tacked to make the row straight and then nailed them down. Start low and work your way up; he'd finish tomorrow and would place the saddle boards on the peak. Then, they'd haul up the ventilator which Mr. Major had fashioned for them, to give a finishing touch. In the barnyard below, chickens and a couple of ducks squawked as someone hurried through them.

Jim looked down, and there was Margie Skene. "What are you doing here?"

"Poppa sent me over with some fish and your mother asked me to stay fer supper. I'm supposed to tell you it's ready."

She bent and roughed up Rusty, who obviously loved her. She kneeled and hugged him and then pulled his tail. He whirled and licked her face.

Heart beating, Jim watched her fondle Rusty as he climbed down. How should he handle this? Over the months he'd had such great debates with himself. Margie did look so pretty right now.

"You've had dogs all along, haven't you?" she asked.

"Oh no, Poppa didn't want no dogs, after the first one ate our chickens."

"Us neither."

Jim paused. "Myself, I always wanted a dog."

"Have you, now?"

Well, take the leap. "You know why I got Rusty last year?"

Roughhousing with the dog, Margie shook her head. "No, why?"

"If you really want to know, I'll tell you why."

She glanced up at him, completely unaware, he realized, of what he was leading up to. But how long could he draw this out? His heart was beating faster than Rusty's tail, and now that the moment was at hand, he didn't know what to do. He looked over to the house. He felt tongue-tied. Persevere, he told himself. "I got Rusty for you."

Margie's eyes opened wide. "Oh no, I'm sorry, Jim, Poppa would never let me have a dog. He hasn't before, why would he now?"

"Margie, Margie," Jim shook his head, "you don't get the idea. If you come live here, I'll give you whatever in the whole wide world you want."

"Live here? What... what exactly are you meaning, Jim?"

He noticed she had gone pale. Well come on, out with it, he virtually yelled at himself. "What exactly I'm asking is, Margie, would you be my wife?"

She stood without speaking for what seemed to Jim an eternity. What would she answer?

After the fight, all summer she had kept her distance, turning away whenever he was in sight. He had wanted to approach her, but then, who knew what she'd say? Proposing was not something he did every day. And after all, it was a lifelong commitment. One thing he did know, his mother was definitely slowing down and the sooner she got help, the better.

Then why not hire a girl from back on the Second? That would take off the pressure. He had actually mentioned it: "Lots of families have too many children, Poppa. We could take an extra girl in to help Momma. She'd eat well, and we got extra beds. The Smiths did that, and Traverses, too. Poor families back on the Second, they're sometimes anxious to get rid of an extra mouth to feed."

"You know your mother. She'd never let anyone else in her kitchen." From his father's look, he knew what the old fella was thinking. Don't talk to me about hiring someone — talk about getting yourself a wife!

So here he was, proposing. They'd known each other for years. Well, with women, they say, you never knew. He just stood, and waited.

Margie took a deep breath. "Well Jim, I guess so. I guess, yes, I will just have to be your wife."

His exultation did finally bring a smile to her serious face.

Chapter Twenty-Four:

August 1860

Jim had gotten stuck with picking up Ned Hayes from the coastal schooner dock at Pabos and bringing him home to his baby daughter. He sure did not want to be there when Ned heard the news about the mistaken baptism.

"Byes, Jim, I can't wait to see my wife," Ned acknowledged as he swung up into the buggy for the long ride back to his wife Hannah and his newborn. "I'm such a lucky man and I got you to thank for all that."

"Me?" Jim asked. Oh-oh, now he'd be blamed for what Ned was about to hear.

"Well, I looked back and I seen how you must'a figured things out. Why else did Hannah bring me them nice meals four year ago, so's we could get to talking? Ye know, I was terble shy in those days. Still am. But not like then."

"Tell me about the Prince coming through Gaspé," Jim said. Anything to change the subject.

"No no, first I got to thank yez. She'll be a fine mother, and already she's a terrible fine wife. And you Jim, I never thought you'd get yourself wedded. But Margie Skene, terble pretty girl. You gettin' on good?"

"Oh yes, good fer shore. Ol' Momma's real happy with

her in the kitchen, I'll tell ya. Though I never thought she'd let another in with her. Now what was that there Prince like, down in Gaspé Port?" He was sure now, he could get him off the subject.

"Oh the Prince? You shoulda come, Jim. After all, you're the fella worked on that bridge, not me."

"Yes, I reckon I should have," Jim admitted. "Good number of fellows there?"

"Oh me son, you never seen the like. Terble pile of fun. All sorts of fellas, and we got to talkin' t'each other. Some down from Fox River, and Haldemand, even some from Grand Valley."

"Did he come ashore? Did he meet the Mayor of Gaspé?"

"No, that there Prince Edward, he stayed on his ship. What a pretty ship. All the flags flying, all new painted, three great masts, even sailors up on the spars for the salute, I never seen nawthin' like it."

"Well, it's his first visit to Canada East."

"Yessir, and byes, ye know, Sir John A. Macdonald was there, George Etienne Cartier, and even that fella Galt. Pretty powerful fellow from what I was told. They all went out to the boat to welcome Prince Edward."

"I wonder why Queen Victoria didn't come?"

. "Well byes, that Queen, she must be so busy running all them countries. So she sent her son. He's the fellow that's going to open the bridge you worked on."

"They call it now the Victoria Bridge, I hear."

"Yes sir. Named after his Momma. He must be so proud."

"Well, I guess he'll be King one day."

"No siree – that old lady, she's gonna live forever."

Jim realized that he had gotten a pretty good picture of the scene, but he egged Ned on to keep talking about it, so as to fill the time until they got back home.

"Now you know, Jim, Hannah told me that if you was gonna pick me up, I'd have to make ya stay to supper. No getting out of it. She's up and about now, ye know after the birth, they have to spend eight days flat on their backs. But that's over. She said it was all right for me to leave for this visit of Prince Edward, and now she's got me back, she's gonna treat you proud."

Jim felt great iron doors closing. Nothing for it but to face up to what was coming.

When they arrived at the house, Ned leapt out of the sulky and hurried to the house. Jim took Lively over to tether him, and went to fetch oats. Better let those two lovey-doveys say hello to each other, he thought.

When he went in, he found Ned already holding the baby girl in his arms. "I reckon, pretty soon we'd better get the Rev. Milne to baptize her, eh Hannah?"

Hannah stood there, looking pale. She and Jim traded looks.

Jim turned to go. "Well, Ned, I'd best be getting home."

"No no no, Jim," Hannah reached out, "you stay, you stay to dinner, you promised now."

Jim had promised nothing, but saw the distress clearly etched into his sister's face. Better stay and pour oil on what would likely be very troubled waters. Ned had taken the baby and was now sitting in a chair, gurgling at her. "Maybe you better speak to him on Sunday, if you're well enough to go to the service."

Hannah opened her mouth, and then closed it again. She looked despairingly at Jim.

Jim nodded reassuringly at her.

"Ned, I've got something to tell yez."

Ned was engrossed in his baby. "How have you been, little girl? Did ya miss me?" he wheedled. "How ya been keepin'?"

"That's it! Ned, she's been terble sick."

Ned looked startled. He turned to face Hannah. "Sick?"

"Yes," she stammered.

"How sick?"

"Terble sick." Hannah looked as if she didn't know how to go on. Jim came over and put an arm around her waist to calm her.

"But she's fine now?" Ned eyed the two of them.

"Yes." With his arm Jim gave her a nudge. "But you see," she went on, "when she was sick, we was so scared."

"I bet you was." Ned looked at them suspiciously.

"Well, I might as well tell you," Hannah said at last. "The Roussys, they came, and they brought the priest up from Port Daniel —"

"The priest?" Ned burst out.

"Yes, well, I told him our agreement, Ned. But the priest wouldn't listen..." She paused, turning pale.

Ned rose, the baby still in his arms. Obviously, the infant felt something, and started to cry. Hannah reached out her arms. Ned swung away and took a pace back. "Go on."

"So... now she's Catholic. Catherine is Catholic," she stammered. "There was nothing I could do."

For the first time Jim heard her name. Now his mother had a new namesake. But Ned was furious.

"Nothing? Didn't you tell the priest our agreement? The boys would be Catholic, the girls Protestant?"

"I told him, Ned, of course, I told him everything. I argued, but the priest wouldn't listen. The Roussys said she should be baptized. What if she died? She wouldn't go to heaven. So what could I say?"

"You could have said, go for Reverend Lyster. He's living up at your brother Joe's."

Her eyes brightened. "Yes, yes, I did. I told them, go get Mr. Lyster. But he said he was away. I don't know whether he was telling the truth."

"The priest? You don't know if the priest was telling the truth?"

"You know the priest, Ned; you don't trust him neither. And before I could say anything, he whipped out his Holy Water, and splat! The child was baptized. She's a Catholic."

Jim shook his head. How seriously some people took their religion! Then, his sister started to cry. Jim put an arm protectively around her. "You know Ned, maybe it's..." But he could think of nothing to say.

Ned came across, and Jim moved away.

"Look Hannah, you did your best." He put an arm around her. "It's not your fault. And let me tell you one thing, my dear wife, no one's gonna blame you, neither. I swear by all that's Holy, it's gonna be a long, long time afore I set foot in a Catholic church, no matter what. And whether it's a boy or a girl, from now on they're all gonna be baptized Protestant! Now we'll talk more about this, let's just get Jim here a nice dinner. He's got the finest horse in Shegouac, no doubt about that, haven't ya, Jim?"

Jim grinned. "No sir, no doubt about that!"

Chapter Twenty-Five: 1861

"Canoe, of course, the only way to travel in those days."

"I think, dear," Catherine interrupted, "you'd gone to Paspébiac to get tar for the roof of the barn we'd built."

Jim loved it when, the first really hot day of summer, his father came out onto the veranda to sit with the family and tell stories from the old days. He'd heard most of them several times, but Ol' Poppa was a wonderful yarner.

Yesterday, the whole family (except for the Robertsons who lived in Cascapédia, too far away) had assembled for the wedding of Jim's nephew John to Margaret Dow. So tonight, to continue the all-too-rare celebrations, Catherine had invited everyone over for a great meal, which she had prepared with Margaret who'd already moved in next door but one with John. They all sat in the cool of the evening, satisfied, stuffed in fact, and in a mood for some good old-fashioned stories. What better entertainment?

"Now it may sound strange," Ol' Poppa went on, "but Paspébiac was all French back then. Charles Robin, he made the place go, kept the fellas in work, like his company does today; wives and children turning the codfish on their flakes and the men mostly out fishing or building ships. And ye know, Paspébiac was pretty wild in them days."

"You must remember," Catherine turned to them, "this

happened the year James and I married. Times was hard then, as you've heard us say far too many times."

"If times was any harder then," cracked Jim's brother Joseph, "how did anyone survive?"

They laughed. In fact, Shegouac now was prospering, Jim reflected. They'd more or less come to terms with the seasonal upsets and harsh conditions. And was not Gaspé the prime port of Eastern Canada with its fourteen foreign consuls?

Thomas Byers came out on the veranda with another large earthenware crock of beer to fill the piggins. "Soon as Mr. Alford starts one of his stories, that calls for a refill!" In the manner of the time, that's how he addressed his own father-in-law.

Mariah frowned at her husband; it was clear that she, like many others, did not approve of the demon drink. Jim thought she overdid it.

His father caught her expression. "That Daniel Busteed up in Restigouche told me they fed patients at his hospital in London two quarts of beer a day. If it's good enough for the sick, it's good enough for us!"

"And Mariah," Catherine spoke up, "we do far too little celebrating and too much work, I'd say."

Jim remembered the evenings when they all gathered on the veranda for stories from books like Grimm's *Fairy Tales*, or Daniel Defoe's *Desert Island*. Jim took his turn reading, but he was never as good as his father.

Sometimes, for the children, James would make up stories of wild animals he apparently knew from his early years, or his time in the Navy, though he never talked about the grisly battles, blood, and mayhem, and the punishments, which Jim figured there'd have been many.

"Well, to get on, I'd been trying to clear land, with Catherine foraging for food. We ate wild roots and what berries she could find. No land cultivated, of course."

"Why not?" asked Robert Byers, now a sturdy teenager.

"You had to have an ox for that. And m'son, whoever could afford an ox in them days? Well, this one time in Paspébiac, I stopped by a general store, and there in the corner, I saw this here little bull calf. Looked dead to me. I went over and I stroked his head, and he opened an eye."

That was a story they all loved. But several had not heard it. Jim sat back and ruffled his dog Rusty's ears.

His father went on to tell how he'd bought the baby bull for thirty shillings "from a weaselly little fella, small eyes, sharp face, as crooked as a ram's horn.... Then I had to get him home by land, because they were watching down by the dock. I slung him round my neck, forefeet on one side, hind quarters on the other; he weighed seventy or eighty pound."

Jim looked up as a fish hawk screamed above: the sky at this hour was peopled with gulls; in the barn, a calf bawled for its mother. In winters, they'd gather about the fire for Bible reading, or stories, but Jim enjoyed this veranda time best.

"Now Paspébiac, that's one helluva long way down to here with a seventy-five-pound calf." James went on about the brigands chasing him most of the way, and when he got to the fight, he told that in detail. "Pitch black, m'son, 'cause o' the overcast, and she started to rain, byes, spring of the year, cold as a frog stuck in ice. That little calf, he was going to freeze to death in no time." He grinned. "But I remember at one point, I felt this here warm water trickle down my back."

"Oh Lord, he was pissing," laughed Jim.

"No road in those days, you know, but around dawn, I saw a couple of houses, up in Hope."

"Is that all?" asked Ann. "You mean Hope's only got settled since then?"

"Not all settled," William objected. "Still lots of places, just woods."

"Get to the end, my dear," said Catherine. "I want them to see what a hateful wife you'd married."

"No you weren't," Ol' Poppa objected. "How I got me over the river, I don't know, but Catherine found me passed out not a hundred yards over there." He jerked his head to where the vegetable garden now stood. "Lord! Was I that happy to see such beauty bending over me, those blue eyes, round cheeks, like an angel."

The family reacted at his praise for their Ol' Momma.

"Keep on, dear, tell them the rest," Catherine prompted.

Jim noticed that his father shifted uneasily, but everyone was watching intently. "Well, you see, when she found out that I'd brought another mouth home to feed, she took off in such a rage! Madder'n two tomcats in a sack!" Jim turned to his mother, surprised. "And here, I'd brought her the one thing that saved our farm."

"As it turned out," Catherine prompted, "Broad did save it."

"Broad? Is that where you got that name, Poppa?" Mariah asked.

"Are those his horns over the door?" one grandchild piped up.

"Yep. Named by Catherine. You see, she soon took a liking to the little fella. Fed it porridge till it got on its feet."

"So Momma," Mariah asked, "you named him Broad?"

"Not 'broad' at the time, though later, he was huge," James said. "Now make sure to tell your children so that they'll know how that ox got his name." Jim saw a tear form which his father brushed away angrily. Maybe thinking about his other ox, Keen, poor Keen, whose bones lay buried back by the stony bridge. Why else should such a happy gathering make his father sad?

* * *

Jim came out with a bucket from having fed the pigs. The old sow had gotten to know him. He had scratched and rubbed her stomach to bring down her milk for the twelve little piglets to have their midmorning drink. As he walked along in front of the barn, he saw Margie hanging clothes on the line. He put his buckets down and went over to help.

"Big pile o' washing today," remarked Margie. "Dunno what you fellas is up to."

"I don't either. I guess some of us like to stay clean." He grinned and picked up the basket with her so she wouldn't have to walk back and stoop every time she hung up a pair of socks.

"You don't need to do this, Jim. This is woman's work."

"I know, I know. But I always like to give you a hand when I can." They worked in silence. "Them piglets sure look fine, I'll tell you that," Jim offered, something on his mind.

Margie rifled in the basket for the next item. It was well known you had to hang your clothes in a certain order. Wrong order, and any other folks passing in their horse and buggies or oxcarts would turn that into a big gossip: that new wife there, she don't even know how to hang clothes on a line...

"Sure is better than doing this in the middle of winter. And today they'll dry a lot quicker." Margie seemed pleased as she picked out more socks.

"Margie I got in my mind a new idea."

"Oh-oh."

"You think you can get your father to row us out this afternoon into the middle of the bay?"

"That's an awful long way, Jim!"

"No no, not the middle, just maybe a mile or two out. You think he might if we gave them one of our piglets to fatten on his own for butchering this fall?"

"I reckon Poppa would do anything for a piglet." Jim knew that her father would have to catch a good few fish to trade for a piglet. "But why ever for would you want Poppa to row you out into the bay?"

"Not just me, Margie. Poppa. And you."

"Me! I never even been in one o' Poppa's boats. And I bet your father never set foot in one either."

"Ol' Poppa's canoed more miles than you'd ever believe."

"Maybe has. But I sure haven't. And what's all this about a canoe?"

"Never mind Margie, I don't want to tell about that now. This here has got to be a surprise. For all of yez. But I want you to come. And I want Poppa to come, and I want your dad to row us out."

That afternoon as they made ready to push out Mr. Skene's fishing boat from Shigawake Brook beach, Jim reflected that a lot of talking had been done to get this accomplished. But he was tickled at what might happen.

Great boulders had tumbled from the cliffs and now lay

worn smooth by spring storms. One dead spruce stretched out its branches, covered in moss, while shoots of small trees clung to crevices crammed with soil. The passage of time was etched into withered trunks leaning lopsided over the bank, while behind, fields with wheat sprouts awaited a warmer sun, now low in the western sky. Gulls were swarming, angry at the disturbance, and out beyond, the hell divers, such sleek but ungainly birds, were fishing like crazed cannonballs piercing the steely hard surface of the grey sea.

"I don't know the why of this pile of craziness, Jim," Will Skene grunted, pushing his heavy boat, "but that piglet you brought over, she looks fine. May and me, we's sure lookin' forward this winter to some nice roast pig, and a good supply of crackling that May makes in the oven."

"Now don't go blaming me, Poppa. It's all Jim's idea. I'm only comin' because I know how Momma likes a nice roast pig."

"And there'll be lotsa roasts when that piglet fattens by autumn," Jim went on, as they finally got the boat out. "Give her all the water from your vegetables, and any peelin's. Maybe some wheat biled up." He came back in to heft Margie in her skirt out through the water to the boat.

His father had been sitting in the prow all the while, shaking his head, gripping the sides with gnarled hands and determined, it seemed, to do whatever his son asked for whatever crazy reason. And anyway, he'd never been against a good adventure, or a surprise, whatever it was.

After Will Skene had rowed a good ways and the Shigawake shoreline was beginning to grow thin in the distance, Jim figured it was time to begin. "Now, Poppa, do you mind the time you told us about that there dream you had when you was out here with Momma afore I was born?"

"You mean, when we were in that canoe?"

"Yep. I heard you tell it a couple of times."

"Well that weren't no dream. More like an imagination thing. Some fellows would say vision." He paused, and waved over the fairly still sea. "The waters were so still, even calmer than now. And I was paddling quietly, Elizabeth sitting up there in the bow of our canoe — but what did you bring that up for?"

"I want you to tell Margie, she's never heard it." Old Will Skene shipped his oars and let the boat drift so they could hear the story.

"Foggy, it were, and so still," James obligingly went on. "I had to guide the canoe by listening to the waves against the shore. That air was so dense, like rain or a big storm coming.

"And out of the mist, now listen to this, I believed I saw some monster of a ship, with no sails! Yes sir, not a sail on it! Not even masts. How did it come by so fast? And the sound: like a sawmill driving it, somehow. I saw people waving at me up at the railing above. I still never heard tell of such a thing."

Jim smiled and lifted his arm to point.

James turned and got the surprise of his life. A speck, coming toward them from the direction of Matapédia, was growing larger. A dull throb began to reach their ears. Jim saw his father stare in astonishment.

Margie, beside Jim, poked him in the side, and nodded, eyes aglow.

"It's the steamer, the steamer from Carleton," Jim explained. "Just started, once a week."

James stared. "What the hell's it doing — coming along over the surface like a real boat?"

Jim beamed. "Just sit tight."

And indeed the steamer, which appeared enormous, came closer. Jim saw his father's eyes widen as he turned, shook his head, and watched as it chugged past them. High above them at the railing, people waved down.

"And look! They're waving down, just like what I saw." He broke out laughing and stood up, trying to reach his son, almost upsetting the boat as it rocked wildly in the wake of the great steamer.

Jim, for himself, was mighty pleased at the reaction. Margie hugged him and gave him a big kiss. He'd succeeded in surprising them all, and most important, delighting his old father.

Chapter Twenty-Six:
November 1862

A violent crack of thunder shook the house. James stirred. All night long he had lain half awake, half asleep, listening to the glorious orchestra of the heavens ring out its tribute to Mother Nature and her extraordinary ways. Usually, he loved thunderstorms: the feel of them coming on, the stillness of the air, the warmth beginning to permeate the currents moving among the trees and over the fields, and then, the great lightning bleaching out massive clouds that rolled their darkness over solitary farmhouses. And then the rain, beating its nourishment into the land, drenching it with new life. But tonight, somehow, all felt different. Feelings of unease bred turbulent nightmares to match the storm outside.

He found himself back in his Micmac canoe, long before he had won the hand of Catherine, making that lonely way to Paspébiac in the freezing spring rain. He had sought shelter under the cliffs on a heap of boulders, pulling the canoe up with him, but those waves, attacking the rocks with a feral intensity, now beat in his mind with ever greater savagery. Soon in this dream he would be pulled from his perch and thrust into the tempestuous seas. And then, choking, suffocating, he would black out, in total fright, and then wake in his bedroom and sit bolt upright.

He turned his head. The bed was empty. Catherine had gotten up. He hoped she wasn't afraid. Usually not. But she had become increasingly frail. Perhaps she was just relieving herself in the chamber pot out in the hall.

New gusts of rain hammered his sturdy house. Inside it felt warm, dry, safe. How he had loved building it with Catherine's brothers, and the help of John Gilchrist, the carpenter from New Carlisle. He must calm himself. He had nothing to fear.

At sunset, he had been doing one of the few jobs allotted him, feeding the chickens and shutting them in the henhouse, when the rolling thunder began with a sharp crack to get his attention, and then rolling onwards and it seemed upwards, high and more distant, through so many layers of cloud piled on cloud, and even higher, until it faded. Then it seemed as if the harsh flash of lightning which preceded each thunderclap came toward them until the whole barnyard was encompassed with a great light, as though some primaeval god was on a rampage letting nothing, not one particle of existence, escape his glare. How amazing, James thought, that this simple globe of earth could produce such wonders, such rain teeming down onto plants, ferns, spruce trees, the slow-growing birch and age-old pine and all living things, replenishing even the springs for thirsty animals. He marvelled at the way it all worked together, winter and summer.

So he had nothing to fear. That is, until he saw by the dawn's illumination, the wraithlike form of Catherine steal into the room and lie down beside him. She remained as one frozen.

"Mother has left us. At last."

"In the night?"

"No, as dawn was breaking." Catherine gave a long pause. He reached out and touched her hand. It felt cold. "Something told me to get up. I crept into her room. Then I decided to sit down by her bed, I don't know why. I reached out and put my hand on hers. And as I did, a great rush of breath shook her body. And then, I just know, her heart stopped."

James absorbed the thought. Eleanor Garrett, née Caldwell, gone into the Great Beyond. Well, probably just as well. It had been a long time coming.

"James, I sat there, very still, with her. And then, a while later, my hand was still on hers, I saw something like a little cloud of mist rise out of her. And then James, it moved across the room, and you know? It slid out under the window. In spite of the storm coming, I had left it open a couple of inches. And I felt certain... there was no point in sitting there any longer. So I came back."

James nodded. "Well, it seemed a peaceful passing."

"It was."

They both lay silent. Much too early to get up and alert the others, though James knew Margie would soon be stirring to make a fire for Jim's tea. Then Jim would go out and do the milking, and come back for the breakfast that Margie would have ready.

"Now my dear, I shall get up and tell Jim. He'll go and get Sam Nelson's mother-in-law, Mrs. Scott, to come and help Margie prepare the body. You just lie here, and try to sleep."

"No James," Catherine spoke sharply, "that is something I do. I've done it often. It's my job."

"I think, in this case, we'll let the others do it. Just keep yourself steady — for advice Margie will need. It's the first body she'll have to deal with, the first of many, I fear. Let her go through it with another experienced woman. Old Isabella Scott, as we all know, has done mostly everyone in Shegouac these last years."

They lay again in silence.

"All right, James," Catherine said. "I'll do as you say."

* * *

Throughout his dinner that noon, Jim watched his wife Margie, who looked washed out. Her jaw quivered as though she might break into tears, and her hand shook as she ate her boiled cod with potatoes and carrots. He'd been talking incessantly, trying to cheer them all up. He'd already gotten the news to the Rev. Mr. Milne and arranged for his grandmother to be buried in St. Andrew's church-yard. No church in Shegouac yet, and no real attempt to build one. But Jim would soon get going onto that.

"Margie's the best helper I ever had," Isabella Scott said, downing her last cup of tea. "Nawthin' like her any-wheres else. You could see she didn't like it, mind, but she did everything she was asked. That Mrs. Garrett? — she's all ready to go, wrapped in her winding sheet, clean and nice."

Margie raised her eyes, smiled briefly, and then began to cry. Jim longed to go and comfort her, hug and wrap his arms around and kiss her, but that was not the way. He nodded his head to one side, and she caught his look. Together they went out onto the veranda, where they sat and watched the rain sheeting off the roof. Holding her tight, he let her cry her eyes out, having held it in so bravely. So strange, he and his wife, having witnessed this brush with the Hereafter, hugging each other like two kids, their love spilling over them like tears.

* * *

That next winter, Jim blew in from the freezing barn to find his father in the kitchen. "Now Poppa, what kind of craziness is this?" he asked with a laugh. His father was struggling with his heavy winter clothes and trying to get the snowshoes to work. He had already put on his Micmac moccasins recovered from the new attic he'd added on thirty years before. God knows how long it had taken him to climb up there. "Fine weather, m'son, I'm going out snowshoeing. I just want to check back by the stony bridge if them oxen are all right."

Now where was the old man's mind? Yes, the weather was good, the snow crisp and the whole hillside shimmered in the glittering sun. But Ol' Poppa — was he back with that day when he'd shot his beloved Keen? Or was he talking about heading into the barn? He didn't need snowshoes for that: the path between the house and the new barn was beaten down, easy walking. But a little bull calf had been born recently — maybe he was thinking of him? "Poppa, if you're worried, I'll go right out to check. The oxen were fine this morning when I went milking."

His father struggled with those long moccasins that came up to his knees. "No sir. Not the barn. Never you mind. I'm just checking back by the stony bridge. Fine day for a walk. Those bears'll be hibernating soon."

"Poppa, look out the window, it's deep snow. The bears

are long asleep. The oxen are safe in the barn. Now don't you worry yourself."

"Don't tell me what to do, Jim, I'm your father. If I want to go snowshoeing, I'll go snowshoeing. Magwés might be out there, too, you never know, and what about One Arm? Where's he got to? They might need help. It's awful cold out. Maybe some hot soup. Yes. Get your wife to heat me up some soup for them, quick-like."

Lord, thought Jim, he's off. Over the dark winter, he'd had one or two periods like this. Most of the time he was fine, but then he'd wake up and his mind would do funny things. Jim was never sure quite how to deal with that.

He went over to his father. "Look Poppa, if I help you get on your moccasins, will you come to the door and look out? You're here at home, you're safe, there's not a Micmac for a hundred miles. You've been dreaming."

The old man tried to rise, and then sat down rather suddenly. "Ship's rocking," he said. "Better be careful, Jim. I think we sighted the French. Must be getting under full sail."

"Well Poppa, I reckon if we're about to meet the French, the best thing would be, batten down the hatches, and hold tight. What do you say?"

"Good thinking." He saw his father look around at the room. "Looks ready for a fight to me."

"We're all ready, yes sir."

"Got to defend the church! That comes first, mind, the church!"

"Yes sir."

"All right then, carry on." His father struggled with the moccasins. Jim knelt beside him, helped get them off, and took his heavy coat to hang up in the porch. "I think with that big battle coming on, Poppa, you'd better take a quick lie-down. These here fights take a lot of energy."

"Right you are, sailor. Well said."

Jim watched his father turn to the stairs, and slowly start up.

Chapter Twenty-Seven:
Winter 1863

The stiff crust of snow lay spread out like a starched apron across the field and up the backside hill that glistened under a low, bright moon. Jim burst out the door laughing with Margie. She was over her morning sickness now and her high spirits infected him. They were off to nephew John's, where he and his wife Margaret had invited his brothers and sisters all to come and meet the new Andrew James, born a week ago. Margie ran on ahead and Jim chased her. What fun they had together, like children again. And after all, at nineteen, was not Margie bustling with youthful energy? They passed the Byers' farmhouse and set off across the next acre to the modest home of John, inherited from his deceased father, also named John. Last November, James had given him that land, and also had designated this piece here to Thomas, Mariah's husband. He'd made a will and helped Catherine — who could neither read nor write — make hers, at the instigation of the Rev. Mr. Lyster, who happened to be also the clerk of Port Daniel. Mr. Lyster had drawn up all the documents, and now, at twenty-four, John Alford owned his own farm and house. And James had let it be known, of course, that young Jim had been named as heir, in both their wills, of the Old Homestead.

Jim and Margie reached John's house to find the others already assembled, having come directly from evensong. No doubt about it, everyone was cheerful, with piggins of beer to hand.

"She'll be right down," John announced. "It's her first day up after the birth. She's determined to show ya." Happy comments greeted this.

"Now before Margaret comes," Jim announced, trying his best not to appear overly rambunctious, though the revelry was continuing, "I need everyone's help."

"Something wrong with the Old Man?" Thomas Byers asked.

They fell silent.

"Oh no, it's about... Well... Y'see, I figure Ol' Poppa's not going to be with us much longer, so we should all get together and figure out a way to give him a present."

"And what might that be?" William Young asked.

Jim took a breath, then launched out: "I think we should get us a church built in Shegouac."

This was met with puzzlement, and some frowns. Jim went on, "We've all heard Reverend Mr. Milne drop hints, and Mr. Lyster, but hints in church go nowhere. Best thing is to start talking, and maybe next winter a pile of us could go cut the foundations, and float 'em down the brook as we did for the school."

His sister Ann Young interrupted, a thing women did not usually do. "Jim, I hate to say this, but with Ol' Poppa not well and Old Momma on her way out, too, we have a lot on our hands. Why not take a few months, and think about it then?"

The room grew quiet as they looked at one another. Thomas Byers mumbled, "Jim, it hurts me to say it, but now is maybe just not the time."

Jim felt his cheeks flush. "Thomas, you saw what happened with the school. That's what everyone said: let's wait. But when we got working, we swung the idea round."

"Like my wife said," Will Young interposed, "I'm not so sure it's the time to start a project like that. Building a church, well, it's a pretty big undertaking."

"So what do I tell Poppa? We're waiting till you die?" Jim still could not get his mind around it.

"I think it's a great idea!" Young John appeared enthusiastic. "It's a plan everyone could get behind..."

"I just have this feeling," Jim urged, "that Ol' Poppa would like nothing more than to know this community has agreed on working together again. I'm not a big churchgoer myself, but everyone else..." He paused. "Poppa's mind might be wandering, and sometimes, he's just not himself. But I just know for sure this'd cheer him up no end."

"It's winter," brother Joe said. "We've got to get through that first. Some families down my way don't even have enough to eat. Not a good time to go soliciting..."

Jim was silent. He'd never expected this. Well, they were wrong.

Perhaps because she saw the look on Jim's face, his older sister Mariah got up and spoke. "Jim, we all know how important Old Poppa is. Look how many children Old Momma has delivered. And how many families Old Poppa gave a helping hand to, over the years. Everyone looks up to both of them. And when they're gone, it's all going to be different." Nods greeted this announcement. "So, Jim, I agree, we just can't wait. It would be wonderful to get talking. We could tell him it's a kind of memorial to him. Something his family can all do, as part of Old Poppa's last wishes."

Jim was pleased that for some reason, his older sister, Mariah, almost twenty years his senior who had helped bring him up, was again on his side.

"Take more than this family," Dan Bisson said.

"Of course, of course, but we gotta start somewhere," John replied.

"All I'm asking is," Jim held Margie's hand for support, "for us just to start putting the word out. I'm telling you, Momma and Poppa, they don't have long..."

"I like the idea," sister Mary Jane said. "If we get talking, I bet in three or four years, that church would get built."

Most were clearly now in agreement, so Jim turned to his host. "Now c'mon John, where is that barrel of rum I brought over in the autumn?"

John, who had been watching the conflict between his aunts and uncles with wide eyes, grinned and leapt to his feet. "Yes sir! But first, here comes Marg, with Andrew James." He opened the door for his wife, now Mrs. Alford.

The proud mother, the former Margaret Dow, entered somewhat unsteadily with a tiny bundle well wrapped up. She looked up and announced shyly, "Your Ol' Poppa and Momma's first *great*-grandchild!"

So tiny, Jim thought as he watched the infant passed from one set of caring arms to another. "It's awfully small."

"Jim! He's not an *it*," Margie came beside Jim and took the baby. "And one of his names is James, after you."

"More after Poppa, I guess," Jim grinned.

"Fer shore, after Grandpa," said John.

Jim took back the tiny infant. How light it was! Imagine,

this tiny piece of living flesh, swaddled in wool, would one day grow up to be a farmer and work the land almost next door. Amazing!

"Well, I can't tell you how tickled Ol' Poppa'll be to see this here great-grandchild," Jim said, to general agreement.

He looked down at the new tiny James in his arms. Such a sweet smell. And such a breadth of years between this and his old father up in that bedroom, sleeping. Even for a brief moment, he conjured up the glorious way in which these tiny creatures were created. And the not quite so glorious way in which they departed. With his own baby on the way, he would be thinking a lot of things like that. During these latter years, his father seemed to be raging so much against this dying of his light. Why not indeed? Old age should rage at close of day.

So similar and yet so different: this feather-light, tender bundle whose bones were still supple and pliant, and the gaunt scarecrow over home whose bones had grown as brittle as his brain, but still filled with feisty longing.

* * *

"You know," Jim began slowly, as they strode happily back home along the beaten path between the houses, "I been thinking where we could place that church. What about that land there below the road, near the new school?"

"You're not talking about Poppa's land, are you?" Margie stooped to scoop up a handful of snow. Was she making a snowball to throw?

"I might be." Jim was testing the waters...

"Jim, Poppa gave land for the school — you're not asking him to slice off a piece more for the church?"

"Wouldn't have to be a big piece, Margie."

"Jim, what good is a church without a churchyard? And a walkway in. And space in front." She let fall the snow, being too cold, and dusted off her hands. "You're getting beyond an acre. You think Poppa's the richest man in Shigawake? Well, he's not. Your poppa is. I mean our poppa," she corrected herself quickly, seeing the flash in Jim's eyes. "I don't see my father just giving and giving. What about someone else handing over their land?"

Jim was silent for a bit. "Look Margie, I'm not saying give. We could take round a collection. We could buy it."

"You want Poppa to sell his best piece of land?"

"Margie," Jim said, "I'm not saying anything, really. I'm just asking you to think it over. You know you're Will Skene's favourite daughter."

"I am not!"

"No? You shoulda seen that look in his eyes when you and me got married. It was like he was losing his own soul. And," Jim went on, "he's a terble fine churchgoer. Every week, he drives down to Port Daniel. I bet he'd be pleased to have a church right here on his doorstep instead."

Margie took that in as they paused at the kitchen door of the Old Homestead.

Well, thought Jim, I probably opened my mouth where I shouldn't. But he knew his wife – she'd turn it over in her mind. And if the idea grew on her, she'd surely act on it.

* * *

Margie and Jim, their cheeks frosty, their eyes sparkling, ears icy, burst into the main room, where James Alford sat sleeping by a dying fire, a throw across his knees.

"Papa, we got the best news!"

James woke with a start, straightened himself and, with an almost regal air, prepared himself. Margie came and set kindling down by the fire as Jim spoke to his father. "Papa, we was just over at John's. We was there for a sight of your first great-grandson. Remember we told you when we left?"

Margie, kneeling at the fire, turned; she didn't want to miss one moment of the look in the old man's eyes when he heard what James had to tell him.

James nodded. "I remember for sure. I came back downstairs; I figured I'd sit here till you came. I want to hear all about it."

"Go on Jim, tell him." The ensuing flames having caught, Margie sat facing; this was going to be a delicious moment.

"Well, Poppa, as you know, the whole family had gathered for the christening."

James nodded.

Jim paused.

"Well, go on Jim," Margie prodded.

"Well... we had a lot of talk about this here new idea."

James lifted his head and looked directly at his son. "What new idea?"

Jim waited an appropriate and lingering moment. "A church."

Growing interest spread across his father's features. "Yes yes, the church.... Why ever for did you bring that up? I thought you were telling me about my new great-grandson."

"I brought it up because, well, we're kind of thinking of making a present for you..." Jim was partly drawing it out, but also finding it difficult to actually make it sound right.

"You've been wanting a church built. And you knew the talk about it. But nothing's happened so far."

"You're not telling me anything new, me son." James's eyes narrowed.

"Well, maybe it isn't much, I guess." James slumped a little because in truth, not that much had been achieved. "But what happened is..." He trailed off.

"Jim!" Margie exclaimed.

"All right, all right." He took a breath. "Poppa, it looks like we're all agreed, we're all behind it, and right away, we're gonna start talking, and somehow, we're gonna get your church built."

James got to his feet, elation written all over his face. Margie leapt across and gave him a big hug, and he shook his son's hand. "Damn fine work, you two. Damn fine."

"Well, 'tweren't much, but..."

"'Twere so, Jim!" Margie said. "Poppa, he worked at the lot of them. First, they's not too keen, but he worked, my Jim, he went at 'em. I'm proud of him."

"You fellas are pretty good at that!" James grinned broadly.

"And your little great-grandson, he's just as fine as any trout in Shigawake Brook," Margie went on.

"Well, I reckon that's two good bunches o' news at one go." James nodded to himself, and then moved slowly across to the stairs.

As he faltered on the first couple of steps, Margie crossed quickly and helped the old man into his bedroom above, up the steep, narrow stairs that turned sharply behind the stove just as decided by James himself and Catherine's brother John in the building of the house forty years previously.

Jim took his place in his father's chair and stared into the flames.

Margie came down shaking her head. "Poor old fella, he sure hates to be like that. He tries not to complain, but I seen it in his face. I bet he used to be some good-lookin' man, and some fine sailor."

After they got into bed that night, the love they made was just glorious. Having seen the baby, the beginning of one life, and another nearing its end, Jim reflected that right now he had everything he could ever want: a father who seemed mighty satisfied, a wife in his arms, enough land to keep him busy for years to come, and a family on the way.

Beside him, Margie felt the same joy. A contented couple, for sure.

Chapter Twenty-Eight:
Spring 1863

Good Friday. After James had heard the family was ready to start on the building of a Shegouac church, he felt better. He knew that once his children got an idea in their heads, they were unstoppable. But tonight, the old fears came pouring over him like the torrents of water over the shingled roof of the Old Homestead.

All week long the house had been buffeted, first by a raging snowstorm on Palm Sunday, so severe that even though it was the beginning of April, the Rev. Milne could not get down to hold his service. Jim and Margie had come back from their long trek down to Port Daniel school, having only said a few prayers of their own, and more especially for their parents.

And now the temperature had risen, and rain beat about the house. Easter Sunday was coming up the day after tomorrow. Oh yes, oh yes, James said to himself, church definitely. Not getting out enough, lately. Couldn't even make the Ash Wednesday service. *Know that ye are dust, and to dust shall ye return.* And as for Palm Sunday last week, well, no. But now that Easter was at hand, he would make a determined effort. So long confined. And confined in this tattered body, this ragged skeleton that must be dispensed with, so he could take on (and the Good Book promised) a body of light.

The Good Book, the Good Book. So what if it lasted two thousand years — hadn't those pagan religions existed much longer? Wasn't everyone now discussing those scientific discoveries refuting God's existence? How dare they doubt? But doubt he did. Trapped there, too. The prison of doubt. How he longed for an escape. A blazing path into wisdom that he could be sure of.

Aha! So that was why, he decided, he had wandered these rooms and hallway at night. Impelled strangely to rise up from his bed and search.

He had moved out of Catherine's bedroom so that she might be better cared for. How much they had shared together! But now, the time for sharing was ending. He shuffled across the room, opened another door, went in, then shuffled back again. The Old Homestead was wrestling with its own angels, the spring storm pelting melted snowflakes against the windows. His own struggles, James knew, were of an altogether different kind. He felt like howling again, howling, as he kept wandering, like a hundred wolves. How else to express his agony, his longing, to find, to know?

In the darkness he bumped into a chair, nearly fell, but fortunately didn't wake Catherine. The collision prompted a paroxysm of anger, why must one bang into things like a village idiot! I can't even stand up and walk straight, he growled as fury built. But something stopped him. Was it the wind whistling around the house? Just like those many nights in the spars of the *Bellerophon*? He was back in his cramped deck with its five feet of headroom, well below the waterline, bounced in his rocking hammock with the other Middies. And clear as a bell, his wondering thoughts came back, as he had pondered the desire to jump ship and to brave those icy waters so many years ago...

"Think of a farm on the cliffs, built from the very trees among which it stands. Think of a wife, broad skirt blowing in the wind, holding a child — your own son. Think of trudging behind sturdy oxen, ploughing furrows in the rich, red Gaspé soil. Think of the companionship of settlers, their pounding hammers erecting your barn, just as you'd help with theirs. Think of the warmth on a frosty night by your fireplace, built from stones picked on these very beaches, while your wife roasts one of the chickens you've both raised."

Well, had he not achieved everything?

Stupid old idiot! What was he doing, how dare he be angry at bumping into a chair! Why was he not praising the Lord above, as would any sane man? Here he was, a true pioneer who had done it all: made his home, raised a fine large family, created a substantial working farm, was that not a life of success? Yes, by any standards, James thought, standing stock-still in his bare feet in his comfortable and warm bedroom...

And then, out of the thunder and the wind howling around the house, he heard from afar the whisper of his name: "James. James..."

He stopped and waited. After a time he found himself answering, "Here I am."

He placed both palms on the windowsill, staring with unseeing eyes into the blackness of the great Chaleur Bay.

"James," the voice came again, not only in the room, but all around, even reaching into his very being.

He opened his mouth to respond, but then the voice seemed to say, *"Oh ye of little faith. Have not I told you, not a sparrow falls from the air but your Father in heaven knows. How much more does He care for you?"*

James lifted his hands to cover his ears. It was terrifying: words from the Bible he'd read so often, now spoken as if all around him and in him, in tones that seemed made of the light itself, though darkness covered all.

"Lord, I hear you."

"Peace I give you, my own peace I leave with you."

James stared, clasped his hands.

"Have faith in God, have faith in me. In my father's house are many mansions. I have gone to prepare a place for you..."

Prepare a place? In the silent room, he beheld a shifting of light as though a veil were lifting. He seemed, indeed, able to see so much more than ever before. His brain and being were filled with knowing, such a knowing that brought on a gentle, all-embracing peace.

He nodded to himself, and made his way back to his bed. Lifting the sheets, he eased himself under the blankets and lay back with his head on the pillow, looking up at the ceiling in darkness. Sweetness filled his taste buds; sound as of a lovely ringing claimed his ears like the chiming of a million silver bells. And the knowing, ah yes, the knowing, how glorious to know, once and for all, that as he went forward, it would not be into the dark unknown, but into the lighted Known, the Welcoming Known of: "I am what I am."

The next day, Jim and Margie saw a whole different attitude, a newly transformed parent. For them now, they could see that he had taken on, at last, his raiment of light.

Afterword

Catherine died soon after James, and in January 1864 the Shigawakers bought a half-acre from Will Skene Sr. and began work on St. Paul's Church. The first recorded service was held in 1865, and the building was finished in 1867.

Jim's first wife, Margie, and their two children, Catherine and Mary Jane, all passed away before 1870; no record of the reason exists. Soon afterwards, Jim married Mary Ann Macpherson and they produced ten children — the eldest, John, and the youngest, Eric, father of the author.

The graves of James and Catherine, and her mother Eleanor Garrett, are no longer marked in St. Andrew's churchyard, New Carlisle, save by a memorial bench placed in 2006 next to the church wall by their great-grandson. And thus they lie undisturbed in the native soil of their beloved Gaspé.

Author's Note

My great grandfather fought in 1805 under Admiral Nelson in the Battle of Trafalgar. When his man o'war, the *Bellerophon*, came to the New World, he jumped ship and built his new home in the Gaspé. His youngest son, my grandfather James, was born in 1835, and my father, Eric, also a youngest son, was born in 1893.

To commemorate these three ancestors, I write this series of largely fictional accounts of a family that helped found a real English community on the shores of the Gaspé Coast, and lived and farmed there for two centuries.

Acknowledgements

While this series is entirely fictional, I have nevertheless enjoyed using real factual events, people, and documents to underpin the story. And with this book, we have moved ahead to oral stories told to living octa- and nonagenarians by their grandparents. This made the writing fun to research, as well as in some ways more difficult.

For example, all the Alford relatives so described herein are real, and the schoolhouse was definitely built in this decade and at the actual spot. And although the dating of the Old Homestead building is correct, the barn was actually built ten years earlier. I hope readers can live with that. The killing of Thomas McMannus and others by the Dragoons remains to this day the most devastating slaughter of striking workers in Canadian history.

The most important source for the facts and dates in this book was Rev. G. Milne's diaries. The <u>Rev. Mr. Milne</u> travelled back and forth between New Carlisle and Port Daniel from 1847 to 1878. Although some of the diaries have gone missing, these daily records of his services and weather conditions and whom he visited give the only detailed picture of life in this part of the Coast for those years, especially the last days of Eleanor Garrett and James and Catherine. The diaries survived through the good offices of Eleanor "Tikey" Blois Hall, now deceased, and the

British Heritage Village and the Restigouche Historical Society, which copied and transcribed them. The story of the baby in the pig-pen comes directly from these diaries.

For the location of each Shigawake farm and its inhabitants, I have to thank Carl and Lois Hayes. Carl would answer my many questions as he threw some of his ten thousand bales of hay from the back of a truck to 130-odd beef cattle. Lois would come in from her garden, having cooked for innumerable relatives that visit, and look up her voluminous notes. They helped in the makeup of the School Commission, and gave me a map of Shigawake as it existed in 1855. I could not have written this without their cheerful and productive help. And especially, I thank them for the story (loosely interpreted herein) of how the Hayes in Shigawake turned Anglican.

The many traditions and practices of early Micmac culture were taught to me by a Native Canadian who became a friend. Roger Pelletier had run the Micmac Museum in Gaspé efficiently, making it a subject of pride for the Micmac nation, and indeed for all Gaspé. But after he had given me more notes and help on this third book, word came from the town of Gaspé that he had shot himself through the heart.

Bill Busteed's family not only built (in 1801), but have continuously occupied, the house Jim visited, a record for the Coast. He was finally forced to move to the Eastern Townships. He filled me in on details of his ancestors, two sisters, and a "medical practitioner."

Mario Mimeault, the distinguished Francophone historian living in Gaspé town, pointed me in useful directions and offered information about prices of the day. He also sent me photocopies of important books.

The British Heritage Village, an important repository of English lore on the Gaspé, and its founder and former chairperson, <u>Joan Dow</u>, and her capable daughter <u>Cynthia</u>, have been a great help and support throughout.

The Restigouche Genealogical Society and its president, <u>Pennie Barbour</u>, provided some of Rev. Mr. Milne's transcripts and gave me helpful advice in several other ways. Pennie also runs the "almondtree" section of the Saga website.

While writing, I was determined to check out facts by other methods. Ted Wright found the foremost "wood dating lab" in Canada, the <u>Mount Allison Dendrochronology Laboratory</u>, located a few hundred miles away. This brilliant team of MAD scientists under their leader, Colin Laroque, descended upon the Old Homestead, took samples, and confirmed my conjectured dates for the buildings.

<u>Paul Piehler</u>, long-time friend and consultant, was helpful in guiding me to sources of Victorian angst reflected in the dilemma of James. Together with Maj-Britt, his wife, they helped me with the more spiritual aspects and especially with the discussions of Bishop Mountain.

My stepson <u>Chris Elkins</u>, now a Montrealer, was a willing and indeed eager helper, racing off with his camera to take pictures of buildings and transcribe plaques for me, some of which, like that of Nelson, have remained in place to this very day.

The great Welsh poet <u>Dylan Thomas</u>, many of whose poems I repeat to illuminate my darkness when the going gets tough, I decided to honour with an homage by burying a couple of his lines in my text: find them who can.

I should mention that <u>Peter Parley</u>'s books were wildfire best sellers in the early 1800s. I thank the departed Mr.

ACKNOWLEDGEMENTS

Parley for his help, and for my quotation from him herein.

I must mention and thank another more distant cousin, Grant Almond, now deceased, who kept my computers running through thick and thin. Jacquie Czernin, the startlingly attractive but unseen host on CBC's Quebec Community Network Radio is also a supporter of these books about her constituency; I thank her and her producer Peter Black. And of course, my Cambridge University friend, David Stansfield, who with his wife Denyse designed my website, and read and corrected the final manuscript. And so important, Cynthia Patterson, a whirlwind supporter of the saga.

Finally, I should acknowledge my former housekeeper for providing me with material from which to shape one of the characters herein.

READERS: I have been blessed by some good advice: Orla Brady, a stunning Irish actress of no little talent, helped with Irish accents and edited some scenes. Diana Colman Webster, a textbook author of substance and my friend from Oxford, proved amazing. Again, the Rev. Susan Klein in the midst of a busy schedule running her large church in Westwood gave me advice on the religious ceremonies and provided general insights. Oren Safdie, the playwright, took time from the London opening of his latest play: *Private Jokes, Public Places*, to read this and give helpful notes. Jennifer Bydwell, a dynamic film executive also had lots of ideas and corrections for me, as did Catherine Evans, now retired but possibly the finest English teacher in all Quebec. My good friend Prof. Danielle Cyr gave a last look over the manuscript, correcting the French as well as the grammar. The lovely Diana Roman, my former assistant, with her sharp eyes and generous spirit helped as a Californian by clarifying some Gaspesian references and modes of speaking. Lynda Robinson Boyd provided help as well as being a welcoming Toronto hostess.

Cousin Ted Wright has been my main partner is this whole endeavour. No mean historian himself, he designs and builds crab traps for *La Fine Mouche*, often supervising a bevy of tough but luxuriously shaped Francophone women. Each morning around five as the sun rose, he set a fire burning in the big iron stove which heats his wing of the Old Homestead before heading out to work. At that time, and at dinner midday, we would thrash out the details of how lives were lived at the mid-century of the 1800s. Acknowledgements such as mine cannot fully express my immense gratitude to him, but more especially for the fun we engender together!

Appendix:
Historical Background

(Note: Differing spellings of present-day Shigawake, and that Catherine could not write.)

Deed of Transfer to Son-in-Law Thomas Byers on September 2nd, 1862

Number 624 Entered and registered at the hour of ten in the forenoon of the first day of September, one thousand eight hundred and sixty two. Province of Canada District of Gaspe. This indenture, made and executed at Chicouac [sic] in the County of Bonaventure, District of Gaspe,

Witnesseth that I James Almond of Shegouac, farmer, have given granted, transferred and made over and by these presents do give grant transfer and make over unto my son in law, Thomas Byers, of Shegouac [sic] aforesaid, Farmer, that certain lot of land situated at Shecouac aforesaid containing thirty superficial acres more or less and bounded on the north by the line of the second concession, south by the Queen's Highway and on the two other sides by the lands belonging to me, James Almond to have and to hold the same for the sole use and benefit of the aforesaid Thomas Byers and his heirs forever hereafter.

Given under my hand and seal at Chigouac [sic] aforesaid this third day of February, one thousand and eight hundred and sixty two. James Almond, signature.

I Catherine Garrett wife of the above James Almond do hereunto set my hand and seal in token of my consent hereby given to the above donation and do by these presents relinquish all right of dower in the same. Catherine (X) Garrett [her mark]
William Gore Lyster, Clerk, John D. Delaney witness.

Deed of Transfer to Grandson John on September 1st, 1862

Number 625 Entered and registered at the hour of ten in the forenoon of the first day of September, one thousand eight hundred and sixty two. Province of Canada District of Gaspe. This indenture, made and executed at Chicouac [sic] in the County of Bonaventure, District aforesaid,
Witnesseth that for and in consideration I James Almond of Shigawake far mer have given granted transferred and made over and by these presents do give grant transfer and make over unto my grandson, John Almond of Shigawake aforesaid Farmer that certain lot of land situated at Chigouack [sic] aforesaid containing thirty three superficial acres more or less and bounded on the north by the line of the second concession on the south by the Bay of Chaleur on the east by lands belonging to me James Almond and in the west by the lands of John Young, to have and to hold the same, for the sole use and benefit of the aforesaid John Almond and his heirs forever hereafter given under my hand and seal at Chedouac [sic] aforesaid,

this third day of February One Thousand Eight Hundred & Sixty Two.

James Almond, signed.

And I Catherine Garrett, wife of the above grantor, James Almond do hereunto set my hand and seal in token of my consent hereby given to the above donation & do by these presents relinquish all right of dower in the same. Catherine (X) Garrett (signed etc)

James Almond's Sale of a Brook Site to Harvey Manderson, 1849

This indenture made 30 day of December, 1850, in the county of Bonaventure and the Province of Canada East

Made the twenty seventh day of October, in the year of our Lord, One thousand Eight Hundred and forty nine, Between James Almond, of the Township of Hope, in the county of Bonaventure and District of Gaspe farmer, and Harvey A. Manderson of Bonaventure, in the county and District aforesaid Millwright, of the other part, Witnesseth That, for and in consideration of the sum of Twenty Pounds, current money of the Province of Canada, to the said James Almond, in hand paid by the said Harvey A. Manderson at or before the execution of these presents, the receipt whereof is hereby acknowledged by the said James Almond, He the said James Almond hath granted, bargained, Sold and confirmed, and by these presents doth grant, bargain, sell, and confirm unto the said Harvey A. Manderson, his heirs and assigns for ever, all that certain piece, parcel or Lot of land, intended for a Millsite or Sites, situated on the West side of the Shedawac [sic] Brook and being a part of lot number forty in the first Range in the Township of Hope in the possession and occupied by the vendor, bounded on the East by the East line of the said lot number forty, on the South and West by a line where fourteen feet perpendicular hight [sic] from the Bed of Brook intersects the highland until it meet the said brook.

The Reverend Mr. Milne's Diaries, 1848–63
(Excerpts)

(*Note again: Different spellings of Shigawake; also that Diaries confirm church services in Port Daniel, and afterwards, in Shigawake school. And finally, see that a new Catherine is born as old Catherine expires.*)

31 Dec 48   Road appeared very bad and snow, drifting much. Left with Mr. Christie about 10 o'clock to try to get to Hopetown for service, as there seemed no chance of getting to Port Daniel. Found the road very heavy and much drifted up, and the wind getting stronger, and snow drifting very much. Saw no likelihood that people would come out. Went a little beyond Assels Bridge, turned back, about an hour from time of leaving till getting home again... day rather worse p.m. and evening.

July 26, 50   Got to Port Daniel at 2 p.m. At 5 p.m. there was a service in the schoolhouse. I read Prayers and Lessons. More than 50 present.

23 Apr 51   D. Bisson called requesting me to go down to visit Mr. Almond at Shigawack [sic], but not able to go, having got cold on Sunday and Monday and had rheumatism in my back.

30 Apr 51   Went to Shiguock [sic] to visit Mr. Almond — found him sitting up and getting better. Spoke with him a considerable time.... Found road through the woods pretty good but very bad through Hopetown and the farther part of Nouvelle and Shigwack [sic], large banks of snow and much water.

Break in Diary (notes lost from 1851–59):

<u>1859 July</u> *Visit by Bishop Mountain*

12   The Bishop landed at 5 a.m. at Point St. Peter and is to be at Port Daniel on Thursday, 14th p.m. for a confirmation. Then we came on and arrived at Paspébiac between 12 and 1. Found all well and in order. Sunday many visitors. Mr. Lyster up. Informed him that he would have to come up tomorrow for examination as the Bishop intended to ordain him on Sunday.

15   Left Mr. Carter's at 9 a.m. Called at Mr. Lyster's and then went on to Shigawake Schoolhouse for service where I read prayers. Mr. Lyster lessons and Bishop confirmed 10 and preached. Lunch at Mr. Thomas Byer's and went on to Hopetown and had service. After service at Hopetown, we came on here and arrived at 5-1/2 p.m. After tea the Bishop examined Mr. Lyster's papers which were sustained and then he was examined in Greek and on Evidences etc. etc. Answered to our Satisfaction.

16   The Bishop expressed his satisfaction with the whole of the arrangements and services.

Continuing Excerpts:

25 June 60 Called to see Mrs. [Eleanor] Garrett.

15 Oct 62 Went to Shigouac [sic] for the Meeting in Mr. Lyster's Mission, <u>which was held in Schoolhouse</u>, all Church Wardens present.

6 Nov 62 Buried at St. Andrew's Church, New Carlisle, Eleanor Caldwell, widow of the late William Garrett in lifetime of Cox, Farmer, who died early yesterday morning at Shigouac, over 90 years old. Very rainy.

28 Feb 63 On way to Port Daniel called at Messrs. McGie's, A. Smiths and Almonds — old Mr. & Mrs. Smith and Mr. and Mrs. Almond, all very poorly.

4 Apr 63 Visited Widow Charlson in Jail for Concealment of pregnancy and murder of child by leaving it to be eaten of Pigs, only a Small part of Head and an arm found in the morning. She seems penitent. Shewed her the greatness of her sin and exhorted her to repent and turn to God for Mercy in Xt.

10 June 63 Went to Shigouac and visited Mrs. Almond, very ill and nothing can be done for her — she wished to have the Holy Communion, but as she cannot eat any bread, could not do it. Explained.

25 Jul 63 Buried at St. Andrew's Church, James Almond of Hope, Farmer, who died on morning of 23rd. Exhortation.

23 Sep 63   Visited Mrs. Almond at Shigouac, now unable to Speak. Baptized... also Catharine (b: 27 Aug 63) Daughter of James Almond of Hope, Farmer, and Margaret Jane Skene, wife, both with sponsors.

6 Oct 63   Buried at St. Andrew's Church, Catharine Garrett of Hope, widow of late James Almond in lifetime of Hope, Farmer, who died on the 4th, aged [blank in journal, 69 in church record].

Victoria Bridge: The Vital Link (Excerpts)

Although the Victoria Bridge was completed by December 1859, the official inauguration was planned only for the summer of 1860. On May 14, 1859 the legislative Council passed a resolution to invite the Queen to come and see the "progress and sincerity of her Dominion" on the occasion of the inauguration of the Victoria Bridge.

Queen Victoria's response, sent on January 30, 1860, was:

> *Her Majesty, unable to come herself, would depute her eldest son and heir to witness those noble advancements in a land, from barbarism to civilization.*

The knowledge that the heir to the throne, Albert Edward, Prince of Wales, would make his first overseas visit, and indeed the first visit of any royal prince to a British colony, created great excitement and in February 1860 the planning committee began to organize the many building projects thought necessary to embellish the city for this auspicious occasion.

The Prince of Wales left Plymouth for North America on July 10, 1860 aboard H.M.S. *Hero*. His suit included the Secretary of State for the Colonies, Her Majesty's Lord Steward, and the Governor to the Prince, Major General the Hon. Robert Bruce.

The *Hero* with its accompanying squadron arrived at St. John's, Newfoundland on July 23. After numerous public functions, the Prince left on the 26th for Halifax, Nova Scotia. On August 2, the royal entourage was feted at St. John, New Brunswick, on August 4 at Fredericton, and on August 9 in Charlottetown, P.E.I.

On August 12, 1860, Lower Canada was first sighted at Gaspé, where a deputation of the Canadian Ministry went aboard to officially welcome the heir apparent. These included the Hon. John Rose, President of the Executive Council, George-Etienne Cartier, Premier and Attorney-General East; John A. Macdonald, Attorney-General West; and A.T. Galt, Minister of Finance.

On Saturday, August 18 His Royal Highness made his official entry into Quebec City...

Source: Montreal: McCord Museum of Canadian History, 1992. Used by permission.

The Phantom Ship

In her book *Treasure Trove in Gaspé and the Baie des Chaleurs (1920s)*, Margaret C. MacWhirter devoted several pages to accounts of such sightings. She wrote:

Among the legends of the Baie des Chaleurs the best known is that of the "Phantom" or Burning Ship.... At certain times, usually before a storm she appears: a ship on fire, rigging and hull enveloped in a mass of flames. She has been seen by many persons at different times.

Paul Almond is one of Canada's pre-eminent film and television directors, and he has directed and produced over 130 television dramas for the CBC, BBC, ABC and Granada Television. He has now turned his talents to writing a series of novels based on his own family's pioneering adventures in Canada. Paul Almond lives on the Gaspé Peninsula in Quebec and in Malibu, California. For further historical background and more about the Alford Saga books, visit Paul online at www.paulalmond.com